DON MARQUIS

The Annotated Archy and Mehitabel

Edited with Notes and Introduction by
MICHAEL SIMS

PENGUIN BOOKS

PENGUIN BOOKS

Published by the Penguin Group

Penguin Group (USA) Inc., 375 Hudson Street, New York, New York 10014, U.S.A.
Penguin Group (Canada), 90 Eglinton Avenue East, Suite 700, Toronto, Ontario,
Canada M4P 2Y3 (a division of Pearson Penguin Canada Inc.)
Penguin Books Ltd, 80 Strand, London WC2R 0RL, England
Penguin Ireland, 25 St Stephen's Green, Dublin 2, Ireland
(a division of Penguin Books Ltd)
Penguin Group (Australia), 250 Camberwell Road, Camberwell, Victoria 3124,
Australia (a division of Pearson Australia Group Pty Ltd)
Penguin Books India Pvt Ltd, 11 Community Centre, Panchsheel Park,
New Delhi – 110 017, India
Penguin Group (NZ), 67 Apollo Drive, Rosedale, North Shore 0632, New Zealand
(a division of Pearson New Zealand Ltd)
Penguin Books (South Africa) (Pty) Ltd, 24 Sturdee Avenue,
Rosebank, Johannesburg 2196, South Africa

Penguin Books Ltd, Registered Offices: 80 Strand, London WC2R 0RL, England

First published in Penguin Books 2006

5   7   9   10   8   6

Introduction and notes copyright © Michael Sims, 2006
All rights reserved

ISBN 978-0-14-303975-4
CIP data available

Printed in the United States of America
Set in Sabon

THE ANNOTATED ARCHY AND MEHITABEL

DON MARQUIS was born in 1878, the second of four children of a physician in Walnut, Illinois. In 1898 he briefly attended Knox College in nearby Galesburg, but he was largely self-educated. As a teenager he began working for local printing offices and newspapers. After short-lived stints on newspapers in Washington and Philadelphia, Marquis moved to Atlanta in 1902 and worked for the *News*, the *Journal*, and *Uncle Remus's Magazine*. Marquis moved to New York City in 1909 and soon became a well-known journalist. In 1912 he launched his now legendary column "The Sun Dial" in the New York *Evening Sun* and four years later Archy and Mehitabel began to appear.

Marquis published three novels—*Danny's Own Story* (1912), *The Cruise of the Jasper B.* (1916), and *Off the Arm* (1930)—and four short story collections. He also collected the episodic adventures of his characters the Old Soak and Hermione and Her Little Group of Serious Thinkers. His several plays include a successful run of *The Old Soak* (1922), in which he himself starred at one point; and *The Dark Hours* (1924), which his second wife later directed in an unsuccessful Broadway production. *Prefaces* (1919) consists of forewords to imaginary books, and *Chapters for the Orthodox* (1934) is religious satire. By far his best known works are the Archy and Mehitabel columns, which he collected into three volumes—*Archy and Mehitabel* (1927), *Archy's Life of Mehitabel* (1933), and *Archy Does His Part* (1935).

Marquis's personal life was plagued with illness and loss. He married his first wife, Reina Melcher, in 1909. They had one son, who lived only six years, and one daughter, who lived only thirteen years. Reina died suddenly in 1923. Marquis married Marjorie Vonnegut three years later; she died in 1936. After years of illness, including strokes that paralyzed him and prevented speech, Don Marquis died in 1937 in New York City.

MICHAEL SIMS is the author most recently of *Adam's Navel: A Natural and Cultural History of the Human Form*, which was a *New York Times* Notable Book and a *Library Journal* Best Science Book. He first wrote about Archy and Mehitabel, as well as other animal characters, in *Darwin's Orchestra: An Almanac of Nature in History and the Arts*. His articles and essays have appeared in many periodicals, including the *Los Angeles Times Book Review*, *New Statesman*, *American Archaeology*, and *Skeptic*. More information is available at www.michaelsimsbooks.com, including links to Archy and Mehitabel Web sites.

Contents

THE ANNOTATED ARCHY AND MEHITABEL

1916

1917

1918

1919

1920

Introduction

A VIEW FROM THE UNDER SIDE

Many books attain classic status primarily because teachers keep them alive for students. Some, in contrast, age into celebrity on their own, because readers continue to find them engaging and relevant. They wind up stuffed into backpacks, read aloud to friends, posted on favorite-quotation Web sites. Such has been the fate of the Archy and Mehitabel books. Long ago the characters outgrew the newspaper in which they were born in 1916.

Don Marquis wrote stories, novels, plays, and "serious" poetry. But by far his best known works are the satirical poems and sketches through which Archy and Mehitabel cavort. A free verse poet reincarnated as a cockroach, Archy reported faithfully to Marquis's newspaper column "The Sun Dial," in the New York *Evening Sun*.[1] He narrated his adventures and those of his friend Mehitabel, an alley cat who once was (or at least claims to have once been) Cleopatra. In New York newspapers and later in magazines and syndication, hundreds of thousands of Americans followed their antics. Many newspaper columns in the early twentieth century featured poems, jokes, news commentary, and recurring characters—but none had been visited by such spirits as these. Generations of readers unacquainted with Marquis's columns have enjoyed collections mined from them, following Archy's sardonic accounts of his adventures with humans, with fellow animals (some of whom are also reincarnates), and even with ghosts and Martians.

No American humorist in the first three decades of the twentieth century was more acclaimed than Marquis. "What a deeply humorous man Don is," wrote fellow columnist Franklin

P. Adams, "and far closer to Mark Twain than anybody I know. . . ."[2] Marquis was already thirty-two when Twain died in 1910, and he was often proclaimed the heir to the grand old man of American humor; one of his many awards came from the Mark Twain Society. Marquis was a finalist three times for the O. Henry Memorial Prize for short fiction and was elected a member of the National Institute of Arts and Letters. He would have been amused to learn that during World War II, after he had been safely dead for several years, the U.S. Navy even christened a carrier the SS *Don Marquis*.

As epigrammatical as Ambrose Bierce in *The Devil's Dictionary*, as irreverent as Lord Byron in *Don Juan*, as happy to puncture humbug as his contemporary H. L. Mencken, Don Marquis at his best stands among the great satirists. In 1973, more than three decades after Marquis's death, E. B. White admitted to a correspondent that he didn't like to see the words *humorist* and *classic* applied to Marquis and his books (perhaps because such terms were applied to himself and his own work), but also made it clear that Marquis's best writing was here to stay:

> "Archy and Mehitabel" is, to my mind, a distinguished work in American letters, and whether it is a classic or not, it doesn't deserve the adjective "minor." There is not a minor word in it.[3]

E. B. White protested the designation *humorist* because it wasn't broad enough to contain Don Marquis. True, much of his daily writing falls into the category of "mere" humor; and, as was the case for every writer paid by the column inch to amuse, not all of it rises above flippancy. We think of humorists as comedians, deriving amusement from topics no more controversial than marital squabbles. Marquis produced plenty of this kind of humor, but he was also a satirist.

"Satire," wrote Philip Roth, "is moral outrage transformed into comic art."[4] Different people might describe a satirist as the watchdog of society, a humorist whose wit is barbed with insight, or a danger to the state. Roth's definition admits plays by Aristophanes in ancient Greece, political caricatures by Honoré Daumier in nineteenth-century France, and stand-up comedy by Lenny Bruce in mid-twentieth-century America. It embraces Stanley Kubrick's film *Dr. Strangelove*, Cintra Wilson's pop-culture criticism, and Aaron McGruder's comic strip *Boondocks*.[5]

Literary taxonomists used to herd every satirist into one of two great phylla, Horatian or Juvenalian. The Latin poet Horace, who lived in the first century BCE, comes across in his satires as mildly amused by his fellow human beings, shaking his head in a will-they-ever-learn sort of way. More than a century later, his countryman Juvenal is distinctly not amused. His satires are born in outrage; he is as morally offended as a television evangelist. Don Marquis employs both styles, sometimes in the same poem. "A man can't write successful satire," wrote Mark Twain to William Dean Howells the year after Marquis was born, "unless he be in a calm judicial good humor. I don't ever seem to be in a good enough humor with ANYthing to *satirize* it; no, I want to stand up before it and curse it, and foam at the mouth—or take a club and pound it to rags and pulp."[6]

Don Marquis often felt the same way. For him, as for his readers, the virtue and risk in his newspaper column was that he could write as the mood struck him. Like earlier satirists such as Pope, Swift, and Voltaire, he found folly and vice depressingly common and couldn't resist flailing them. The Archy and Mehitabel series wrestles with the signature issues of its era—unemployment, Prohibition, unionization, barriers of class and race, the growing influence of science and technology, the League of Nations, isolationism versus internationalism, the progress of World War I, and the religious yearning behind spiritualism.

To ripen toward inclusion in the world's shared culture, however, satire must avoid the historical dead end of mere topicality. Newspaper editorials and barroom quarrels—however effectively they mock the buffoonery du jour—seldom age well. They tend to be long on complaint and short on art. When craft lifts the protest into art, it has a chance of surviving.

But if the work outlives its creator, it faces another hazard: its allusions become increasingly antiquated. The Archy and Mehitabel adventures appeared between 1916 and 1936. For many twenty-first-century readers, especially students, they already teem with references as archaic as Voltaire's. In the present volume, readers will find a broad selection of the Archy and

Mehitabel columns (many of them never before reprinted), annotated with biographical and historical context, in the order of their original newspaper publication. This narrative format not only demonstrates the growth of Marquis's characters and themes; it also chronicles his fascinating era.

A NEW OUTLOOK UPON LIFE

i will write you a series of poems showing how things look to a cockroach

Don Marquis prefaced Archy's debut in "The Sun Dial" with an account of their first meeting. On March 29, 1916, his column opened with its usual brief jibes at the world around him—at a prominent judge, at the Mexican bandit Pancho Villa, at scarlet fever.[7] Then he told his readers about a strange phenomenon that he had witnessed a couple of weeks before: "We came into our room earlier than usual in the morning and discovered a gigantic cockroach jumping about upon the keys." There is no further reference to Archy's large size; in the rest of the series he is able to quickly scurry out of sight on those rare occasions when anyone notices him.[8]

Marquis describes the now classic scene in which he witnessed the cockroach's herculean efforts:

He would climb painfully upon the framework of the machine and cast himself with all his force upon a key, head downward, and his weight and the impact of the blow were just sufficient to operate the machine, one slow letter after another. He could not work the capital letters, and he had a great deal of difficulty operating the mechanism that shifts the paper so that a fresh line may be started. . . . After about an hour of this frightfully difficult literary labor he fell to the floor exhausted, and we saw him creep feebly into a nest of the poems which are always there in profusion.

And then Marquis walks over to his own typewriter and reads Archy's first words to appear in print—at least in this lifetime:

expression is the need of my soul
i was once a vers libre bard
but i died and my soul went into the body of a cockroach
it has given me a new outlook upon life
i see things from the under side now

It is true, as some commentators have remarked, that there was a practical side to the creation of Archy. Free verse was at its faddish height and ripe for mockery, and its short unrhymed lines permitted the deadline-haunted Marquis to fill column inches quickly. A longtime newspaperman, Marquis knew also that variety on the page draws a reader's eye and promises a lively mix. "In the very act of spoofing free verse," wrote E. B. White of Marquis, "he was enjoying some of its obvious advantages."[9] Typographical stunts may have lured browsers to the column, but such effects didn't make the series memorable. The characters did.

The mystery novelist Rex Stout once explained that his character Nero Wolfe differed from other detectives that he wrote about because he wasn't invented: "He was born. A born character arrives completely created."[10] Archy arrived this way. Marquis didn't consciously sit down to invent a character who might serve his artistic and commercial needs; he was the last to realize the insect's significance. His description of Archy's first appearance is true in the way that dreams are true. One day a cockroach showed up on the desk in his mind, and Marquis stood aside and watched to learn what it would say. The most artistic side of Don Marquis is distilled into Archy's cynical humor and artistic struggles. Skeptical, world-weary, Archy nonetheless yearns to communicate his response to life and to the mystery of consciousness embodied.

Archy laments the state of the world but no longer expects reform. Poetry is his solace and irony his defense. "His thought is spun of contempt and holy anger," wrote Bernard DeVoto of Archy, "down some dizzy slant of the mind where only he could keep his feet—happily, he had six."[11] Yes, but let's not forget that these conceptual fireworks arrive inside a versatile wit that is no less amusing for sometimes being gallows or gutter humor. The Archy and Mehitabel stories—many in the form of poems, but usually still narratives—are marvelously funny, even if their comedy sometimes becomes, as Richard Schweid remarks, "a humor as sharp as the grave."[12]

Marquis turns his sardonic view itself into an art form. A pharaoh's mummy awakens after arid millennia to find Prohibition denying him relief. When Archy tires of his high-flying soul being trapped in such an earthbound form, he attempts suicide, but he can't figure out how a cockroach can kill itself. Archy and his creator play many roles. Often Marquis casts himself as an exploitative boss and the cockroach as a long-suffering employee who appeals for raises—in the form of larger type and more edible scraps around the office—and finally strikes for better working conditions. Archy converses with ghosts and hornets, mollusks and birds. Marquis mutters asides about everyone from Kaiser Wilhelm to Shakespeare; karma and kismet come up as often as unemployment and hunger. At one point Archy admits that his favorite sport is theology. "A human being so largely and kindly planned," wrote columnist and friend Christopher Morley after Marquis's death, "moves always in widening rings of irony."[13]

Through the reincarnated cockroach, Marquis could also express the sense of fleeting time that haunted him. His long-range view of history, frequently including prehistory, fueled his melancholy. He felt that human life was a mess and always had been, that greed and ignorance destroyed the civilizations of the past and probably will destroy the current ones. "every time i die," sighs Archy, "it makes me more of a fatalist." John Batteiger, a journalist and Marquis bibliographer whose detective work contributed greatly to the present volume, writes that over the years Marquis exposed "a progressive heart and an increasingly cynical soul."[14] A smaller version of the same heart and soul animates the cockroach who throws himself bodily against the keys of Don Marquis's typewriter.

Despite high hopes for his own art and occasional indulgence in self-pity, Archy is a Cynic philosopher who obsessively watches other creatures and even plays Boswell for Mehitabel. The cat, in contrast, sings about herself. She belts out the themes of Don Marquis the tippler, the tavern habitué and bon vivant. Hedonist, reprobate, Mehitabel pipes rhyming stanzas about free love, the burden of reproduction, back-alley heartbreak, and the need to dance away your sorrows. Many songs carry the refrain that despite the paradoxes of reincarnation and the villainy of toms she remains ever a lady. Quick to resent and quick to draw blood, Mehitabel would have wreaked havoc among Old Possum's cats, even Growltiger and the Great Rumpuscat. T. S. Eliot's rarefied London is a long way from the garbage cans of Shinbone Alley.[15] Old Deuteronomy must not have his nap disturbed, while Mehitabel dances to keep from freezing because she has nowhere to sleep.

Mehitabel's essentially static character—no reader expects her to find true love or repent her ways—is indicated by the Dickensian catch-phrases that surround her in our memory. Like Mr. Micawber or Sairey Gamp, she walks onstage accompanied by pet phrases: *toujours gai*, "a dance in the old dame yet," and that Vonnegutian tic *wotthehell*. She is funny and outrageous and poignant, but she doesn't learn anything, even though this is her ninth (and presumably her final) life. She goes where chance leads her, from the ancient Nile to Jazz Age Hollywood, pausing occasionally to forgive herself: "the things that i had not ought to / i do because i ve got to."

In his choice of background for his protagonists, Marquis further prepared the stage for irony and satire. When human, Archy was a poet, a philosophical and artistic man of no social importance; in one poignant aside, he even remembers how homely a man he was. Mehitabel, in contrast, has fallen from a greater height. Once swaddled in privilege as the powerful Cleopatra, she now scrounges for a fishbone dinner:

> a cockroach which you are
> and a poet which you used to be
> archy couldn t understand
> my feelings at having come
> down to this

Longtime Marquis fans may be surprised to learn in the present volume that in his initial appearance, as printed in the *Evening Sun*, Archy describes Mehitabel merely as "that cat," although he names his rival poet, Freddy the rat. For the first six weeks Mehitabel remained nameless. When Marquis gathered the poems together for the first book, in 1927, he inserted her name into the earlier poems in order to establish her from scene one as worthy of sharing the marquee.

"Only fantasy was wide or versatile enough to contain him," wrote Bernard DeVoto of Marquis; "his mind kept escaping through cracks in the sane, commonplace world out into dimensions that were loops and whorls and mazes of the unpredictable."[16] Escaping through a narrative crack, Marquis was able to create characters and write about topics otherwise too hot to handle. Mehitabel's questionable morality, disdain for motherhood, and irreverent mouth would not have been tolerated in a human character in a 1916 newspaper—just as that wily fox Reynard gets away with comments that would have resulted in legal action had they been about human beings. Few books tell us more about Medieval society than the Reynard story cycle, and Archy and Mehitabel likewise immortalize their era.

"Fantasy," observed V. S. Pritchett, "states what realism will obscure or bungle."[17] It has always been the habitat where humans and animals commune. Beasts caper through mythology and folklore. We have long seen family resemblances in other creatures, usually beginning by interpreting their behavior in terms of our own. We impose symbolic delusions: coyotes skulk, eagles rule. We can barely imagine a scavenger—a hyena, say, or a vulture—as hero. It is as if each animal is born into a rigid social caste. The title of Disney's movie *The Lion King* is almost redundant; we know that a lion will be brave, strong, and authoritative. This is why the Cowardly Lion in *The Wizard of Oz* is funny, and this kind of thinking makes a philosophical cockroach funny. We even fantasize about exchanging forms with other creatures—yet another way that Don Marquis turned to a venerable tradition when he first spoke in the voice of Archy. The metamorphoses in Ovid, like those in Marquis, often involve a human being who turns into an animal but continues to think like a human. The freedom, the goad to imagination, in this theme has lured writers from Apuleius to Kafka.

Archy and Mehitabel belong to an ancient and noble family in this class of fictional characters: animals that writers have created in order to explore—and comment from within—their outsider view of human society. Readers of Aesop or Bidpai or La Fontaine immediately understand why Marquis reincarnated his socially conscious narrator as a cockroach rather than as an eagle or a lion. Because they frequent garbage cans, cockroaches must constitute the animal peasantry. Like Tom and Huck's, Archy and Mehitabel's adventures and opinions would have been completely different had they come from upper-class characters.

Marquis's clever use of reincarnation as the bridge between species, however, permits him to employ animal stereotypes without being trapped inside them. Returned to embodiment as a cockroach, Archy now occupies the lowest rung of the natural and social ladder, but his consciousness is still human. Marquis needed this kind of viewpoint character. Like Mark Twain before him and John Steinbeck after him, he examined the American experience from outside the drawing-room window. Viewing life "from the under side"—reviled, persona non grata—Archy embodies a populist sermon against the myth that social status limits perception or relevance. He scurries around the feet of New Yorkers like Gulliver in Brobdingnag, and like Gulliver he alternately laughs and groans over the antics of the giants. Marooned in a new era and a new body, the former poet is a visitor to his own world.

THE BONDAGE OF RHYMING

> before i became a cockroach
> i was a free verse poet
> one of the pioneers of the artless art

As long ago as 1667, John Milton prefaced *Paradise Lost* with a manifesto about the time-honored virtues of unrhymed verse. Invoking Homer and Virgil on his own behalf, the contentious Puritan argued that "true musical delight" in poetry rejects "the troublesome and modern bondage of rhyming." Of course, Milton was talking about book-length heroic verse, not squibs hammered out by arthropods, but the admonition still applies. Poetry does not demand rhyme.

Milton employed blank verse, unrhymed iambic pentameter, which he and Shakespeare established as the voice of serious poetic utterance in English poetry. ("Of Man's First Disobedience and the Fruit / of that Forbidden Tree. . . .") In its regular meter, however, even blank verse is not totally "free." Our insect anarchist requires absolute liberty for his expression. In his first appearance Archy declares that he is a "vers libre bard"; later he describes himself as in the epigraph above. Anglophone poets and critics use the French *vers libre* and the English *free verse* interchangeably. Rejecting predictable meter or even patterns of line length, free verse depends upon language's natural rhythms, primarily—in a Germanic language such as English, at least—through the alternation of stressed and unstressed syllables. Proponents of free verse argue that poetry's rhythms are more natural, its nuances more precise, when poets are liberated from the need to carve lines into matching structures that may distort image and meaning. *Leaves of Grass* is probably the most familiar example of free verse prior to the twentieth century's flowering. Walt Whitman, however, was not the first to employ this method in English; you can see it used to brilliant effect in the King James translation of the *Psalms* and the *Song of Solomon*.

Marquis's use of the phrase "artless art" reminds us that he created Archy to parody the vogue for free verse. Good free verse isn't artless—although, like abstract painting, it looks at first glance as if anyone can do it. By 1916 this misconception was inspiring a torrent of unrhymed, meter-free writing. But the era also produced much strong and original free verse by writers such as Ezra Pound, E. E. Cummings, and Amy Lowell (whose work Marquis particularly disliked). The year before Archy arrived, Edgar Lee Masters published his influential volume of elegiac free verse, *Spoon River Anthology*, and T. S. Eliot inaugurated the Modernist era with his free-verse "Love Song of J. Alfred Prufrock."[18] Also in 1915 Kafka brought invertebrate vermin to twentieth-century literature by having Gregor Samsa awaken as a beetle—*not*, as some writers have claimed, as a cockroach.[19] It is worth pointing out, however, that Kafka's story had not yet been translated into English when Marquis invented Archy.

Although Marquis composed plenty of free-verse poems that he did not credit to a cockroach with a typing disability, it is the insect, not the newspaperman, who flatly proclaims himself a vers libre poet. Marquis was certainly not opposed to rhyme and usually found it crucial in his bag of tricks. Unforeseen rhyme is a staple of comic verse. Shortly after Mehitabel appears on the scene, she begins caterwauling stanzas that are much funnier because of their sometimes tortuous rhyme scheme. In the Archy poems, Marquis turns to rhyme whenever he wants to— probably whenever the first couple of lines arrived rhyming and he surrendered to their momentum. He explained it on the first occasion—April 10, 1916—by casually remarking of Archy that "he was a rhymester too." Glib facility was Marquis's trademark from newsroom to saloon, but it required that he trust inspiration. And spontaneity was no guarantee of quality, as a few of the Archy and Mehitabel columns (not reprinted here) demonstrate.

Because Archy calls himself a free-verse poet, we tend to think of all his contributions to Marquis's column as poems. Actually some are poems, some sketches, and some transcriptions of songs, usually but not always Mehitabel's. Archy dislikes restrictive categories. Like Wagstaff, Groucho Marx's college president in *Horsefeathers*, he could sing, "Whatever it is, I'm against it." He even lives a bandit's life on the frontier between poetry and prose. He couldn't survive without enjambment, the continuation of verse from one line to the next with no pause such as a grammatical break or a rhyme.

Christopher Morley described Marquis's choice of lower-case for Archy's writings as a waggish stunt that once begun could not be discontinued.[20] True, but it was also a reasonable outgrowth of the premise, and it afforded Marquis an opportunity to do what Alfred Hitchcock advised filmmakers to do: exploit the setting. Lowercase invites other experimentation, such as Archy's parody of the Simplified Spelling movement. Language-conscious writers create narrators who exist within and because of their unique manner of expression; witness Alex DeLarge in *A Clockwork Orange* or Christopher Boone in *The Curious Incident of the Dog in the Nighttime*—or even Huckleberry Finn. Archy's voice doesn't merely report his character. It helps fashion it.

THE TYRANNY OF CIRCUMSTANCE

While preparing a biographical essay about Marquis, Christopher Morley once complained that he was having trouble sorting fact from fiction. "It is true that I have invented for myself a good many experiences which I never really had," replied Marquis. "But they were all experiences which belonged to me by right of temperament and character. . . . I was despoiled of them by the rough tyranny of Circumstance."[21] He insisted that he balanced accounts by omitting many real-life incidents because they were lies told about him "by the slinking facts of life." His unpublished autobiographical fragments include the admission, "I must begin being honest by telling you that I shall lie a little here and there."[22] He so loved speaking through characters that he wrote his memoir in the third person. Therefore it is prudent to note that, although most of the following incidents can be confirmed, a handful may be embroidered.

The most outrageous story that Marquis told about his life, however, was true. Donald Robert Perry Marquis was born in the Illinois hamlet of Walnut, west of Chicago, on July 29, 1878. In his unpublished memoirs, Marquis wrote that he was born at three o'clock in the afternoon, "during an eclipse of the sun—not merely on the same day, but during the eclipse itself."[23] For once Marquis was not pulling the reader's leg. The eclipse's path of totality was south of Walnut, but the town definitely witnessed it.[24] Marquis cherished this ancient omen as a parallel to Comet Halley attending the birth and death of Mark Twain.

Marquis's father was from Ohio, his mother from Virginia. When he was born the American Civil War had been over for only thirteen years and scars were still fresh. The abuses of Reconstruction constrained relations between his father's and mother's families. It was not a progressive era. Proposed laws and constitutional amendments advocating racial and gender equality were struck down by the Supreme Court in 1878. Some physicians were recommending whiskey and tobacco as defense against the yellow fever epidemic that would claim fourteen thousand American lives during the year. Yet change was in the air. Marquis—who reached adulthood before automobiles were common or airplanes even in existence, whose grandfather fought in the War of 1812—grew up to write poems in which Archy is interviewed by Martians who contact him via radio.

Appropriately for a writer whose best-known creation types with his entire body, Marquis was born in the same year that the typewriter leaped forward technologically with Remington's introduction of the shift key. Mark Twain had only recently become the first prominent author to deliver a typewritten manuscript to a publisher.[25] Archy can't work the shift key that would enable him to capitalize words, and he can barely manage the carriage return. (See the columns for August 17 and 23, 1916.) Had the newfangled typewriter not existed, Marquis might have had to reincarnate his poet as a rat or some other creature that might grasp a pen. *Freddy* and Mehitabel? Inconceivable.

When praising the Archy and Mehitabel chronicles, few readers comment upon their offhand violence. Characters maul and maim each other. Mehitabel faces mayhem every day, from dark alleyways to suburban lawns. Archy flees numerous threats—often from Mehitabel herself. Several characters die in this saga, most of them unpleasantly.

At a young age Marquis was exposed to violence and hypocrisy, and he didn't lose his hatred for or his fascination with either. His father was a physician, although he never achieved financial success in Walnut. Several years before Don's birth, he was called to the deathbed of a pregnant woman, where he discovered that she had been beaten. He found the weapon—an iron stove leg—hidden nearby, and her husband went to prison for the murder. By the time that Marquis was five or six years old, the old man had been released from prison and would stand up before the local Baptist congregation and gleefully lament his despicable sinning before he learned to love Jesus.

Disturbing events surrounded young Don as they did so many children of his era. When he was about twelve years old, he and a friend found the body of a man who had hanged himself. The man had misjudged the height of the tree limb that served as gallows and "had danced himself to death," wrote Marquis; when they found him "he was dead, but still dancing."[26] In

Walnut Marquis saw on display the corpse of a man who had been shotgunned during a drunken rampage. Later he witnessed the 1906 Atlanta race riots, whose horrific events inspired his short story "Carter," which describes the brutal treatment of a mixed-race man and finally his murder at the hands of a mob. Later Archy would work a lynch mob into his review of the movie *The Three Little Pigs*, and describe how clams were forming the Ku Klux Klam to battle the alleged threat of oysters.

Other circumstances planted seeds that would flower in Marquis's writings. When he was five or six years old, the Marquis family moved into a three-story house owned by a spiritualist. The landlady occupied the top floor herself—along with, she claimed, numerous spirits. Don and his brother David agreeably pretended to hear ghostly rapping. David and his friends also feigned a conversion to spiritualism, even holding séances—including one for a deceased dog. Prankish humor was part of the family heritage.

Historians consider the spiritualist movement to have begun in upstate New York in 1848, when three sisters began snapping their toe joints and claiming that the resulting raps were produced by ghosts. By the time that Don Marquis encountered his clairvoyant landlady, the movement had been gaining force for more than three decades. Through séances, in which a medium would channel a ghost on demand, spiritualism seemed to offer to an increasingly materialistic age some encouraging evidence of life beyond the grave.

Injustice, hypocrisy, and violence haunt the lives of Archy and Mehitabel as they did the youth of their creator. Marquis was always skeptical about spiritualism, too, which may be why he employed it as the centerpiece of the Archy and Mehitabel chronicles.

"DON MARQUIS, THE NEW HUMORIST"

Like most aspiring writers, Marquis started out working odd jobs. He plucked chickens and delivered groceries; he sold clothes and sewing machines; he taught briefly in a country school. But he began writing at a young age. Reminiscing about early influences, he recalled yearning to emulate the jokey

columns of Eugene Field. In Marquis's youth Field would have
been writing his "Sharps and Flats" column for the Chicago
Morning News.[27] He ranged from lampoons of Chicago's nou-
veau riche to homilies in mock rural dialect, and often threw in
poems such as the one now called "Wynken, Blynken, and Nod."

Marquis was still a teenager when he wandered into a printing
office and quickly found himself helping to edit the regional
weekly. "Besides the local news and editorials," he recalled, "I
started a column, consisting of verse, sketches, jokes, character
studies, and so forth. I didn't get paid anything for this work; I
was more than gratified to get the opportunity of doing it."[28] Af-
ter only three months at Knox College in nearby Galesburg, and
brief newspaper stints in Washington and Philadelphia, Marquis
moved to Atlanta in 1902 as associate editor of the Atlanta
News. He was permitted to contribute signed (but unpaid)
tidbits—poems, observations—only after he had completed writ-
ing editorials. In 1904 he moved to the Atlanta *Journal*, where
his signed work was still basically unpaid.

Atlanta provided another crazy true story worthy of the natal
eclipse. A runaway circus lion simply walked in through the
open door of the bar where Marquis was drinking. This aged,
toothless beast yawned with boredom and flopped onto the
floor, but in Marquis's variations on this anecdote he promoted
the lion to a Fiendish Cat from Hell with whom he nonetheless
shared a convivial drink. Years later the lion was still showing
up in his writing.

In Atlanta Marquis met Joel Chandler Harris. A popular hu-
morist, Harris specialized in regional dialect tales such as those
of Br'er Rabbit and Br'er Fox, told by the slave Uncle Remus to
the son of a plantation owner. Although employing American
characters—human and animal—the original stories told by
slaves were based on African folklore. In early 1907 Harris
launched *Uncle Remus's Magazine* and hired Marquis as asso-
ciate editor. The magazine got off to a promising start, immedi-
ately publishing such popular authors as O. Henry and Jack
London. Marquis wrote book reviews, editorials, poems, and
short stories—so many that he signed some with initials or vari-
ations on his three given names. Much of this writing appeared
in his first regular column, "A Glance in Passing." Harris's ani-

mal characters may have helped inspire Archy and Mehitabel.

From early in his career Marquis often fell into the trap of phonetically misspelling words for humorous effect—spelling *was* as *wuz*, for example, or *specially* as *speshually*. The rationale for this gimmick collapses when a reader realizes that even when people misspell words they don't do so phonetically—and there is no rationale at all for stories in which a presumably omniscient narrator reports words that someone else spoke. Joel Chandler Harris used this style consistently. So did many other humorists of the era, especially those we now call the Literary Comedians, most of whom posed as unlettered jesters and cracker-barrel philosophers. Josh Billings, the pen name of Henry Wheeler Shaw, had been the chief perpetrator of *faux-naïf* dialect humor, most famously with his 1860 "Essa on the Muel" and his long-running parody of *The Farmer's Almanac* entitled *Josh Billings' Farmer's Allminax*. (Archy works in a double joke about language when he criticizes the boss's "joshbillingsgate" in the poem on April 10, 1916.) Another American practitioner of this sort of humor was Charles Farrar Browne, best known for his writings under the pseudonym Artemus Ward. Each of them—like Mark Twain, who eclipsed them all—began in the diverse and competitive world of newspapers.[29]

Soon Marquis demonstrated the independent thinking that would issue from the mouth of Archy nine years later. He mocked John D. Rockefeller's frequent claim that he was rich because Providence smiled upon him; Marquis credited instead "that divinely appointed organization, the oil trust." He declared flatly that "The Russian government permits, if it does not directly encourage, the massacre of the Jews." One widely quoted editorial was a proclamation that critics ought to abandon their messianic vigil for the Great American Novel because Mark Twain had already written it in *Huckleberry Finn*. This was by no means the literary consensus at the time. It would be decades before Ernest Hemingway proclaimed Twain's novel the fountainhead of American fiction.

In 1907, at the *Uncle Remus* office, Marquis met a young writer named Reina Melcher, who had sold a story to the magazine. His next move was fateful; he invited her out for an ice cream soda. Within a year they were married. A few weeks later Joel Chandler Harris died, and Marquis began to lose interest in the fledgling publication that had been largely an extension of Harris's own personality. Soon Marquis (with Reina following) moved to a setting that would ignite his imagination, that would embrace him and make him famous, the town with which Archy and Mehitabel are associated to this day—New York City.

"I began to like New York on account of what I intended it should do for me later," Marquis recalled about his early days in the city.[30] He came of age during the heyday of the great American newspapers. In the last decades of the nineteenth century they had made advances in printing (see notes for the September 4, 1916 column), in reproduction of illustrations, and even in distribution, and had become the voice of a tumultuous democracy. New York was home to many competing papers, each with its own style and market—the *Times*, the *Tribune*, the *Mail*, the *Sun*, the *Evening Sun*, the *Post*, the *Globe*, the *Press*, the *World*, the *American*, and others. Neither radio nor television even existed as a word yet; their later inroads on newspaper readership were unimaginable.

Consequently it was also a good time to be a columnist. Over the next few years Marquis was friend and colleague—and rival—to most of the legends. Franklin Pierce Adams, known as F.P.A., was writing his popular "Conning Tower" column. Christopher Morley held forth from "The Bowling Green." (Both columns appeared in a succession of papers.) Alexander Woollcott wrote columns and essays for various newspapers and the *New Yorker*. These men were not academics but they were literary-minded. They reviewed books and plays; Morley edited *Bartlett's Familiar Quotations*. This was the era that preceded Robert Benchley, Dorothy Parker, James Thurber, and E. B. White.

It was a riotous time. The muckrakers were finding no shortage of civic and corporate muck. Ida Tarbell's 1904 history of the Standard Oil Company helped lead to its dissolution, and Upton Sinclair exposed the inhumane practices of the meatpacking industry in his 1906 novel *The Jungle*. President Theodore Roosevelt was busting trusts and posing for photographs advertising his manliness. Houdini was exposing the spiritualists who were hoodwinking the grieving and credulous, including Arthur Conan Doyle, creator of the supremely rational Sherlock Holmes. Archy's very existence as a character owed much to spiritualism, and he would comment on this topic many times.

On his first day in New York, exploring the newspaper district, Marquis stumbled upon Lipton's bar, in the triangle where Park Row and Nassau Street met. He swung open the door and walked into newspaper lore. Over the years, wherever he lived, Marquis accumulated admiring friends. He liked to drink and he wrote many an ode to saloons and bars. During his lifetime his tipsy anti-Prohibition character Clem Hawley, the Old Soak, became a household name (and went on to theater and film) through his harangues against the evils of temperance. Marquis was famed as a good listener and a man always willing to lend a dollar or buy a drink. He also possessed a quick and capacious memory. Ministers were surprised to find how much of the Bible this heretic seemed to have on file in his brain, and rival F.P.A. called Marquis his favorite Shakespeare concordance.

In 1912 a review of his first novel, *Danny's Own Story*, was headlined "Don Marquis, the New Humorist." A few months later he was invited to edit a magazine page at the *Evening Sun* and then moved to the editorial page with a column called "The Sun Dial." Finally Marquis had the journalistic home for which he had so long yearned. He began filling it with material he had been saving, and it was an immediate success. "I began to create characters," he recalled, "through whom I might comment upon or satirize current phases of existence, or whom I might develop for the sheer pleasure of creation."[31] The best known characters to regularly visit his column were the Old Soak and the flighty Hermione, whose pseudo-intellectual Little Group of Serious Thinkers in Greenwich Village smugly embraces every craze from spiritualism to free verse. Both characters were already successful when, in March of 1916, Archy jumped onto the keys of Don Marquis's typewriter.

THE CREATOR OF A COCKROACH

After he retired from his full-time column in 1925 to write more fiction and drama, Marquis admitted, "I got to seeing my column as a grave, twenty-three inches long, into which I buried myself every day. . . ."[32] His other writings demonstrate his restlessness and ambition. Always drawn to the easy humor of dialect, but lacking Twain's mastery of it, Marquis has the narrator of *Danny's Own Story* tell a colloquial tale that includes itinerant actors, con men, and other types familiar from *Huckleberry Finn*. In *The Cruise of the Jasper B.*, his second novel, he satirizes adventure stories. Other books besides the Archy and Mehitabel volumes were drawn largely from columns; *The Almost Perfect State* is a hodgepodge on the general theme of utopian societies. Marquis also adapted the Old Soak columns into a successful Broadway comedy, at one point acting the role of Clem Hawley himself.

Like Archy, Marquis could have claimed theology as his favorite sport. He devoted considerable energy to his solemn Crucifixion drama *The Dark Hours*. Closer to the spirit of Archy is his 1934 semi-novel *Chapters for the Orthodox*, which consists of twelve adventures set mostly in New York City and starring Jehovah, Satan, Jesus, and other biblical characters. Although the book has funny and provocative moments, many scenes go on too long, reminding us that for Marquis newspaper columning imposed a constructive brevity.

Marquis's last years were fraught with loss and illness. His first wife, their daughter and son, his second wife—each pre-deceased him. He had twice been a devoted husband and was a famously doting father. Bereft, Marquis began suffering strokes. His third, in 1936, left him barely able to move and almost entirely unable to speak. He spent his last year and a half cared for by his two sisters, whom he had previously supported for their entire lives. He died on December 29, 1937.

Newspapers around the country, especially in New York, ran affectionate obituaries. In a gesture that would have made Marquis guffaw, Christopher Morley visited the undertaker who had embalmed his old friend's body and instructed him to remove the too-dressy suit and replace it with Marquis's favorite brown tweed. Morley swapped Marquis's necktie with the one that had been around his own neck. In early January, E. B. White wrote to James Thurber about Marquis's death, describing their fellow humorist as "one of the saddest people of our generation." He enumerated Marquis's sufferings and added, "What a kick in the pants life gave that guy!"[33]

It is axiomatic that clowns have painted smiles for a reason. "Gravity and levity," remarked Christopher Morley, "were so mixed in Don's mind that it puzzled even himself. . . ."[34] Humor, whether in despair or camaraderie, was not just Don Marquis's profession. It was his creative medium. Under false names he typed notes to fellow columnists—seeking romantic advice, submitting awful poems, claiming to be an outraged reader or a lawyer suing for libel. After Marquis's death, Morley and other friends tearfully reminisced about his pranks. Marquis's narrator in *Sonnets to a Red-Haired Lady* admits, "My dreams I hedge about with bitter wit." Apparently this attitude was true until the end. During Marquis's long inarticulate decline, his sisters reported that sometimes they found him laughing quietly to himself—but no longer able to explain the joke.

Just as Marquis was himself influenced by the Literary Comedians, so have his style and his characters already influenced generations of writers and other artists. James Thurber patterned his early newspaper columns on those of Marquis and Franklin P. Adams.[35] E. B. White insisted that his own writing was influenced more by Marquis than by literary heavyweights such as Hemingway.[36] When he moved to New York City, White was in awe of Marquis and his generation of columnists, and he wrote that he "would hang around the corner of Chambers Street and Broadway, thinking: 'Somewhere in that building is the typewriter that archy the cockroach jumps on at night.'"[37]

In 1949, prior to writing an affectionate tribute to Marquis for Doubleday's omnibus volume, White reread all three Archy collections. Soon he began writing his own story about a talking animal, and his hero was also an invertebrate writer. In letters he specifically compared Charlotte the spider to Mehitabel the cat. When a film studio representative wrote White about plans for an animated adaptation of *Charlotte's Web*, White was anxious to avoid the imposition of some kind of moral upon his novel. "I would hate to see Charlotte turned into a 'dedicated' spider: she is, if anything, more the Mehitabel type—toujours gai."[38] But surely the philosophical ancestor of Charlotte—who is compassionate, opposed to injustice, and able to extract words from her very essence at great personal toll—is actually Archy.

Don Marquis the aspiring dramatist might be pleased to know that Archy and Mehitabel began capering across stages in 1954 and haven't stopped yet. In that year composer George Kleinsinger and lyricist Joe Darion, who was later famous for *Man of La Mancha*, premiered in New York City a musical entitled *Archy and Mehitabel*. Variations of it still make the rounds of regional theater. Soon afterward they produced an album entitled *Archy and Mehitabel: A Back-Alley Opera*, with Carol Channing giving voice to Mehitabel and Eddie Bracken as Archy. In 1957 a revamped musical appeared on Broadway as *Shinbone Alley*, the result of a collaboration between Kleinsinger, Darion, and a little-known comedian named Mel Brooks. The Broadway version starred Bracken again as Archy but replaced Channing with Eartha Kitt, who would round out her sex-kitten phase by portraying Catwoman on the 1960s *Batman* TV series. Unfortunately the Broadway version betrayed the spirit of its own inspiration by portraying Archy in love with Mehitabel; when the show closed after forty-nine performances, Marquis purists were not distraught. The musical appeared on television in 1960. Then in 1971 *Shinbone Alley* achieved permanent form as an animated film directed by John Wilson.

There have been other artistic responses to Marquis's characters. Taking homelessness as his official theme, composer Andrew Stiller set Mehitabel's midnight dance with Boreas to violin—"the traditional fiddle of the danse macabre," he explained—and gave Mehitabel herself musical voice through accompanying soprano. The opera premiered in 1989. The stage musical still reappears in theaters around the world—including in Australia in late 2005—and actor Gale McNeeley has been honing his one-man performance piece for years.

Unlike many newspaper columnists, Don Marquis never claimed to be a prophet, but he was positively oracular when he complained that it looked like he was going to be remembered as the creator of a cockroach. Like Arthur Conan Doyle, who ranked his phenomenally popular detective far below his historical novels, Marquis eventually found the demand for

Archy and Mehitabel tiresome. He actually killed Archy a couple of times, only to have him migrate into the body of another cockroach.

Few of Don Marquis's other characters seem to possess what show business people call legs. His novels and short stories are mostly forgotten. The Old Soak is inescapably pickled in his gin-mill era. Hermione and her pretentious coterie can still be relevant in our gullible age, but they too appear to be mummifying into museum exhibits. So far only Archy and Mehitabel have joined the rowdy club of characters who escape their creator's mortality and find themselves embraced by the world and posterity.

1. The *Evening Sun* was the less well-behaved sibling of the *Sun*, a morning paper once edited by the legendary Charles Dana. Marquis began his column at the *Evening Sun*. In 1920 *The Sun* merged with the *New York Herald*, at which time the *Evening Sun* dropped the adjective and became a new version of *The Sun*. In 1922 Marquis moved to the *New York Tribune*, where his column was called "The Lantern."
2. Bernard DeVoto, "Almost Toujours Gai," in *Harper's*, March 1950. Reprinted in DeVoto's collection *The Easy Chair* (Boston: Houghton Mifflin, 1955).
3. Dorothy Lobrano Guth, ed., *Letters of E. B. White* (New York: Harper & Row, 1976), p. 649. Letter to Edward C. Sampson, dated May 31, 1973. The title "Archy and Mehitabel" refers specifically to the first collection, published in 1927, but it is often used to denote the entire series.
4. Philip Roth, "The Hurdles of Satire," *New Republic*, September 9, 1957.
5. For the origins of satire, see Gilbert Highet, *The Anatomy of Satire* (Princeton, NJ: Princeton University Press, 1962). For an introduction to and anthology of satire in America, and to the context for Marquis's work, see Henry C. Carlisle, Jr., *American Satire in Prose and Verse* (New York: Random House, 1962). See also Edward A. Martin, *H. L. Mencken and the Debunkers* (Athens, GA: University of Georgia Press, 1984), especially Chapter 8, "A Puritan's Satanic Flight: Don Marquis, His Archy, and Anarchy." Horace and Juvenal are available in countless editions.
6. Quoted in Justin Kaplan, *Mr. Clemens and Mark Twain: A Biography* (New York: Simon & Schuster, 1966), p. 169.

7. The entire text appears as the first entry in this volume, with notes.

8. For Archy's likely species, turn to the note for the poem on October 12, 1916.

9. E. B. White, "Don Marquis," in *The Second Tree from the Corner* (New York: Harper & Row, 1954). An earlier, less polished version appeared as his "Introduction" to *The Lives and Times of Archy and Mehitabel* (New York: Doubleday, 1950).

10. John McAleer, *Rex Stout: A Biography* (Boston: Little, Brown, 1977), p. 247.

11. DeVoto, "Almost Toujours Gai."

12. Richard Schweid, *The Cockroach Papers: A Compendium of History and Lore* (New York: Four Walls Eight Windows, 1999), p. 100.

13. Christopher Morley, "O Rare Don Marquis," in his column "The Bowling Green," *Saturday Review*, January 8, 1938.

14. John Batteiger, www.donmarquis.com. His Web site provides an excellent introduction to Marquis and his various creations.

15. Shinbone Alley is where Archy reports, in later poems, that Mehitabel is living. It became the title of a musical and animated film, as discussed later in this essay. It is an actual alley in New York City, connecting Lafayette Street, across from Jones Alley, with Bleecker Street, across from Mott Street. See the "Forgotten New York" Web site, http://www.forgotten-ny.com/Alleys/Soho/soho.html. Truly obsessive Marquis devotees may wish to know that there are references to Shinbone Alley on Merle Haggard's 1971 album *A Tribute to the Best Damn Fiddle Player in the World*, in the song "Stay a Little Longer" and on the Spin Doctors' 1991 album *Pocket Full of Kryptonite*, in the song "Shin Bone Alley."

16. DeVoto, "Almost Toujours Gai."

17. V. S. Pritchett, "A Dandy," in *Complete Collected Essays* (New York: Random House, 1991); p. 929. An essay on Max Beerbohm.

18. On free verse see especially these sources: T. S. Eliot, "Reflections on Vers Libre," *New Statesman*, March 3, 1917; reprinted in *To Criticize the Critic and Other Writings* (New York: Farrar, Straus & Giroux, 1965). Paul Fussell Jr., *Poetic Meter and Poetic Form* (New York: Random House, 1965). Karl Shapiro and Robert Beum, *A Prosody Handbook* (New York: Harper & Row, 1965).

19. Kafka describes Samsa's insect form as *ungeheuren Ungeziefer*, roughly "monstrous vermin," and wisely avoids identifying it more fully. Nabokov in his lectures on "The Metamorphosis" argues from textual description (even employing diagrams) that Samsa awoke as a dung beetle. See Vladimir Nabokov, *Lectures on Literature*, ed. by Fredson Bowers (New York: Harcourt Brace Jovanovich, 1980).

20. Christopher Morley, "Archy—From Abdera." *Saturday Review*, May 15, 1937, in his "Bowling Green" column.

21. Quoted in Edward Anthony, *O Rare Don Marquis* (New York: Doubleday, 1962), p. 43.

22. Anthony, p. 44.

23. Anthony, p. 21.

24. See NASA's Web site: http://sunearth.gsfc.nasa.gov/eclipse/SE history/SEpath/SE1878Jul29T.html.

25. Mark Twain, "The First Writing Machines," in "From My Unpublished Autobiography," *Harper's Weekly*, March 18, 1905.

26. Anthony, pp. 29–30.

27. The *Morning News* was renamed the *Record* in 1890, when Marquis was twelve.

28. Anthony, p. 66.

29. For more on the Literary Comedians, see David B. Kesterson, "The Literary Comedians and the Language of Humor." *Studies in American Humor*, vol. 1 [New Series], no. 1 (June 1982), 44–51. For general background on later American humor, see Norris W. Yates, *The American Humorist: Conscience of the Twentieth Century* (Ames, IA: Iowa State University Press, 1964), especially Chapter 11, "The Many Masks of Don Marquis." Numerous anthologies of humor include selections by and commentary upon Marquis.

30. Anthony, p. 117.

31. Anthony, p. 139.

32. Marquis, "Confessions of a Reformed Columnist," *Saturday Evening Post*, December 29, 1928, p. 62.

33. Letter to James Thurber, dated January 8, 1938. In Guth, *Letters*, p. 171.

34. Morley, "O Rare Don Marquis."

35. Harrison Kinney, *James Thurber: His Life and Times* (New York: Henry Holt, 1995), p. 267.

36. Guth, ed., *Letters*, p. 574. Letter to William K. Zinsser, dated December 30, 1968.

37. E. B. White, "Here Is New York," reprinted in *Essays of E. B. White* (New York: Harper & Row, 1977), pp. 125–6. This is one of the rare occasions on which White, the most important commentator on Archy, failed to capitalize the cockroach's name.

38. Guth, ed., *Letters*, p. 613. Letter to Gene Deitch, dated January 12, 1971.

Suggestions for Further Reading

BOOKS BY DON MARQUIS

Danny's Own Story. Garden City, NY: Doubleday, Page & Co., 1912.

Dreams & Dust. New York and London: Harper & Brothers, 1915.

The Cruise of the Jasper B. New York and London: D. Appleton and Co., 1916.

Hermione and Her Little Group of Serious Thinkers. New York and London: D. Appleton and Co., 1916.

Prefaces. New York and London: D. Appleton and Co., 1919.

The Old Soak and *Hail and Farewell.* Garden City, NY, and Toronto: Doubleday, Page & Co., 1921.

Carter and Other People. New York and London: D. Appleton and Co., 1921.

Noah an' Jonah an' Cap'n John Smith: A Book of Humorous Verse. New York and London: D. Appleton and Co., 1921.

Poems and Portraits. Garden City, NY, and Toronto: Doubleday, Page & Co., 1922.

Sonnets to a Red-Haired Lady (By a Gentleman with a Blue Beard) and *Famous Love Affairs.* Garden City, NY, and Toronto: Doubleday, Page & Co., 1922.

The Revolt of the Oyster. Garden City, NY: Doubleday, Page & Co., 1922.

The Old Soak's History of the World, with Occasional Glances at Baycliff, L.I., and Paris, France. Garden City, NY: Doubleday, Page & Co., 1924.

The Dark Hours: Five Scenes From a History. Garden City, NY: Doubleday, Page & Co., 1924.

The Awakening & Other Poems. London: William Heinemann

Ltd., 1924. (First U.S. edition published 1925 by Doubleday, Page & Co.)

Out of the Sea: A Play in Four Acts. Garden City, NY: Doubleday, Page & Co., 1927.

The Almost Perfect State. Garden City, NY: Doubleday, Page & Co., 1927.

Archy and Mehitabel. Garden City, NY: Doubleday, Page & Co., 1927.

Love Sonnets of a Cave Man, and Other Verses: Garden City, NY: Doubleday, Doran & Co., 1928.

When the Turtles Sing, and Other Unusual Tales. Garden City, NY: Doubleday, Doran & Co., 1928.

A Variety of People. Garden City, NY: Doubleday, Doran & Co., 1929.

Off the Arm. Garden City, NY: Doubleday, Doran & Co., 1930.

Archy's Life of Mehitabel. Garden City, NY: Doubleday, Doran & Co., 1933.

Master of the Revels: A Comedy in Four Acts. Garden City, NY: Doubleday, Doran & Co., 1934.

Chapters for the Orthodox. Garden City, NY: Doubleday, Doran & Co., 1934.

Archy Does His Part. Garden City, NY: Doubleday, Doran & Co., 1935.

Sun Dial Time. Garden City, NY: Doubleday, Doran & Co., 1936.

Sons of the Puritans, edited by Christopher Morley. New York: Doubleday, Doran & Co., 1939.

The Lives and Times of Archy and Mehitabel. New York: Doubleday, Doran & Co., 1940. An omnibus edition comprising the three previous collections.

The Best of Don Marquis, edited by Christopher Morley. New York: Doubleday, Doran & Co., 1946.

The Lives and Times of Archy and Mehitabel. New York: Doubleday, Doran & Co., 1950. An omnibus edition comprising the three previous collections, with the addition of an introduction by E. B. White.

Archyology: The Long Lost Tales of Archy and Mehitabel,

edited by Jeff Adams. Hanover and London: University Press of New England, 1996.

Archyology II (The Final Dig): The Long Lost Tales of Archy and Mehitabel, edited by Jeff Adams. Hanover and London: University Press of New England, 1998.

BIOGRAPHICAL AND CRITICAL WORKS

This list omits articles and most books already cited in the endnotes to the Introduction.

Anthony, Edward. *O Rare Don Marquis*. New York: Doubleday, 1962.

Batteiger, John. www.donmarquis.com.

Lee, Lynn. *Don Marquis*. Boston: Twayne, 1981.

McCollum, William, Jr. *Selected Letters of Don Marquis*. Stafford, VA: Northwoods Press, 1982.

A Note on the Text
and Format of This Edition

This book is the first to present the adventures of Archy and Mehitabel in the order in which Don Marquis wrote them. Its extensive selection has been compiled from newspaper files rather than drawn from the text of a previous edition. To orient readers, the date of each poem's first publication appears at the top of the page—year on the left page, month and day on the right. Marquis compiled the original volumes without regard for chronology and omitted entries he considered too stale for reprinting. In an annotated edition, however, topicality is a gateway rather than a barrier, because the notes explain historical, cultural, and biographical allusions.

Few of these works bore any title in their newspaper incarnation except for the recurring subhead "A Communication from Archy," because the cockroach jostled for attention alongside other material. Even when collecting parts of a series, such as Archy's strike, Marquis disregarded their original order and retitled entries. At times he merged columns that originally appeared on different dates or separated those that originally appeared on the same date. When one of Archy's contributions included a title on its first appearance, it is retained here. For the majority, however, a chronological format demanded a new title for each work; to minimize editorial presumption, each consists of a word or phrase taken directly from the poem. Two poems have been slightly shortened. In the January 27, 1917 column, the ellipsis indicates the excision of a long-winded tangent. In the February 26, 1918 column, several more definitions of poetry have been omitted.

Readers familiar with the three collections published during Marquis's lifetime and the two small posthumous collections (see

"Suggestions for Further Reading") may notice some differences. The poem "Cleopatra," dated August 28, 1916, for example, includes several lines about religion that either Marquis or his editor excised for book publication in 1927.

ON CAPITAL LETTERS

Outside Archy's own text, the names Archy and Mehitabel, like all other proper names, are capitalized. Marquis himself capitalized them in his column. Archy specifically asked others to do so, as you can see in his August 2, 1922, postscript (reprinted here for the first time) to the poem about Warty Bliggens. Archy was by choice a free-verse, not a lower-case, poet; he did not incorporate his shortcomings as a typist into his artistic manifesto.

Titles are also capitalized herein. Marquis capitalized titles in the column because they weren't provided by Archy, and occasionally the title is even Marquis's reply to Archy's following remarks. On rare occasions, however, a capitalized word or a punctuation mark appeared in the original newspaper publication. Because upper-case typing was a physical impossibility for Archy, the editor has corrected these typesetter's errors (actually errors only in this context), as well as the rare obvious misprint, without comment. Some of Archy's communications to Marquis were signed *archy* or *archy the cockroach* and some were not; for consistency this edition omits his signature.

There has been no other editorial tinkering.

The Annotated Archy
and Mehitabel

ARCHY THE FREE-VERSE COCKROACH

On September 11, 1922 the *New York Tribune* ran a large illustration of Archy to welcome the famous cockroach— and his creator, Don Marquis—as they moved to the *Tribune* after years at the *Evening Sun* and the *Sun*. For Archy's outraged response to this portrayal, see the poem for September 18, 1922. *(Image courtesy of John Batteiger.)*

1916

MARCH 29

Expression Is the Need

THE SUN DIAL

The Query of the Hour

Justice Hughes,[1]
What are your views?

• • •

When Villa[2] is captured, they will take him to Washington and read to him all the laudatory remarks the members of the Wilson Administration made about him a couple of years ago and watch him laugh himself to death.

• • •

The Scarlet Fever germ is cross
And full of cranky notions,
And everywhere he takes his seat
He raises red emotions.

• • •

Dobbs Ferry possesses a rat which slips out of his lair at night and runs a typewriting machine in a garage. Unfortunately, he has always been interrupted by the watchman before he could produce a complete story.

It was at first thought that the power which made the typewriter run was a ghost, instead of a rat. It seems likely to us that it was both a ghost and a rat. Mme. Blavatsky's[3] ego went into a white horse after she passed over, and someone's personality has undoubtedly gone into this rat. It is an era of belief in communications from the spirit land—there is Patience Worth[4] and there is the author of the Letters of a Living Dead Man,[5] and there are many other prominent and well-thought of ghosts in touch with the physical world today—and all the other ghosts are becoming encouraged by the current attitude of credulity and are trying to get into the game, too.

• • •

We recommend the Dobbs Ferry rat to the Psychical Research Society. We do not pretend to know anything about the Dobbs Ferry rat at first hand. But since this matter has been reported in the public prints and seriously received, we are no longer afraid of being ridiculed, and we do not mind making a statement of something that happened to our own typewriter only a couple of weeks ago. We came into our room earlier than usual in the morning, and discovered a gigantic cockroach jumping about upon the keys.

• • •

He did not see us, and we watched him. He would climb painfully upon the framework of the machine and cast himself with all his force upon a key, head downward, and his weight and the impact of the blow were just sufficient to operate the machine, one slow letter after another. He could not work the capital letters, and he had a great deal of difficulty operating the mechanism that shifts the pages so that a fresh line may be started. We never saw a cockroach work so hard or perspire so freely in all our lives before. After about an hour of this frightfully difficult literary labor he fell to the floor exhausted, and we saw him creep feebly into a nest of the poems which are always there in profusion.

• • •

Congratulating ourself that we had left a sheet of paper in the machine the night before so that all this work had not been in vain, we made an examination, and this is what we found:

expression is the need of my soul
i was once a vers libre bard
but i died and my soul went into the body of a cockroach
it has given me a new outlook upon life
i see things from the under side now

thank you for the apple peelings in the wastepaper basket
but your paste is getting so stale i cant eat it
there is a cat here at night i wish you would have
removed she nearly ate me the other night why dont she
catch rats that is what she is supposed to be for
there is a rat here she should get without delay
most of these rats here are just rats
but this rat is like me he has a human soul in him
he used to be a poet himself
night after night i have written poetry for you
on your typewriter
and this big brute of a rat who used to be a poet
comes out of his hole when it is done
and reads it and sniffs at it
he is jealous of my poetry
he used to make fun of it when we were both human
he was a punk poet himself
and after he has read it he sneers
and then he eats it
i wish you would have that cat[6] kill that rat
or get a cat that is onto her job
and i will write you a series of poems
showing how things look
to a cockroach
that rats name used to be freddy
the next time freddy dies i hope he wont be a rat
but something smaller i hope i will be the rat
in the next transmigration and freddy the cockroach i
will teach him to sneer at my poetry then
dont you ever eat any sandwiches in your office
havent had a crumb of bread for i dont know how long
or a piece of ham or anything but apple parings
and paste leave a piece of paper in your machine
every night you can call me archy

• • •

We have left a piece of paper in our machine every night since,
as Archy requested. But up to date nothing has come of it. We
begin to fear that Freddy, his rival bard, has caught Archy un-
awares and eaten him. It is an interesting problem—and one we

refer to the transmigrationists—as to whether Freddy's personality would be influenced by Archy's after Freddy had eaten Archy.

But the whole thing, we must admit, has left an unpleasant impression on us. Are poets never to be at peace with one another? We will have to put the case of Freddy and Archy up to some of Hermione's friends.

DON MARQUIS

MARCH 31
Just Cockroaches

Archy, the *vers libre* cockroach, has been banging out copy on our typewriter again. When we came to work this morning we found the following poem:

i wish i had more human society
these other cockroaches here are just cockroaches
no human soul ever transmigrated into them
and any soul that would go into one of them
after giving them the once over
would be a pretty punk sort of a soul
you cant imagine how low down they are with no
esthetic sense and no imagination or anything like
that and they actually poke fun at me because I used to
be a poet before i died and my soul migrated into a
cockroach they are as crass and philistine as some
humans i could name their only thought is food but
there is a little red eyed spider lives behind your
steam radiator who has considerable sense
i dont think he is very honest though i dont know
whether he has anything human in him or is just
spider i was talking to him the other day and was
quite charmed with his conversation
after you he says pausing by the radiator
and i was about to step back of the radiator ahead
of him when something told me to watch my step

and i drew back just in time
to keep from walking into a web
there were some cockroach legs and wings
still sticking in that web
i beat it as quickly as i could up the wall
well well says that spider you are in quite a hurry archy
ha ha so you wont be at my dinner table today then
some other time cockroach some other time
i will be glad to welcome you to dinner archy
he is not to be trusted but he is the only insect
i have met for weeks that has any intelligence if you
will look back of that locker where you hang your
hat you will find a dime has rolled there i wish you
would get it and spend it for doughnuts a cent at a time
and leave the doughnuts under your typewriter i get tired
of apple peelings i nearly drowned in your ink well last
night dont forget the doughnuts

archy

We are trying to fix up some scheme whereby Archy can use
the shift keys and thus get control of the capital letters and
punctuation marks. Suggestions for a workable device will be
thankfully received. As it is Archy has to climb upon the
frame of the typewriter and jump with all his weight upon the
keys, a key at a time, and it is only by almost incredible exer-
tions that he is able to drag the paper forward so he can start
a new line.

APRIL 7
Something to Say

thank your friends for me for
all their good advice about how to
work your typewriter but what i have
always claimed is that manners and methods
are no great matter compared
with thoughts in poetry you cant hide

gems of thought so they wont flash
on the world on the other hand if you press
agent poor stuff that wont make it live
my ego will express itself in spite of
all mechanical obstacles having something
to say is the thing being sincere
counts for more than forms of expression thanks
for the doughnuts

April 10
Simplified Spelling

Archy, our cockroach into whose body has migrated the soul
of a poet, is thoroughly in sympathy with the efforts of the Sim-
plified Spelling Board.[1] As he has to jump on the keys of the
typewriter headfirst every time he makes a letter, the fewer the
letters the less toll for Archy. He tells us he was a rhymester too
before he took to *vers libre;* and we find on our machine to-day
the following expression of his sentiments:

the simplified speling bords stand
          4 the shorter and uglier word
they want the old fashund stuf cand
          joshbilingsgate[2] stuf is preferd

and i in the noshun rejoic
          it shud hav bin dun long b4
4 my ego in finding a voic
          is making my cranium sor

i find it a heluva strain
          2 butt[3] in2 yor colum by hek
and i think in the end that my brain
          wil telescope in2 my nek

in the small of my bak theres a kink
          and the rapid sukseshin of shocks

is putting my chin on the blink
    and merging my nees with my hocks

but the thing that most hurts me i swear
    is more than a fizical wo
tis the fact that the forid i wear
    is becuming uncomonly lo[4]

i wunc had a brow that was hi
    with the thots in it lofty and wide
but now it sags over my eye
    and theres nothing important in side

heres luk 2 the simplified bord
    may they finish the work theyve begun
my hart with that harts in akord
    my mind and thare minds r as 1

April 26
Hell

listen to me i have
been mobbed almost
theres an old simp[1] cockroach
here who thinks he has
been to hell and all
the young cockroaches make a
hero out of him and admire
him he sits and runs his front
feet through his long white
beard and tells the story one
day he says he crawled into a yawning
cavern and suddenly came on a
vast abyss full of whirling
smoke there was a light
at the bottom billows
and billows of yellow smoke

swirled up at him and
through the horrid gloom he
saw things with wings flying
and dropping and dying they veered
and fluttered like damned
spirits through that sulphurous mist

listen i says to him
old man youve never been to hell
at all there isn t any hell
transmigration is the game i
used to be a human vers libre
poet and i died and went
into a cockroach s body if
there was a hell id know
it wouldn t i you re
irreligious says the old simp
combing his whiskers excitedly

ancient one i says to him
while all those other
cockroaches gathered into a
ring around us what you
beheld was not hell all that
was natural some one was fumigating
a room and you blundered
into it through a crack
in the wall atheist he cries
and all those young
cockroaches cried atheist
and made for me if it
had not been for freddy
the rat i would now be
on my way once more i mean
killed as a cockroach and transmigrating
into something else well
that old whitebearded devil is
laying for me with his
gang he is jealous

because i took his glory away
from him dont ever tell me
insects are any more liberal
than humans

———

*Archy the cockroach has struck for a raise in salary—he says
he wants his stuff printed in minion or brevier, after this, instead
of in nonpareil type. We don't believe in encouraging rebellion.
One more murmur out of Archy and he goes into agate.*[3]

MAY 10
Freddy Is No More

listen to me there have
been some doings here since last
i wrote there has been a battle
behind that rusty typewriter cover
in the corner
you remember freddy the rat well
freddy is no more but
he died game the other
day a stranger with a lot of
legs came into our
little circle a tough looking kid
he was with a bad eye

who are you said a thousand legs
if i bite you once
said the stranger you won t ask
again he he little poison tongue said
the thousand legs who gave you hydrophobia
i got it by biting myself said
the stranger i m bad keep away
from me where i step a weed dies
if i was to walk on your forehead it would
raise measles and if
you give me any lip i ll do it

they mixed it then
and the thousand legs succumbed
well we found out this fellow
was a tarantula he had come up from
south america in a bunch of bananas
for days he bossed us life
was not worth living he would stand in
the middle of the floor and taunt
us ha ha he would say where i
step a weed dies do
you want any of my game i was
raised on red pepper and blood i am
so hot if you scratch me i will light
like a match you better
dodge me when i m feeling mean and
i don t feel any other way i was nursed
on a tabasco bottle if i was to slap
your wrist in kindness you
would boil over like job and heaven
help you if i get angry give me
room i feel a wicked spell coming on

last night he made a break at freddy
the rat keep your distance
little one said freddy i m not
feeling well myself somebody poisoned some
cheese for me im as full of
death as a drug store i
feel that i am going to die anyhow
come on little torpedo come on don t stop
to visit and search then they
went at it and both are no more please
throw a late edition on the floor i want to
keep up with china we dropped freddy
off the fire escape into the alley with
military honors

MAY 11
Up or Down the Scale[1]

there is a good deal
of metaphysical discussion going on
amongst my own little group here
i said freddy the rat was no
more he expired at the moment he
slew that tarantula well he had
once been a human and had
transmigrated into a rat just
as i had transmigrated into a
cockroach the question now
is where will freddy turn up next will
he go up or down the scale and
that has led to the further question as
to what is up and what is down
producing considerable dissension all the
spiders claim they are higher in
the scale than the cockroaches and that
lazy cat mehitabel[2] looks on superciliously
as if confident that she has it on
all of us spiritually speaking
well all i have to say is that in
my case a soul got out of a vers libre
bard into a cockroach but i have
known cases which are exactly the
reverse if you get what i mean
not that i would name any names

MAY 23
Raise in Salary

well this goes into
brevier instead of nonpareil
if you keep your promise thank

you for the raise in salary boss
but i find i have not
anything of great moment
to say[1] how often that
happens when a man becomes
conspicuous he has used all
his best stuff winning fame in
small type or some other
inconspicuous way and in
poverty and obscurity has put his
soul into his work suddenly fame
and success come and he gets promoted
to big type on account of his
merits and lo and behold his
great thoughts desert him thank you
for the raise i hope the common fate
will not overtake me boss i will
strive to deserve the raise
hereafter

MAY 29
An Easy Mark

listen to me that
fellow who was in to see
you the other day bulling you
about your stuff
is no true friend you got
so proud of yourself on
account of what he
said you gave him a copy
of your book and
autographed it for him i thought
he was a shine so
i hopped into the
cuff of his trousers and
went out with him

he sold that book for
ten cents at a second
hand place and
treated himself to a
drink on the river front
he cursed because if
you had not written your name
in the book he might
have got fifteen cents for
it he said you are an
easy mark

MAY 30
Grind Down the Laboring Man

well i note you
put me back into nonpareil
again monday after raising me
to brevier all right boss
all right grind down
the laboring man there will come
a day of reckoning i don't have
to do this you know as far
as the food is concerned that
you have been giving me i lived before
i ever got into your column must close now
as mehitabel the cat is
scratching her claws against
the desk in a meaning sort of way
yours hastily

JUNE 8
Just for This, You Go in Agate, Archy

see here boss i am no kicker nor
growler nor do i want more than is coming
to me but after raising me to brevier one
day you slammed me back into nonpareil
again what i want to know is this if you
think the stuff is rotten why do you
use it at all and if you think it is o k
why not give it a show here i am
trying to build up a public for
myself and you too and look at the
appreciation i get all right boss all right
but i warn you that you are queering your
own game i dont ask for brevier this time
but you might at least give me minion if
i make good in minion then raise me think
it over boss think it over i am making no
threats of quitting but you think it over

JUNE 17
Desk All Cleaned Up

well boss now youve got
your desk all cleaned up for the
first time since ive known you what
am i going to do for
a safe retreat in times of dire
need formerly i could crawl under a
bushel of poems and mehitabel the
cat could not find me this
room is as bare as the inside of
a drum you might at
least have left me a tobacco can i

feel as visible as a hyphen and not
half so sure of myself

JUNE 19
Capitals

I THOUGHT THAT SOME HISTORIC DAY
SHIFT KEYS WOULD LOCK IN SUCH A WAY
THAT MY POETIC FEET WOULD FALL
UPON EACH CLICKING CAPITAL
AND NOW FROM KEY TO KEY I CLIMB
TO WRITE MY GRATITUDE IN RHYME
YOU LITTLE KNOW WITH WHAT DELIGHT
THROUGHOUT THE LONG AND LONELY NIGHT
I'VE KICKED AND BUTTED (FOOT AND BEAN)
AGAINST THE KEYS OF YOUR MACHINE
TO TELL THE MOVING TALE OF ALL
THAT TO A COCKROACH MAY BEFALL
INDEED IF I COULD NOT HAVE HAD
SUCH OCCUPATION I'D BE MAD
AH FOR A SOUL LIKE MINE TO DWELL
WITHIN A COCKROACH THAT IS HELL
TO SCURRY FROM THE PLAYFUL CAT
TO DODGE THE INSECT EATING RAT
THE HUNGRY SPIDER TO EVADE
THE MOUSE THAT %) ?)) " " " $$$ ((gee boss
what a jolt that cat mehitabel made
a jump for me
i got away but she unlocked the shift key
it kicked me right into the
mechanism where she
couldn t reach me it
was nearly the death of little
archy that kick spurned me right
out of parnassus[1] back into
the vers libre slums i lay

in behind the wires for an hour after
she left before i dared to get
out and finish i hate
cats say boss please lock the shift
key tight some night
i would like to tell the story of
my life all in capital
letters

JUNE 28
Why Not Commit Suicide

well boss from time
to time i just simply
get bored with having
to be a cockroach my
soul my real ego if
you get what i mean is
tired of being shut
up in an insects body the
best you can say for it is that it
is unusual and you could
say as much for mumps so
while feeling gloomy the
other night the thought came
to me why not
go on to the next stage as
soon as possible why not
commit suicide[1] and
maybe be reincarnated in
some higher form of life why
not be the captain of my
soul the master of my fate and
the more i pondered over it the
more i was attracted to
the notion well boss you would
be surprised to find

out how hard it is for a
cockroach to commit suicide unless
you have been one
and tried it of course i
could let mehitabel the
cat damage me and die that
way but all my finer sensibilities
revolt at the idea i jumped out
the fourth story window and
a wind caught me and blew
me into the eighth story i
tried to hang myself with a
thread and i am so light i
just swung back and forth and
didnt even choke myself shooting
is out of the question and poison
is not within
my reach i might drown myself
in the ink well but if
you ever got a mouthful of it you
would know it was a
thing no refined person could go
on with boss i am going to
end it all before long and i
want to go easy have you
any suggestion yours
for transmigration

JULY 12
Writing All By Itself

whoever owns the typewriter
that this is sticking in will confer
a favor by mailing it to
mister marquis
well boss i am somewhere in long
island and i know now how

it got its name i
started out to find the
place you are commuting from and
after considerable trouble and being for some
days on the way i have lost myself but
at twilight last evening i
happened to glance towards a lighted
window in a house near the railway and
i saw a young woman writing on a typewriter i
waited until the light was out and crawled
up the side of the house and through a
hole in the screen fortunately there was a
piece of paper in the machine it was my only
chance to communicate with you and ask
you to hurry a relief party when
the house got quiet i began to write
the foregoing a moment ago i was
interrupted by a woman s voice what
was that noise she said nothing at all
said a man s voice you are always
hearing things at night but it
sounded as if my typewriter were clicking she
insisted go to sleep said he then
i clicked it some more henry get up she said
there s some one in the house a moment
later the light was turned on and
they both stood in the doorway of the room now
are you satisfied he said you
see there is no one in here at
all i was hiding in the shadow under the
keys they went back into
their bed room and i began to write
the foregoing lines
henry henry she said do you hear that
i do he says it is nothing but the
house cooling off it always cracks that way
cooling off nothing she said not a
hot night like this then said henry it
is cracking with the heat i tell you

she said that is the typewriter clicking well
he said you saw for yourself the room was
empty and the door was locked it can t
be the typewriter to prove it to you
i will bring it in here he did so the
machine was set down
in the moonlight which came in one of
the windows with the key side in the
shadow there he said look at it and see
for yourself it is not being operated by any one
just then i began to write the foregoing
lines hopping from key
to key in the shadow and being anxious
to finish my
god my god cried henry losing his nerve
the machine is writing all by itself it
is a ghost and threw himself face
downward on the bed and hid his face in the
pillow and kept on saying my god my
god it is a ghost and the woman screamed
and said it is
tom higginbotham s ghost that s whose ghost
it is oh i know whose
ghost it is my conscience tells me i
jilted him when we were studying
stenography together
at the business college and he went into
a decline and died and i have always
known in my heart that he
died of unrequited love o what a
wicked girl i was and he has come
back to haunt me
i have brought a curse upon you henry chase
him away says henry trembling so the bed
shook chase him away mable you coward you
chase him away yourself says mable and both
lay and recriminated and recriminated
with their heads under the covers hot
night though it was while i wrote

the foregoing lines but after
a while it came out henry had a
stenographer on his conscience too and
they got into a row and got so
mad they forgot to be scared i will
close now this house is easily seen from the
railroad station and the woman sits in
the window and writes i will be behind the waste
paper receptacle outside the station door
come and get me i am foot sore and weary
they are still quarreling as i
close i can do no less than
say thank you mable and henry in
advance for mailing this

JULY 25
We Rushed Forward and Swatted

We are something of a fly-swatter.[1] We took it up seriously as a
duty some weeks ago; later it became a pleasure; now it is a
habit.

All the flies have long since been slain in the house in which
we live, all the flies that used to loaf around the front porch
have been slain; we have even killed the flies in the garage,
where the lawn mower is kept.

•   •   •

By the time the flies began to disappear, fly-swatting had be-
come a sport with us. Others develop their golf and their tennis
and all that sort of thing, but we rejoiced in our skill as a fly-
swatter. We got so that we scorned to kill a fly sitting; we would
take him as he went humming and whirling through the air.
Flies began to give out, and at night we would go out after light-
ning bugs. The necessity to swat something grew upon us; it be-
came a sort of monomania. The joy of swatting vanished, so
that we no longer felt happy when we swatted, but we felt un-
happy if we were not swatting.

•   •   •

We were sitting on the veranda on Sunday wishing that a fly or insect of some sort would come along and grieving for new insects to conquer when we saw coming up the gravelled drive-way, which reaches all the way from the garage to the hold in which they are going to put gas pipes some day, an insect. Our heart bounded with the passion of the chase. A speckled hen of a phlegmatic disposition cut her eye at him as he went by; she strolled along after him for two or three yards; we thought every moment that she would make a dash at him and we would be robbed of our prey. But perhaps she was too lazy; perhaps she recognized him as belonging to a species that she had eaten of before and found to disagree with her; at any rate she let him go by unscathed.

· · ·

The insect moved as if he had sore feet. We are no entomologist; we can't tell a rod away what brand an insect belongs to, except in a very rough, general sort of fashion. But this varmint was brown, and it was easy to see that he was sad. He moved gingerly, he came along cater-cornered, like a lame pup; we could not see his face; his head hung down dejectedly. Evidently he was an insect who had just suffered some discouraging experience. This, no doubt, should have moved us to pity. But when the mania for swatting grips a man he forgets pity. We rushed forward and swatted.

· · ·

He died, and as he was dying we recognized him. He strove to speak, his lips moved feebly: we hope that they moved with a murmur of forgiveness, for it was Archy.[2]

· · ·

We buried him among the roots of a rosebush. It would scarcely be in good taste to express our grief publicly—unless we did it in verse. And we do not feel like verse today. Some people may be able to hic jacet one of their best friends and then go about their business as usual, talking of it the while, but these things cut deeper with us. He had come out to see us; it had taken him weeks to make the trip; weeks of toil and trouble and even danger, and just as he was crawling to our feet we slew him.

· · ·

We buried him in a little golden casket that used to be the case
of a safety razor; no marauding chicken there idly scratching
there shall find and desecrate his remains.

AUGUST 2

My Naked Soul

> well boss here i
> am a cockroach still boss
> i have often been disgusted
> with life but now i am
> even more disgusted
> with death and transmigration i
> would rather not inhabit
> any body at all than
> inhabit a cockroachs
> body but it seems i
> cant escape it that
> is my destiny my doom my
> punishment
> when you struck me that
> terrific blow a few
> days ago and i
> died there at
> your feet my first
> sensation was one of glad
> relief what body will
> the soul of archy transmigrate
> into now i asked
> myself will i go
> higher in the scale of
> life and inhabit the
> body of a butterfly
> or a dog or a
> bird or will i sink
> lower and go into the

carcase of a poison
spider or a politician
i sat on a blade of
grass and waited and wondered
what it would be i
hoped it wouldnt be
anything at all too soon
because if you remember
it was a hot
day and as i sat
on that blade of grass
in my naked soul and
let my feet hang over i
was deliciously
cool try it some of
these hot nights leave
your body in the
bed and go up on the
roof in your
spirit and float around
like a toy balloon its
great stuff well while
i was sitting there
thinking what i
would inhabit next if
it was up to me
personally i had
a swooning sensation
and when i came
to i was in the
flesh again dad gum
it i lifted first
one leg and then
another to see what i
was this time and
imagine my chagrin and
disappointment when i
found myself inside

another cockroach the
exact counterpart of the
one you smashed whats
the use of dying if
it dont get you
anywhere i was so
sore i went and
murdered a tumblebug i
suppose as a cockroach
i was not good enough
to be promoted
and not bad enough to
be set back boss a
thing like that makes a
fellow feel awful humble i
came back to town in
that special delivery letter i
would rather dodge
the thing
they cancel stamps with
all day than walk again
say boss
please thank my friends
for all the kind
words and flowers i
must close in haste there
is a new rat
in your office since i
was here last i
wish you would sprinkle a
little cereal in the
bottom of the waste paper
basket

AUGUST 5

AUGUST 4
On My Recent Demise

ive been looking at
some of the letters
received on my recent demise
they reconcile me
to my fetters
i am typing with tears
in my eyes
it is worth an
occasional parting
even death at the hand
of a friend
to return and find
hearts that are smarting
at the thought
of ones untimely end

AUGUST 5
Ballade of the Under Side

by archy

the roach that scurries
skips and runs
may read far more than those
that fly
i know what family skeletons
within your closets
swing and dry
not that i ever
play the spy
but as in corners
dim i bide

i can t dodge knowledge
though i try
i see things from
the under side

the lordly ones the
haughty ones
with supercilious
heads held high
the up stage stiff
pretentious guns
miss much that meets
my humbler eye
not that i meddle
perk or pry
but i m too small
to feel great pride
and as the pompous world
goes by
i see things from
the under side

above me wheel
the stars and suns
but humans shut
me from the sky
you see their eyes as pure
as nuns
i see their wayward
feet and sly
i own and own it with
a sigh
my point of view
is somewhat wried[1]
i am a pessimistic
guy
i see things from the
under side

l envoi[2]
prince ere you pull a bluff
and lie
before you fake
and play the snide
consider whether
archy s nigh
i see things from
the under side

AUGUST 12
Aeroplane[1]

well boss i have had
some experiences you know that
fellow with the teeth that glitter
and the eyes that glitter who
comes in to see you and
who has been talking about his aeroplane
for six months you thought he
was always a liar and
so did i he is the kind of a liar who
looks so much like a liar no one
believes him when he tells the
truth i thought i would call
his bluff so i crawled into
his outside breast pocket the other day
and went out to a place near mineola
with him he really has an aeroplane he
went up in it the next morning and
i went along boss i must have
picked out the wrong position i sat
on top of one of the planes thinking i would see
more of the country boss
dont ask me for any sensations the
only thing i felt was wind i felt

like a sigh in a cyclone i had
about as much control of myself as a
bullet that is going through the
barrel of an airgun i dont want
to rub anything in boss but it
was as hard to hang onto as the water
wagon² which is a simile
you may be able to appreciate i
dug all my feet and claws
and teeth in but the wind rushed by
me like a church scandal going
through a little village i would have
felt nausea if
my stomach hadnt been scared to death
it was only a question of time before i
would let loose thank heaven i thought i am
not an elephant i didnt
want to die again so soon just because
i can come to life again is
no reason for overworking a good thing too
many deaths and transmigrations look
vulgar and ostentatious
and when i did let go i must have
been two miles high around and
around i spun whirling like a flake of
soot that has been flipped
off of a devils wing between the
worlds and is spinning back home to
hell and beneath me it looked
like hell there was a vast expanse of water
with the sun making it
seem like melted metal i suppose i said
i will get all my feet wet now and
take my death of cold if a fish
dont eat me and just then i saw
beneath me a great fish grinning as if
he had heard a joke on the
bottom of the sea and come up to
laugh at the cosmos get that

cosmic stuff boss it goes great in some
circles i lit on one of his great white teeth
and waited for the gulp that should land
me in his interior department oh
lord i said if i ever see dry land i
will never mock at that jonah story[3]
again i dont want to die in
midocean and be reincarnated as a
sardine or as an oyster
a cockroach isnt much but
he has a look in in society where
an oyster is never mentioned except as an
article of food but if it
must be it must be kismet and karma and
that bunch of bullies vote us the way they
please we are only instructed delegates
in the universal convention every
time i die it makes me more of a fatalist and
i waited for him to gulp but
he didnt gulp i hopped over to
the next tooth to the right as you go in
and investigated and finally climbed
out where his upper lip would have been if he had
had one and worked up to his eye it was
glassy in death i was floating on a dead shark
and it was all the more unpleasant
because he had not had any dental work done for a
long time or else he had adenoids or maybe
he had died of ptomaine poisoning boss what i am
delicately trying to convey is
that he had been dead so long he had a right to
be ashamed of it just then i
heard human voices and looking around i saw
two young men in bathing suits and
a motor boat a shark a shark cried one
of them put her about the motor is still
busted said the other row row for your
life but wait said the first one this
shark seems deceased bill lets haul him to land

and say we slew him right o tom says
bill it will make a hit with all the girls he
attacked us says tom and i jumped into the water and
cut his throat with my jackknife you
did eh says bill what was i doing then put two
slashes into him which they did one for each and
fastened him to the stern of their boat with a
line and as they towed him to the beach with
me sitting listening they fixed
up an awful lie talk about ovations boss when they
came to the beach they got one the
more i see of human nature the less i know
whether to despise it for being so easily
gulled or for being so ready to
gull by the time they had told
that story eight times each believed that
he was telling the truth although he
still thought maybe the other one was lying well
i left those two heroes
surrounded six deep by girls and came to
town in a little bunch of dress goods samples a
commuters wife has been trying to make
him remember to match my
sympathies being with the shark poor feeble old
thing he had likely perished of old age
to be killed a second time is hard luck but
this is the truth of a story that you
may read another version of in
the news columns

AUGUST 17
Back to the Starting Point

i see where one
of your correspondents asks how
does archy get the carriage on his
typewriter back to the

starting point again when he
wants to begin a new
line i release the spring
with my left hind
leg and butt the thing over
with my head yes i am bald but my
baldness is on the outside
of my head not on the inside
like some i could name

AUGUST 18
Lightning Bug

a lightning bug got
in here the other night a
regular hick from
the real country he was
awful proud of himself you
city insects may think
you are some punkins
but i don t see any
of you flashing in the dark
like we do in
the country all right go
to it says i mehitabel the
cat and that green
spider who lives in your locker
and two or three cockroach
friends of mine and a
friendly rat all gathered
around him and urged him on
and he lightened and
lightened and lightened you
don t see anything like this
in town often he says go to it
we told him it s a
real treat to us and

```
we nicknamed him broadway
which pleased him
this is the life
he said all i
need is a harbor
under me to be a
statue of liberty and
he got so vain of
himself i had to take
him down a peg you ve
made lightning for two hours
little bug i told him
but i don t hear
any claps of thunder
yet there are some men
like that when he wore
himself out mehitabel
the cat ate him
```

AUGUST 23
The Next Line

"I don't want to appear inquisitive," says D. S. H., "nor do I wish to embarrass archy, but as a sincere friend and a true admirer and in the cause of science I wish to learn how archy gets the roll turned for the next line? This would appear too much of a task for a being that is bald headed on the outside, even. Can it be that he has a harness rigged up for mehitabel and hitches her to the ratchet and she turns the—a—a—shall I call it trick? That would be a reasonable excuse for having that infernal cat around."

He braces his head against the frame of the machine, puts his hind legs against the cogwheel and kicks the thing til he hears it click into the next notch.

DON MARQUIS

AUGUST 25
Be Beautiful

well boss did it
ever strike you that a
hen regrets it just as
much when they wring her
neck as an oriole but
nobody has any
sympathy for a hen because
she is not beautiful
while every one gets
sentimental over the
oriole and says how
shocking to kill the
lovely thing this thought
comes to my mind
because of the earnest
endeavor of a
gentleman to squash me
yesterday afternoon when i
was riding up in the
elevator if i had been a
butterfly he would have
said how did that
beautiful thing happen to
find its way into
these grimy city streets do
not harm the splendid
creature but let it
fly back to its rural
haunts again beauty always
gets the best of
it be beautiful boss
a thing of beauty is a
joy forever
be handsome boss and let

who will be clever is
the sad advice
of your ugly little friend

AUGUST 28
Cleopatra

boss i am disappointed in
some of your readers they
are always asking how does archy
work the shift so as to get a
new line or how does archy
do this or do that they
are always interested in technical
details[1] when the main question is
whether the stuff is
literature or not what difference does it
make how a thing is
produced the thought
content is the thing the koran was written
on the white bones of dead
sheep picked up by mahomet in the desert
so i have heard but
some of it is great stuff in spite
of that so i have heard from a little
hot footed spider that came
over from smyrna in a crate of figs i
met him down on the water front but
i don't take much stock in his religion after
you have migrated a few times all
religions get to looking
alike to you i get a slant
at them from an angle
not possible to many which
reminds me i wish you would leave that new
book of george moores[2] on the floor

mehitabel the cat and i want to
read it i have discovered that
mehitabels soul formerly inhabited a human also at
least that is what mehitabel is
claiming these days it may
be she got jealous of my prestige anyhow
she and i have been talking it over in a
friendly way who were you
mehitabel i asked her i was
cleopatra[3] once she said well i said i
suppose you lived in a palace you bet she
said and what lovely fish dinners we used to
have and licked her chops mehitabel would sell
her soul for a plate of fish any
day i told her i thought you were
going to say you were the favorite wife of
the emperor valerian[4]
he was some cat nip eh mehitabel but
she did not get me

SEPTEMBER 1
The Queens I Have Been

mehitabel the cat claims that
she has a human soul
also and has transmigrated
from body to body and it
may be so boss you
remember i told you she accused
herself of being cleopatra once i
asked her about antony[1]

anthony who she asked me are
you thinking of that
song about rowley and gammon and
spinach heigho for anthony rowley[2]

no i said mark antony the
great roman the friend of
caesar surely cleopatra you
remember j caesar[3]

listen archy she said i
have been so many different
people in my time and met
so many prominent gentlemen i
wont lie to you or stall i
do get my dates mixed sometimes
think of how much i have had a
chance to forget and i have
always made a point of not
carrying grudges over
from one life to the next archy

i have been
used something fierce in my time but
i am no bum sport archy
i am a free spirit archy i
look on myself as being
quite a romantic character oh the
queens i have been and the
swell feeds i have ate
a cockroach which you are
and a poet which you used to be
archy couldn t understand
my feelings at having come
down to this i have
had bids to elegant feeds where poets
and cockroaches would
neither one be mentioned without a
laugh archy i have had
adventures but i
have never been an adventuress
one life up and the next life
down archy but always a lady
through it all and a

good mixer too always the
life of the party archy but never
anything vulgar always free footed
archy never tied down to
a job or housework yes looking
back on it all i can say is
i had some romantic
lives and some elegant times i
have seen better days archy but
whats the use of kicking kid its
all in the game like a gentleman
friend of mine used to say
toujours gai kid toujours gai he
was an elegant cat he used
to be a poet himself and he made up
some elegant poetry about me and him

lets hear it i said and
mehitabel recited

persian pussy from over the sea
demure and lazy and smug and fat
none of your ribbons and bells for me
ours is the zest of the alley cat

over the roofs from flat to flat
we prance with capers corybantic
what though a boot should break a slat
mehitabel us for the life romantic

we would rather be rowdy and gaunt and free
and dine on a diet of roach and rat

roach i said what do you
mean roach interrupting mehitabel
yes roach she said thats the
way my boy friend made it up
i climbed in amongst the typewriter
keys for she had an excited

look in her eyes go on mehitabel i
said feeling safer and she
resumed her elocution

we would rather be rowdy and gaunt and free
and dine on a diet of roach and rat
than slaves to a tame society
ours is the zest of the alley cat
fish heads freedom a frozen sprat
dug from the gutter with digits frantic
is better than bores and a fireside mat
mehitabel us for the life romantic

when the pendant moon in the leafless tree
clings and sways like a golden bat
i sing its light and my love for thee
ours is the zest of the alley cat
missiles around us fall rat a tat tat
but our shadows leap in a ribald antic
as over the fences the world cries scat
mehitabel us for the life romantic

persian princess i dont care that
for your pedigree traced by scribes pedantic
ours is the zest of the alley cat
mehitabel us for the life romantic

aint that high brow stuff
archy i always remembered it
but he was an elegant gent
even if he was a highbrow and a
regular bohemian archy him and
me went aboard a canal boat
one day and he got his head into
a pitcher of cream and couldn t get
it out and fell overboard
he come up once before he
drowned toujours gai kid he
gurgled and then sank for ever that

was always his words archy toujours
gai kid toujours gai i
have known some swell gents
in my time dearie but i canned her
off or she would be going
yet

September 4
Unpunctuated Gink

say boss i had
a great idea last night i thought
if i could operate a
typewriter why not a
linotype machine[1] i went down into
the composing room
and started to hop from key to key
and a guy said to me wheres
your union card
get out of here or you will get
into the paper
in a way you dont like you will
get a nice hot bath
in that little pot of type metal do
you get me you may con the editorial
staff but no unpunctuated
gink can sling his joshbillingsgate
around here see
raus or i will spread you on
the minutes and not charge
any overtime for it
either so i came away

SEPTEMBER 6
Butting These Keys with My Head

say boss its a good
thing for you
that you dont pay me any wages for
the stuff i write
for you if you did
i would have to have them raised all
these strikes are getting
me feverish and excited one of
my long pieces in your column
often costs me twelve or
fifteen hours of steady
labor and i am drowsy
all the next day butting these
keys with my head is no snap boss
anything i got for it would
be underpaying me i wish you would
buy a pear and leave it under the
metal typewriter case where the rats
cant get to it

SEPTEMBER 8
Drunken Hornet

well boss i had a
great example of the corrupting
influence of the great
city brought to my notice recently a
drunken hornet blew in here
the other day and sat down in the
corner and dozed and buzzed not a
real sleep you know one of those wakeful
liquor trances with the
fuzzy talk oozing out of it to hear

this guy mumble in his dreams he was right
wicked my name he says is crusty bill
i never been licked and i never will and
then he would go half way asleep
again nobody around here wanted to
fight him and after a while he got
sober enough to know how drunk he had
been and began to cry over it and get
sentimental about himself mine is a wasted
life he says but i had a good
start red liquor ruined me he says and
sobbed tell me your story i
said two years ago he said i was a country
hornet young and strong and handsome i
lived in a rusty rainspout with my
parents and brothers and sisters and all was
innocent and merry often in that happy
pastoral life would we swoop down
with joyous laughter and sting the school
children on the village green but on an evil
day alas i came to the city in a crate
of peaches i found myself in a market
near the water front alone and friendless in the
great city its ways were strange to
me food seemed inaccessible i thought
that i might starve to death as i was buzzing
down the street thinking these gloomy
thoughts i met another hornet
just outside a speak easy[1] kid he says
you look down in the mouth forget
it kid i will show you how to live without
working how i says watch me he says just
then a drunken fly came crawling out
of the bar room in a leisurely way my new
found friend stung dissected and consumed that fly
that s the way he says smacking his lips
this is the life that was a beer fly
wait and i will get you a cocktail fly this
is the life i took up that life alas the

flies around a bar room get so drunk drinking
what is spilled that they are helpless all a
hornet has to do is wait calmly until
they come staggering out and there is his
living ready made for him at first being
young and innocent i ate only beer flies but
the curse of drink got me the mad life began
to tell upon me i got so i would not eat a
fly that was not full of some strong and heady
liquor the lights and life got me i would
not eat fruits and vegetables any more i scorned
flies from a soda fountain
they seemed flat and insipid to me
finally i got so wicked that i
went back to the country and got six innocent
young hornets and brought them back
to the city with me i started them in the
business i debauched them and
they caught my flies for me now i am in
an awful situation my six hornets from the
country have struck and set up on their own
hook i have to catch my flies myself
and my months of idleness and
dissipation have spoiled my technique i
can t catch a fly now unless he is dead drunk
what is to become of me alas the curse
of alcoholic beverages especially with each
meal well i said it is a sad story
bill and of a sort only too
common in this day of ours it is he says i
have the gout in my stinger so bad
that i scream with pain every time i spear
a fly i got into a safe place on the
inside of the typewriter and yelled out at him
my advice is suicide bill all the time
he had been pitying himself my sympathy had
been with the flies

September 12
Cheer Up Cheer Up

i can t see for the
life of me what there is
about crickets that makes people
call them jolly they
are the parrots of the insect race
crying cheer up cheer up
cheer up over and
over again till you want to
swat them i hate one of these
grinning skipping smirking
senseless optimists worse
than i do a cynic or a
pessimist there was
one in here the other day i was
feeling pretty well
and pleased with the world when
he started that confounded
cheer up cheer up cheer up stuff
fellow i said i am
cheerful enough or i was till
a minute ago but you
get on my nerves it s all right
to be bright and merry
but what s the use
pretending you have more
cheerfulness than there is in the
world you sound
insincere to me you insist on
it too much you make
me want to sit in
a tomb and listen to the
screech owls telling
ghost stories to the tree toads i
would rather that i heard a door squeak have

you only one record the sun
shone in my soul today before
you came and you
have made me think of the
world s woe groan
once or i will go mad your
voice floats around the world like
the ghost of a man
who laughed himself to death
listening to funny stories
the boss told i listen to you
and know why shakespeare
killed off mercutio so
early in the play it is only
hamlet that can
find material for five acts
cheer up cheer up cheer up he
says bo i told him i
wish i was the
woolworth tower i would fall
on you cheer up cheer up cheer
up he says again

SEPTEMBER 13
White Powder

boss i dont want to
be importunate or nag you or
anything like that but
working nights and sleeping by day as
much as i do i dont get
time to hustle up any
grub for myself wont
you please leave
something behind the radiator it has
been three days since i ate i might
have dined on an apple core last night

but there was white powder
sprinkled near it and over it i
have my enemies boss a little scrap of
dried beef would be appreciated

SEPTEMBER 16
My Ultimatum

boss this is my
ultimatum unless you have
made arrangements
for more regular meals for
me by monday
september 18 i will
quit you cold and go out and
live in a
swiss chess i have nothing
to arbitrate

SEPTEMBER 18
Swiss Cheese

thank you boss for the
swiss cheese i hardly hoped
for a whole one i
took up quarters in it at once
the little galleries and caves and
runways appealed to
my sense of adventure after
i had made a square
meal i lay down in the inner
chamber for a nap feeling
safe i had hardly composed my limbs
for slumber when i heard
a gnawing sound and squeaks

of glee cautiously i
approached the north gallery a mouse
was there i hastily
retreated thinking i would make
my escape by way of one of the
windows on the south facade another
mouse was there the citadel
in short was attacked on all sides mice
mice mice coming nearer and nearer
their cold blooded squeaks and the champing
of their cruel teeth made the night
hideous minute after minute i lay
in the stokehold
until the slow minutes grew into
intolerable hours of agony great drops
of perspiration broke through the callous
on my brow i prayed for
dawn or the night watchman suddenly
into my retreat protruded a whisker it
was so near it tickled me closer and
closer it came it twitched i knew
that it had felt me a moment more and
all would be over just as
i prepared myself for another
transmigration mehitabel the cat
bounded into the room and i was saved
if you get me another cheese please
put a wire cage over it

SEPTEMBER 19
Katydid

boss is it not awful
the way some female
creatures mistake ordinary
politeness for sudden
adoration

i met a katydid in a
beef stew in ann
street the other evening her
foot slipped and she
was about to sink
forever when i pushed her a
toothpick since i
rescued her the poor silly
thing follows me about
day and night i always felt
my fate would be a
poet she says to me how lovely
to be rescued by one i
am musical myself my
nature is sensitive to it so
much so that for
months i dwelt in a grand
piano in carnegie hall i
hope you don t think
i am bold no i said you
seem timid to me you
seem to lack courage entirely the
way you dog my footsteps
one would think you
were afraid to be alone i do
not wish any one any
ill luck but if
this shrinking thing got
caught in a high wind and
was blown out to
open sea i hope she would
be saved by a ship
outward bound for
madagascar

SEPTEMBER 21
Suicide Club, Part 1

boss i ran onto a queer bunch
in the back room of a saloon on william street
the other night there were six of them
two cockroaches
a grass hopper
a flea
and two crickets
they have what they call a suicide club
not the sort our old
friend r l s[1] made famous
the members of which intend to kill
themselves but each member of this
club has committed suicide already
they were once humans
as i was myself
at least i was a poet
after they killed themselves their souls
transmigrated into the bodies
of the insects mentioned
and so they have got together and
formed a club the other night the grass
hopper told why he had killed himself
it was a misunderstanding
with one i loved he said
which impelled me to the rash act
she and i were walking down a country
road and i got some gravel in one
of my shoes shortly afterward we
boarded a trolley car would you
mind i asked her if i took my shoe off
and shook out the gravel
help yourself she said
just as i got my shoe off we passed
a glue factory

i hastily put the shoe on again by the
time it was on again we were well past
the glue factory
the period during which the shoe was off
and the period during which we
were passing the glue factory exactly
synchronized
she did not see the glue factory
and refused to believe there had been
one in the neighborhood i could
never explain a month later
i killed myself tough luck
old top said the flea i will now
tell you why i took the fatal
plunge to be continued

SEPTEMBER 22
Suicide Club, Part 2

continued from thursdays
paper yes said the flea i will
tell you how it was i
committed suicide and transmigrated
into the body of an insect i was
the india rubber man in a circus side
show and fell in love with a
pair of beautiful siamese twins
public opinion was against
me marrying both of them
although both of them loved me as i
loved them both you
must choose between them said the
manager what god has joined together
let no man put asunder i said but
public opinion was too much for me
but the surgical operation which

severed them changed their
dispositions you cant fool with
a freak without running some such
risk when they were cut apart one of
them eloped with the surgeon
who had done the work and the other
married an interne in the
hospital they had a double
wedding and i slew myself that night
well said one of the crickets i will
now tell you how i shuffled off
this mortal coil and
transmigrated into the
body of a cricket and became a member
of this suicide club to be
continued

SEPTEMBER 23
Suicide Club, Part 3

continued from yesterdays
paper yes said the first cricket i
will tell you how it was i
committed suicide and
my soul transmigrated into the
body of an insect and i became a
member of this has been club my father
belonged to a religious sect which
forbids shaving and i was
brought up in that way no
razor ever touched my face when i was
forty years old i had a beard that hung
down to my knees it was red and
glossy i went around the country
posing as a doctor for a medicine
company hitting the tank towns in a
wagon and giving a spiel and

playing on the banjo i did well as
my beard attracted
crowds and was happy and
prosperous until one day a
malignant old man who
had just bought six bottles of tonic[1]
for five dollars made of roots herbs
and natures own remedies
containing no
mineral ingredients and brewed from
juniper leaves hazel roots choke
cherries and the bark of the
wild cohosh exactly
as the indians made it for a
thousands years
in the unpathed forests before the
pale face came said to me mister
can i ask you a question yes i
said i have nothing to conceal i am on
the level if one wine glass full before
meals does not give you an appetite
take two or three
mister he says the question is
personal go ahead i says i am the
seventh son
of a seventh son a soothsayer and a
seer i can tell by the way
you chew tobacco you have liver
trouble i will make a
special price to you fourteen
bottles for ten dollars cash no he said
it is about your beard it grew i told
him through using this medicine
my chin was bald at
birth it is a specific for erysipelas
botts neuralgia stomach trouble loss
of appetite hearts disease dandruff and
falling hair thirty bottles to you
for twenty dollars and i will throw

in an electric belt
mister he said i only want to ask
you if you sleep
with all your beard outside
of the covers or
under the covers when you go to
bed at night and he give me an evil
grin and went on i
never thought of it
before i had just gone to bed and slept
as a rule but that night when i
climbed into bed i thought of the old
mans question i spread all my
beard outside of the covers and it
was immediately apparent to me
that i did not have the habit of
sleeping with it that way then i put it
under the covers and was
no less certain that i did not
sleep with it that way i worried
about it till morning and each way i
put it seemed at
once to be the wrong way
the next night it was the same
thing i could not keep from
thinking about it i got no sleep at all
and became the mere shadow of my
former self it so preyed upon me
that at last i saw i must either
shave off the beard or end it all but i
could not shave off the beard
without deserting the religious principles
instilled into me by my father and so i
took the fatal plunge hard lines said
the second cricket i will
now relate the circumstances which
led up to my suicide to be
continued

SEPTEMBER 26
Suicide Club, Part 4

continued from last
saturdays paper well said the
second cricket the way i happened to
commit suicide and undergo
transmigration and
thus qualify for a member of this club
was this when i was a
human i was wedded to a lady whose
mother had a very strong
and domineering character she
lived with us night after
night i would lie awake thinking
up schemes to get even
with her i thought up
some lovely schemes but when
morning came my nerve would
leave i never had the courage to
put them into execution finally
the thought came to me that if i was
a ghost i could haunt her and
she would have no come back i slew
myself but alas my soul transmigrated
into the body of a cricket and
if you had ever seen that strong and
bitter old woman slaying spiders and
crickets you could realize
the despair that has settled down on me
since too bad said one
of the cockroaches i will now narrate the
events which led up to my
determination to
take the leap into the
darkness to be continued

SEPTEMBER 27
Suicide Club, Part 5

continued from tuesdays
paper i cant say the first of the
two cockroaches remarked that i
had any good reason for
slaying myself i had done everything
else at least once i was a
young man possessed of a
considerable fortune which it was my only
occupation to dissipate when
everything else palled i
took up theology i made a bet
with another student that the soul
was not immortal the only way to
settle it was to die and find out we both
did well fellows we both lost mine
proved to be immortal for here i am but his
was not it completely disappeared and
has never been heard of again
which shows you never can tell and
yet i am still interested in
games of chance my story said the
second cockroach breaking in is far more
interesting and far sadder i will
narrate it to be
concluded in my next[1]

SEPTEMBER 30
Killing Off the Sparrows

boss what is all this talk about
killing off the sparrows
i hold no brief for any bird for

all of them are greedy
insectivorous beasts but why is it
that everyone is sore on the sparrow all
birds put it across on their enemies
when they can but the sparrow
puts it oftener because
he packs the punch
i have an idea that the reason they all
pick on the sparrow is because he is
not beautiful but it discourages him just as
much to get killed as if he were
a nightingale you ought to
know how it is yourself boss if a
fat man falls down or has to chase his hat
or anything of that sort everyone
laughs but if a slim and elegant apollo
sprains his ankle
everyone says too bad too bad lots of
people try to step on cockroaches
boss just because they are not as pretty
as humming birds they think nothing
of the soul within i am
for the sparrow if he is a better
fighter let him win out it isnt
right for humans to take sides in these
wars between birds somebody is
always stepping in and trying to ball
up evolution i stand for the great flock of
sparrows who represent the common
people boss the plain
people[1]

OCTOBER 12
My Last Name

boss i just discovered what
my last name is i
pass it on to you i belong to the
family of the blattidae[1] right o
said mehitabel the cat when i told her
about it they have
got you sized up right you blatt out
everything you hear
i gleaned the information from
a bulletin issued by the
united states department of
agriculture which you left on the
floor by your desk it was entitled
cockroaches and written by
c l marlatt[2] entomologist and acting
chief in the absence of the chief and he
tells a dozen ways of killing roaches boss
what business has the united states
government got
to sick a high salaried
expert onto a poor little roach
please leave me some
more cheerful literature also please
get your typewriter fixed the keys are
working hard again butting them as i
do one at a time with
my head i get awful pains in my
neck writing for you

NOVEMBER 6
Where Is Archy?

HAS ANY ONE SEEN ARCHY?

"Where is Archy?" ask a score or more of his friends. And we are obliged to confess that we don't know. Has any one seen a Vers Libre Cockroach with a sore head and a dejected manner lately?

• • •

Frankly, we fear the worst.

• • •

Archy came to us a couple of weeks ago with his head hanging down. This is no figure of speech. His head was hanging down and his neck was wried and lumpy. He asked for a leave of absence. We refused it. There were words. He left anyhow. We fear the worst.

• • •

Archy, writing all his communications by the slow and painful process of butting his head against one typewriter key after another, developed a callous on his skull at the same time that his neck muscles began to weaken. He asked us for some sort of head harness, such as football players wear.[1]

• • •

After thinking the request over, we refused it. We cannot afford to encourage contributors in the idea that it is possible to get anything in the way of material recompense out of writing for the Sun Dial.

• • •

Buy Archy headgear and next some other poet would want a lead pencil, a pad of paper or even a theatre ticket.

• • •

Once that sort of thing starts there's no telling where it may run to before it stops.

• • •

"Archy," we said, "is the glory you get worth nothing to you? We're astonished to find you so materialistic! How about art for art's sake?"

. . .

"Well, boss," he said, "if you won't get me the harness so I can write without screaming every time I hit a letter, at least let me lay off for a week or two."

. . .

We thought it over. And decided against it. Begin to treat contributors as if they were human and there's no telling . . . there's no telling . . . it runs into drinks and lunches the first thing you know.

. . .

"Back to the mine!" we cried. . . . Then is when he left us. . . . We still think we did right.

. . .

Still, if any one sees a Free Verse Cockroach with a low-hung calloused brow and a wried neck wandering at large, lost and in distress, we will be glad to be informed of his whereabouts.

DECEMBER 20
Arrest That Statue

i was up to central
park yesterday watching some
kids build a snow man when
they were done and had
gone away i looked it
over they had used two
little chunks of wood for
the eyes i sat on one
of these and stared at
the bystanders along came a
prudish looking
lady from flatbush she
stopped and regarded the
snow man i stood
up on my hind legs in
the eye socket and
waved myself at her

horrors she cried even the
snow men in manhattan
are immoral officer arrest
that statue it winked
at me madam said the cop
accept the tribute
as a christmas present
and be happy my own
belief is that some
people have immorality
on the brain

DECEMBER 28
Happy Inspirations

excuse me if my
writing is out of alignment i
fell into a bowl of
egg nog the other
day at the restaurant down
the street which the doctor
says he is glad to
hear you are keeping away
from and when i
emerged i was full of happy
inspirations alas they
vanished ere the break of
day i am sure they
were the most brilliant and
witty things that ever
emanated from the mind of
man or cockroach or poet i
sat inside a mince pie
and laughed and laughed at
them myself the world seemed all
one golden glory boss
i came up the

street to get all this
wonderful stuff onto paper for
you but when i tried to
operate the typewriter
my foot would slip and
by the time i had control
of the machine again
the thoughts had gone
forever it is the
tragedy of the artist

1917

JANUARY 2
That Cockroach Glide

boss you oughta been
here last night we
had a ball on
top of your desk in honor
of your getting it cleaned
for 1917 three
cockroaches a katydid
two spiders and a
peruvian flea that came
in with the decayed
gentleman who tried to sell
you his autobiography in
poetical form the
other day and compromised by
borrowing a dime finally
a thousand legs came along
and made a hit by
dancing a dozen different
dances all at once each
pair of legs keeping step to a
different tune what we
need here worst of
all is two or three crickets
for an orchestra i
am inventing a new

step called that cockroach
glide

JANUARY 27
Archy Gets His Statue Made

Some months ago the friends of Archy, unable to conceal
their interest any longer, began to send insects to us by mail.
The idea was, perhaps, that Archy condemned to the society of
humans and poets, might be languishing for the lack of associ-
ations more distinctly entomological. At any rate, there was one
week during which we received, in trust for Archy, boxes con-
taining the following insects:

One croton bug, alive.
One small roach, gone before.
One small mutilated roach, gone quite a long way before.
One grasshopper, alive and voting.
One large roach, alive and suffering from overfeeding, in a
box which contained also a piece of toast, plastered over with
welsh rabbit.
One small red and black spider, gone before.
One infinitesimal smear, purporting to be the physical re-
mains of a defunct flea.

• • •

None of these things was acknowledged at the time. It was ev-
ident that some little group of serious drinkers were spoofing us,
and using Archy as a peg to hang their practical wit upon. We
had no bird to feed the insects to, and we did not dare or care to
encourage the spread of the pastime by noticing it in print. We
sent Archy into the silences for a few weeks, hoping that when
he emerged again the Cockroach Shower would have ceased.

• • •

But we received last week a pedestrian statue of Archy,
which, because of its artistic excellence, we are obliged to
notice—and acknowledge. It is by Mrs. Helena Smith Dayton,
and represents Archy as we ourself have always imagined him
to be—a bit of the scholar, with the scholar's stoop, a bit of the

pedant, the highbrow, determined to mix with lowbrows on terms of equality—a superior insect, resolutely democratic for the moment because of what he might learn—a distinctly literary creature, reaching out to life for literary purposes only, and interested in nothing not susceptible of being ground into grist in the literary mill—not a cockroach reaching up into art from life, but a cockroach consciously condescending to life and leaning toward it from the pedestal of art—a bug being vulgar now and then with an effort and solely for the sake of capturing the franchise of the majorities—a supercilious cockroach hiding his superciliousness under the affectation of being hail-fellow-well-met with all sorts and conditions of men, a spy scurrying among the lower classes, so-called, for the purpose of reporting them amusingly to his particular clientele . . . ; he thinks sincerely that he is seeing life from the under side, whereas he brings to the examination of the under side his literary preconceptions and prejudices.

JANUARY 30
Statue of Myself

say boss but its great to
be famous when i saw that pedestrian
statue of myself on your desk i reflected that not
every one is privileged to see his
monument erected before he dies nor
after either for that matter it
gave me the feeling that i was looking at my own
tombstone erected in memory of my good
deeds how noble i will have to be to live up
to all that i felt just as a person might
feel who was hearing his own funeral
sermon preached over him i
stared at the statue and the statue stared at
me and i resolved in the future to be
a better cockroach of course it doesnt flatter me
any my middle set of legs arent really

that bowed but the intellectual look
on my face is all there

MARCH 3
Going to War or Just Going to Hell

well boss i have
been down to washington to see
if i could find out whether
we were going to war or
just going to hell anyhow i
was looking for statesmen to my
surprise i found quite a
number of cockroaches in
charge of affairs cockroach mann
cockroach
kitchin need i specify further it
made me ashamed of the cockroach
tribe more anon

MARCH 29
More or Less Neutral

well boss there are
some great questions before us these
days such
as which shall i be a militarist or
a pacifist as between the two things i
am more or less neutral some days i
say on with the dance let war be
unconfined i
am a militarist other days i shout let
loose the dogs of peace and the
average i strike is one of complete
neutrality between the two last evening

after
you left some of the gang gathered
on your desk a couple of cockroaches
a red eyed
spider a mouse with a set of german
military
whiskers who is believed to be a
spy a big blue bottle fly that has been
asleep behind the radiator all winter
and we had
all decided on militarism when in blew a
hornet what is the question before
house he
asked and when we told him he said if
this bunch is
for militarism count me a pacifist
or vice versa he said
anything for trouble i especially hate
spiders my grandfather got tangled up
in a web little red eye do you want
any of my
game i have not said a word remarked
the little red
eyed spider stranger go in peace you
hadn t better
say a word either said the hornet
i give you
warning that wherever i look i
create a barred zone i
will sink you without visit or search
stranger
said little red eye i never brag but
my bite
is poison where my tongue stabs a
life ceases if i was to spit on the floor a
poison flower would bloom there i
never boast myself
said the hornet i am a quiet person
but it is

only fair to tell you that i can lick my
weight in
german measles declare yourself
spider whatever you
are i am the other thing stranger said
the spider i
advise you to begin nothing that you are
not able to carry to a conclusion i feel
sorry for you stranger i hate to see an
innocent thing from the suburbs get
entangled with
a concentrated essence of pestilence like
myself come come said the hornet let
the note writing
cease i dare you dare me to do what asked
the spider dare
you to live any longer said the hornet
and they
went at it then the results were fatal
to both the
hornet stung the spider to death
and died of his own
wounds crying out for water to
the last watching
that fight made me more neutral
than ever if
possible

MARCH 30
Between Him and His Masterpiece

boss why dont you get a
ribbon put into your typewriter it is only
after the most desperate exertions that
i am able to pound out these few lines i
had to get a sheet of carbon paper
and insert it between two sheets of white paper

and fix it in the machine in order to
write at all[1] and would never have got it
done if it hadnt been that mehitabel the
cat and all the rest of the gang
around here helped me i had something
important i wanted to write you but all this
frightful physical labor has driven it out
of my mind it is always so with the
artist by the time he has overcome the
difficulties that lie between him and
his masterpiece
he is tired i wish you would get me an
electric typewriter and why not have me
endowed so i would not have to worry about
material things at all i would like to write
and eat and sleep and not work at anything else

APRIL 16
War Times[1]

well boss we may
be legally at war but
i am derned if i can
make myself feel like it was war
times wait says mehitabel the
cat till the food shortage comes then
you will know it is war
times all right as far as food is
concerned i answered her it is war time
most of the time with me
anyhow boss i don't like to be always
hinting but if you could
establish something more like a
regular ration for me i would feel
more like devoting myself to my
art

April 17
Agate for You, Archy, Just to Curb Your Pride

thank you boss for
printing me up near the
top of the column the
other day i
am not a vain cockroach but
it does me good
to feel that merit will finally
be recognized if i
could only attain
brevier type now my cup
would be full you
may hear little more from
me for some days as
i am engaged on a literary
work of some importance it is
nothing more nor less
than the life story of
mehitabel the cat she is
dictating it a word
at a time and all
the bunch gather around to listen but
i am rewriting it as i go along
boss i wish we
could do something
for mehitabel she is
a cat that has seen
better days she has
drunk cream at fourteen
cents the half pint
in her time and now she
is thankful for a
stray fish head from a
garbage cart but she is
cheerful under it all toujours

gai is ever her word
toujours gai kiddoo drink she
says played a great
part in it all she
was taught to drink
beer by a kitchen maid she
trusted and was
abducted from a luxurious home
on one occasion in a
taxicab while under
the influence of beer which
she feels certain had been
drugged but still her
word is toujours gai my
kiddo toujours gai wotto hell
luck may change

APRIL 19
The Story of Mehitabel the Cat

well boss i promised to tell you
something of the life story of
mehitabel the cat archy says she i
was a beautiful kitten and as good
and innocent as i was beautiful my
mother was an angora you dont
look angora i said your fur
should show it did
i say angora said mehitabel it must
have been a slip of the tongue my
mother was high born and of
ancient lineage part persian and part
maltese a sort of maltese cross
i said archy she said please
do not josh my mother i
cannot permit levity in connection

with that saintly name she knew many
troubles did my mother and
died at last in a slum far from
all who had known her in her better
days but alas my father
was a villain he too had noble blood
but he had fallen into dissolute
ways and wandered the
alleys as the leader of a troupe of
strolling minstrels stealing milk
from bottles in the early mornings
catching rats here there and
everywhere and only too frequently
driven to the expedient of dining on
what might be found in
garbage cans and suburban
dump heaps now and
then a sparrow or a robin fell to my
fathers lot for he was a mighty hunter i
have heard that at times he even
ate cockroaches and as she said
that she spread
her claws and looked at me with her
head on one side i got into the works
of the typewriter mehitabel i
said try and conquer that wild and
hobohemian strain in your blood archy
she said have no fear i have dined
today but to resume my
mother the pampered beauty that she
was was eating whipped cream one
day on the back
stoop of the palace where she resided
when along came my father bold
black handsome villain that he was and
serenaded her his must have been a
magnetic personality for in spite of
her maiden modesty and
cloistered upbringing she responded

with a few well rendered musical
notes of her own i
will not dwell upon the wooing suffice
it to say that ere long they
not only sang ducts together but
she was persuaded to join
him and his troupe of strollers in
their midnight meanderings alas that
first false step she
finally left her luxurious home it was
on a moonlight night in may i have
often heard her say and again and
again she has said to me that she
wished that robert w chambers could
have written her story or maybe john
galsworthy in his later and
more cosmopolitan manner well to
resume i was born in a stable in
greenwich village which was at
the time undergoing transformation
into a studio my
brothers and sisters were drowned
dearie i often look back on my life and
think how romantic it has all
been and wonder what fate saved
me and sent my brothers and sisters
to their watery grave archy i
have had a remarkable life go
on telling about it i said never
mind the side remarks i became
a pet at once continued
mehitabel but let us not make the first
instalment too long the
tale of my youth will be reserved
for your next chapter to be continued

MAY 8
A Pampered Kitten

well i said to
mehitabel the cat continue
the story of your life i
was a pampered kitten for
a time archy she said but
alas i soon
realized that my master and
mistress were becoming
more and more fond of a
dog that lived with
them in the studio he was
an ugly mutt take it from
me archy a red eyed little bull
dog with no manners i
hope i was too much of a lady
to show jealousy i have
been through a great deal
dearie now up and now down
but it is darn seldom
i ever forget i was a
lady always genteel archy
but this red eyed mutt was
certainly some pill and those
people were so stuck on
him that it would have made
you sick they called him
snookums and it was snookums
this and snookums that and
ribbons and bells and porterhouse
steak for him and if he
got a flea on him they called a
specialist in only one
day archy i hear my
mistress say snookums ookums
is lonely he ought to

have some one to play with
true said her husband every
dog should be brought up along
with a baby a dog
naturally likes a child to
play with we will have no
children said she a
vulgar foolish little child
might harm my snookums we
could muzzle the child said
her husband i am sure
the dog would like one to
play with and they
finally decided they would get
one from a foundling home
to play with snookums if
they could find a child
with a good enough pedigree
that wouldnt give any
germs to the dog well
one day the low lived mutt
butted in and tried to
swipe the cream i was drinking even
as a kitten archy i
never let any one put anything
across on me although i
am slow in starting
things as any real lady
should be dearie i let
this stiff snookums get
his face into the saucer
and then what i did
to his eyes and nose with
my claws would melt the
heart of a trained
nurse the simp had no
nerve he ran to his
mistress and she came after
me with a broom i

got three good scratches
through her silk stockings
archy dearie before i
was batted into the
alley and i picked myself
up out of a can full
of ashes a cat without a
home a poor little
innocent kitten alone
all alone in the great and
wicked city but i never
was one to be down
on my luck long archy my
motto has always been
toujours gai archy toujours
gai always jolly archy
always game and thank god
always the lady i
wandered a block or
two and strayed into
the family entrance of
a barroom it was my
first mistake mehitabels
adventures will be continued

MAY 11
Mehitabel the Cat Has Struck

well boss i am
sorry to report that
mehitabel the cat has
struck no more story archy
she said last night
without pay art for arts
sake is all right but
i can get real
money in the movies the

best bits are to
come too she says my life
she says has been a
romantic one boss she has
the nerve to hold out
for a pint of
cream a day i am sick
of milk she says and
why should a lady author
drink ordinary milk cream
for mine she says
and no white of egg beaten
up on top of it either i
know what my dope
is worth boss it is
my opinion she has the
swell head over getting into
print i would hate
to stop the serial
but she needs a
lesson listen archy she said
to me what i want
with my stuff is
illustrations too the next
chapter is about me taking
my first false step well
archy i either get an
illustration for that or else
i sign up with these
movie people who are always
after me you will be
wanting to sing into a phonograph
next i told her
my advice is to
can her at once i will fill
the space with my own
adventures

MAY 14
It Was Beer

to continue the story
of mehitabel the cat
she says to me when i
walked into that
barroom i was hungry and
mewing with despair
there were two men sitting
at the table and
looking sad i rubbed
against the legs of one
of them but he never moved
then i jumped up on
the table and stood
between them they both stared
hard at me and
then they stared at each
other but neither one
touched me or said anything
in front of one of
them was a glass full
of some liquid with
foam on the top of it i
thought it was milk
and began to drink from the
glass little did i
know archy as i lapped
it up that it was beer the
men shrank back from me and
began to tremble and shake
and look at me
finally one of them said to
the other i know what you
think bill what do i
think jeff said the

other you think bill that
i have the d ts said the
first one you think i
think i see a cat drinking
out of that beer glass but
i do not think i
see a cat at all that is all
in your imagination it
is you yourself that
have the d ts no said the
other one i dont think
you think you see a
cat i was not thinking
about cats at all i
do not know why you mention
cats for there are no
cats here just then a
salvation army lassie came
in and said you
wicked men teaching that poor
little innocent cat to
drink beer what cat
said one of the men she
thinks she sees a cat
said the other and
laughed and laughed
just then a mouse ran
across the floor and i
chased it and the salvation
lassie jumped on a
chair and screamed jeff
said bill i suppose now you
think i saw a
mouse i wish bill you
would change the
subject from animals said
jeff there is nothing
to be gained by talking

of animals mehitabels
life story will be
continued in an early number

MAY 17
A Saucer Full of Beer

for some weeks said
mehitabel the cat continuing the
story of her life i
lived in that barroom and
though the society was
not what i had
been used to yet i
cannot say that it was
not interesting three
times a day in
addition to scraps from
the free lunch
and an occasional mouse
i was given a saucer
full of beer sometimes i
was given more and
when i was feeling
frolicsome it was the custom
for the patrons to gather
round and watch me
chase my tail until
i would suddenly fall
asleep at that time
they gave me the
nickname of pussy cafe but
one day i left the
place in the pocket
of a big fur
overcoat worn by
a gentleman who was

carrying so much that i thought
a little extra burden would
not be noticed he got
into a taxi cab
which soon afterwards
pulled up in front of
a swell residence uptown
and wandered up the
steps well said his
wife meeting him in the
hallway you are here
at last but where is my
mother whom i sent you to
the train to meet
could this be she asked
the ladys husband
pulling me out of his
coat pocket by the neck and
holding me up with a
dazed expression on his face
it could not said his
wife with a look of
scorn mehitabels life
story will be continued
before long

JUNE 7
The Cat Is Sore at Me

well boss mehitabel the
cat is sore at me she says
that it was my fault
that you cut off her story
of her life right in
the middle and she
has been making my life a
misery to me three

times she has almost clawed
me to death i wish
she would eat a poisoned
rat but she wont she
is too lazy to catch one well
it takes all sorts of
people to make an
underworld

JUNE 15
Comma Boss Comma

say comma boss comma capital
i apostrophe m getting tired of
being joshed about my
punctuation period capital t followed by
he idea seems to be
that capital i apostrophe m
ignorant where punctuation
is concerned period capital n followed by
o such thing semi
colon the fact is that
the mechanical exigencies of
the case prevent my use of
all the characters on the
typewriter keyboard period
capital i apostrophe m
doing the best capital
i can under difficulties semi colon
and capital i apostrophe m
grieved at the unkindness
of the criticism period please
consider that my name
is signed in small
caps period[1]

                 archy period

JUNE 30
Lawn

boss i must say
you are some gardener i
gave that hand
nourished lawn of yours the
once over the other
day and the only
question in my mind is
whether you will
cut the grass yourself
with a safety razor or send for a barber

JULY 7
Workman Spare That Bathtub[1]

boss i saw a
pitiful sight yesterday i
was crawling across the
ruins of an old house that
the workmen are tearing
down up town and
i saw a middle
aged man sitting on a
pile of bricks with
his gray hair in his hands he
was weeping and moaning
and i gathered from his
remarks that the place was once
a boarding house where
he had spent
many happy years i caught
a few strophes of his
song of woe as

follows
o workman spare that bathtub o
that bathtub made of zinc
that bathtub in the boarding house
that i lived in for years
fond recollections of
my youth surge oer
me when i think
upon that bathtub in that
boarding house and i
choke up with tears
when splashing of a sunday
morn a peevish voice and surly
would tell me to make
haste and be
myself again adorning
throughout the week it
had few friends
but o on sunday morning
that bathtub in the
boarding house was
busy bright and early
how well i can remember how
as i tripped down the hall
the boarders heads would
be poked out along the
corridor
the sound of some one singing
upon my ears would fall
and sounds of others waiting
and getting very sore
o workman spare that
bathtub to me it does
bring back
the merry days when i was
young and all the world was pink
o workman spare that bathtub
from ruin and from rack
the bathtub in the

boarding house
the bathtub made of zinc

JULY 27
Washington D C

washington d c july
23 well boss here
i am in washington
watching my step for fear
some one will push me
into the food bill[1] up
to date i am the only thing
in this country that
has not been added to it by
the time this is
published nothing that
i have said may be
true however which is a
thing that is constantly happening
to thousands of
great journalists now in
washington it is so hot here that
i get stuck in the asphalt
every day on my
way from the senate press
gallery back to
shoemakers where the
affairs of the nation
are habitually settled by
the old settlers it
is so hot that you can
fry fish on the
sidewalk in any part of
town and many people
are here with fish to fry
including now

and then a german
carp i am lodging on
top of the washington
monument where i can
overlook things
you cant keep a good bug
from the top of
the column all the time i
am taking my meals with
the specimens in the
smithsonian institution when i
see any one coming i hold
my breath and look like another
specimen but in the
capitol building there
is no attention paid to me
because there are so
many other insects
around it gives you a
great idea of the
american people when you
see some of the
things they elect after july
27 address me care
st elizabeth hospital
for the insane i am going out
there for a visit with
some of your other
contributors

AUGUST 1
Archy in Washington

well boss from official
circles here I learn
that things could not well be worse
with regard to the war situation and that

this is no time for
pessimism as we have
the enemy licked to a
frazzle everything
is gloom and america
is about to save the
world there is no
hope anywhere and we
should all feel cheerful because
things are going better than
could be expected the
administration is very
angry at the people who are
giving out cheerful
reports and at the same time
wishes to emphasize the fact that
pessimism is part of the
propaganda of our enemies the
way russia is acting now has cheered
everybody up wonderfully and
all seems lost it hampers the
administration frightfully for conflicting
reports to be sent to the
country and I am authoritatively
informed that what the
secretary of war said
yesterday will be denied by the
secretary of the navy
tomorrow it is of the utmost
importance that the people
should realize that
the department of publicity is
doing all it can to
suppress such rumors as it has
not started itself the
situation here is full of
depression and recent reports
from returned observers
say that all is well I am keeping

in touch with everything
that is about to happen and will
let you know from day
to day what the news was about to be
so you can have plenty of time
to deny it in advance
of its publication

AUGUST 20
To Help Win the War

i was asking
myself the other day
what i could do to help
win the war and
like a flash the answer came to
me i can help with
the food problem by keeping
out of the canned goods and
this will not only be better
for the country but
more comfortable for myself there
are thousands and thousands
of other insects all over
the country who
can render a similar service

SEPTEMBER 24
Out of the Cockroach Body

boss i have had a terrible time
since i last wrote you as i
told you long ago i was originally a
vers libre poet and my
soul after leaving that body

migrated into the
body of a cockroach before that
happened i did not believe in the
doctrine of transmigration of
souls but after it happened
how could i refuse to credit it well
it gave me a great deal of interest
in all psychic matters and it
struck me not many weeks ago that
if it were possible for a soul
to leave a poet that way and go into
the body of a cockroach
at the poets death it might be
possible to manage it without death the
truth is that i got tired of being a
cockroach and wanted to be
human again i practised and practised
until i found myself able to get out
of the cockroach body and
naked on the air of heaven ride but it
is not all that it is cracked up to be
there is nothing that can get so
cold as a soul these autumn nights
when it has no body and no blankets
and in winter it is worse yet after i
had gained proficiency i began
to look around for a human to
get into but as far as i could
learn every human was filled with
a soul already but i began to
make longer and longer trips away from
my cockroach body imagine my
consternation and surprise one day
some weeks ago upon returning to the
cockroach body which i had left to find
that it had been squashed and swept out
with a broom i looked at the fragments
with horror it was a very discouraged

looking set of remains but there i
was out in the world with
no shelter all sould up as you might
say and no place to go it may strike you
as nothing to worry about and it
wasnt so bad for a day or two but there
is a horrid sense of helplessness
about it if you are interested in
psychic research and that
sort of thing you can get a
little fun for a while appearing in
seances and balling up the messages
but believe me psychic research is more
interesting when you are the human calling
up the spirits than when you
are the ghost too often
they make you the goat that
soon palled on me and i wandered for
weeks the most lonely thing in new york
city at last in despair i
got into the carcass of another cockroach
again of about the same size and
general appearance of my old frame but
the whole affair has had a most
depressing effect on me imagine taking
all that trouble to get away from
being a cockroach and then get
shoved back into one by
fate again i think i will
stick to the old homestead for a
while how do i know but what the next
time i might get into the body of a
flea or a communist

OCTOBER 13
A German Periscope

well boss after a series of
adventures more thrilling than anything
that ever happened to
sindbad the sailor i
found myself clinging to
the top of a german
periscope 300 miles off the
coast of new england any moment the
vessel might submerge and
it would take me hours to wade ashore suddenly
i saw a fleet of
vessels coming in our direction heavens it
was a flock of ships carrying american
soldiers and supplies to france had the
submarine seen it yet i asked
myself i must save that covey
of transports at all costs in a
moment my plan was laid i climbed
onto the lens of the periscope and began
to run rapidly back and forth across it with an
undulating movement as if
i were a ship presently i heard a voice in german
floating up the tube of the periscope which i
translate for the
convenience of your readers heinie[1] said the
voice look out the periscope and see if
any transports are about high high
your ayeness i mean aye aye your highness said
heinie and a moment later he
exclaimed i see a queer ship
shaped like a cockroach skooting over the
waters of the atlantic fool let me look you
have been inhaling too much oil said the
commanding officer i redoubled my

efforts to look like a ship it is too true said
the commanding officer the americans
have launched some
terrible new invention in the foreground
is a
vessel like a cockroach and behind it is
a fleet i can scarcely make out but
likely they are all composed of these
new hellish inventions what fiendish
practices they put into operation
against us
poor innocent submarines let us
sink at once and do it as
spurios as possible an instant later the
vessel had sunk and i was on my way
to the
bevy of american ships i had
just saved

OCTOBER 19
Patience Worth[1]

Archy, our well known vers libre cockroach, who has
skipped merrily on from incarnation to incarnation, is planning
to interview Patience Worth in the near future.

NOVEMBER 1
Beware the Demon Rum[1]

well boss on these
rainy days i wish i was
web footed like a jersey mosquito no
one has yet invented
an umbrella for cockroaches i was
over across the street

to the barroom you used to
frequent before you reformed today
and it was raining outside i
pulled a piece of cheese
rind over my head to
protect me from the weather and
started for the door as i
passed by one of the booths a man
who was sitting in it said to
his companion please call a
taxi for me where do you want to go
said his companion i am
bad again said the man i want to
go to some place where they
treat nervous diseases
at once you look all right
said his companion i may look all
right said he but i don't see
all right i just saw a piece
of cheese rind crawling along the
floor and as i passed by i
said to myself beware the demon rum
it gives your brain a quirk
it puts you on the bum
and gives the doctors work

NOVEMBER 8
Sounds Like a Jolly Gang

well boss i had one gay
time last night i ran
onto a book worm in one of
the tomes on your desk and
found him a friendly
little cuss come he said to
me with his little eyes
shining brightly through his

horn rimmed glasses let us
make a night of it let us
have a gay evening lead on
says i we will go says
he to the annual
exhibit of the new york
microscopical society at the
american museum of natural
history they have there
some treponema pallidum[1] some
models of amoeba and
paramoecium and some
pediculus capitis the deuce you
say said i yes said he it
will be a rare treat
indeed there are also some
ziroons there showing their
pleochroic halos the
nerve of them i said do
the authorities know it my
word yes says he the department of
health is responsible for
it come let us hasten there is
also a fine selection
of diplococci to say nothing
of the protococcus nivalis and
a specimen of phlogopite
from canada it sounds like a
jolly gang i said will there
be anything to drink
at this party i understand
he said that cerebro spinal
fluid will flow
like water the gay dogs i
said guide me to
it professor its always
fair weather when good fellows get
together i must warn
you he says that one

is not allowed to feed the
animalculae well when we
got there what do you
suppose the bunch was
germs boss germs just
ordinary germs pardon me i said
i will associate
with insects humans and
ghosts but not knowingly
with germs you must excuse me
one must draw the line somewhere
these friends of yours look
like alien enemies to me they
may have noble names but
their blood is thin
so i left
him flat and dropped into
a beef steak pie in one
of these arm chair restaurants for
a bite to eat and a
warm bath before
going to bed
that book worm was
out for some wild
evening boss its strange how
many of these quiet
looking little high brows have
bohemian tastes

NOVEMBER 12
Interest in Science

boss my interest in science
is keen but my
sympathy with scientists is
declining very rapidly the
more i see of them the less i

want them to see
me i heard a couple of
entomologists talking the
other day you want to be sure
and get over to the brooklyn
museum on thursday evening he said
there is going to be a
lecture on a new
kind of killing bottle good
said the second one i will
surely be there if there is
anything that is needed for
the cause right now
it is a new killing bottle i
looked at him and he
seemed a kind hearted man too
just thoughtless likely
i thought what is sport to
you old fellow is
death to us insects morality
is all in the point
of view if the cockroaches
should start to killing the
humans just to study them there
would a howl go up from
danville illinois to
beersheba palestine even germans
are not gassed for study but
only in the way of
business and battle many would
think twice about stepping
on a pacifist who would
send any number of potato bugs
to their funeral pyre without
remorse justice as maurice
maeterlinck points out is not
inherent in the universe and what
man has put there he
uses when he uses it at all

strictly for his own
purposes the world is so sad that
the only way to live
with it is to laugh at it

NOVEMBER 14
He Cried into His Beer

as i go up and down the town
hither to and fro i gather many a
smile and frown and talk of
thus and so i lately
listened and i heard two chaps
their luck bewail life did not get
a pleasant word they
told an awful tale for one of them
had just been fired he
glummed and wondered why he cried
into his beer
aspired
to punch the boss his eye too
true the other one exclaimed this
world s a burning shame the
game of living has been framed it is
a rotten game and ever as they railed
at fate and wooed the sombre muse
they steadily absorbed a great
sufficiency of booze but neither one
that cursed his luck and beat his burning bean
would blame the downfall on the truck
that passed his lips between
and as i listened there i thought it were
more candid far to give its dues to what they bought
across the varnished bar they should indeed
be far more frank about their hard lucks boss
they should remark
each genial tank unto their bosses faces

you can t expect a man to drink as much as i do boss
and have much time to work and think
and put the job across
oh boss you ask too much of me
i do the best i can but who can lush
continually and be a working man
you can t expect a man to booze from morning
until night and feel quite nimble
in his shoes and add his figures right oh boss
you ask too much of us we have no flair for toil
we d rather daily dally thus-imbibing joyful oil
you can t expect a man to souse
and do work for your business house so do not be unjust
twere more like reason if they said such words
unto their bosses than tear the hair
and beat the head and blame luck
for their losses

NOVEMBER 19
Prudence

NO, ARCHY . . . AGATE, TO REBUKE YOUR
INCREASING PRIDE

dear boss i have worked
pretty hard over the
following poem not only to
make it rhyme but
also butting it out on the
typewriter with my head one
letter at a time so wont you please
just this once set it in
large type i get awfully tired of
butting out poems and seeing
them always printed in

nonpareil let me have brevier
just this once boss

Prudence

i do not think a prudent one
will ever aim too high
a cockroach seldom whips a dog
and seldom should he try

and should a locust take a vow
to eat a pyramid
he likely would wear out his teeth
before he ever did

i do not think the prudent one
hastes to initiate
a sequence of events which he
lacks power to terminate

for should i kick the woolworth tower
so hard i laid it low
it probably might injure me
if it fell on my toe

i do not think the prudent one
will be inclined to boast
lest circumstances unforseen
should get him goat and ghost

for should i tell my friends i d drink
the hudson river dry
a tidal wave might come and turn
my statements to a lie

NOVEMBER 23
Too Romantic to Work

well boss mehitabel the cat
has turned up again after a long
absence she declines
to explain her movements but she
drops out dark hints of a
most melodramatic nature ups and downs
archy she says always ups and downs
that is what my life has
been one day lapping
up the cream de la cream and the
next skirmishing for
fish heads in an alley but
toujours gai archy toujours gai no
matter how the luck broke i have had a
most romantic life archy talk
about reincarnation and transmigration
archy why i could tell you things of who
i used to be archy that would make
your eyes stick out like a snails one
incarnation queening it with a tarara on
my bean as cleopatra archy and
the next being abducted as a poor
working girl but toujours gai archy toujours
gai and finally my soul has migrated to
the body of a cat and not even a persian or
a maltese at that but where have you been
lately mehitabel i asked her never mind
archy she says dont ask no questions
and i will tell no lies all i
got to say to keep away
from the movies have you been in the
movies mehitabel i asked her never mind
archy she says never mind all i got to
say is keep away from those

movie camps theres some mighty
nice people and animals connected with them
and then again theres some that aint i
say nothing against anybody archy i am
used to ups and downs no matter
how luck breaks its toujours gai
with me all i got to say
archy is that sometimes a cat
comes along that is a perfect gentleman and
then again some of the slickest furred ones
aint if i was a cat that was the
particular pet of a movie star archy and
slept on a silk cushion and had
white chinese rats especially
imported for my meals i would try to live
up to all that luxury and be a
gentleman in word and deed mehitabel i said
have you had another unfortunate romance i am
making no complaint against any
one archy she says wottell archy wottell even
if the breaks is bad my motto is toujours gai
but to slip out nights and sing and frolic
under the moon with a lady and then cut her
dead in the day time before your rich
friends and see her batted out of a studio
with a broom without raising a paw for her
aint what i call being a
gentleman archy and i am
a lady archy and i know a gentleman when
i meet one but wottell archy wottell toujours
gai is the word never say die
archy its the cheerful heart that wins all i
got to say is that if i ever get that
fluffy haired slob down on the
water front when some of my gang
is around he will wish he had
watched his step i aint vindictive archy i
dont hold grudges no lady does but i

got friends archy that maybe would take it
up for me theres a black cat with one ear
sliced off lives down around old slip is a
good pal of mine i wouldnt want to
see trouble start archy no real lady
wants a fight to start over her but
sometimes she cant hold her friends back
all i got to say is that boob with his silver
bells around his neck better sidestep old slip
well archy lets not talk any more about my troubles
does the boss ever leave any pieces of sandwich
in the waste paper basket any more honest
archy i would will myself to a furrier for a
pair of oysters i could even she says eat you
archy she said it like a joke but there
was a kind of a pondering look in her eyes
so i just crawled into the inside of
your typewriter behind the wires it
seemed safer let her hustle for a
mouse if she is as hungry as all that
but i am afraid she never will she
is too romantic to work

NOVEMBER 27
I Knew a Ghost

the longer i live the more i
realize that everything is
relative even morality is
relative things you would not do
sometimes you would do other
times for instance i would not consider
it honorable in me as a
righteous cockroach to crawl into a
near sighted man s soup that
man would not have a sporting chance but
with a man with ordinarily good eye

sight i should say it was
up to him to watch his soup himself and
yet if i was very tired and hungry
i would crawl into even a near
sighted man s soup knowing all the
time it was wrong and my necessity would
keep me from reproaching myself too
bitterly afterwards you can
not make any hard and fast rule
concerning the morality of crawling into
soup nor anything else a certain
alloy of expediency improves the
gold of morality and makes
it wear all the longer consider a
ghost if i were a ghost i
would not haunt ordinary people but i
would have all the fun i wanted to with
spiritualists for spiritualists are
awful nuisances to ghosts i knew a
ghost by the name of clarence one
time who hated spiritualists with a
great hatred you see said clarence they
give me no rest they have got my
number once one of those psychics gets a
ghost s number so he has to come
when he is called they work him till
the astral sweat stands out in beads
on his spectral brow they seem to think
said clarence that all a spook has to do
is to stick around waiting to dash in
with a message as to whether mrs millionbucks
pet pom has pneumonia or only wheezes
because he has been eating too many
squabs clarence was quite
bitter about it but wait he says till
the fat medium with the red nose
that has my number
passes over and i can get my
clutches on him on equal terms there s

going to be some initiation beside
the styx several of the boys are
sore on him a plump chance i have
don t i to improve myself and pass on
to another star with that medium
yanking me into somebody s parlor to
blow through one of these little tin
trumpets any time of the day or night
honest archy he says i hate the sight of a
ouija board would it be moral he
says to give that goof a bum tip on the
stock market life ain t worth
dying he says if you ve got to fag
for some chinless chump of a psychic
nor death ain t worth living
through would it be moral in me to
queer that simp with his
little circle by saying he s got an
anonymous diamond brooch in his pocket
and that his trances are rapidly developing
his kleptomania no clarence i said it
wouldn t be moral but it
might be expedient there s a ghost
around here i have been trying to get
acquainted with but he is shy i think he is
probably afraid of cockroaches

December 3
That Ghost That Loafs

well boss i have
finally succeeded in getting into
touch with that
ghost that loafs around here he
is a sort of a tired out
timid kind of a ghost and
says he wants it understood that he

is doing no haunting he hangs
around your office nights because it is
quiet he says and he hopes you
wont be harsh with him and
put him out he is hiding from a
bunch of spiritualists he
says one medium in particular who
has been working him nearly to
distraction he told me some of
his experiences with
spiritualists and it is a
most pathetic tale which i
will communicate to
you later

DECEMBER 8

Superior

the high cost of
living isn t so bad if you
dont have to pay for it i met
a flea the other day who
was grinning all over
himself why so merry why so
merry little bolshevik i asked him

i have just come from a swell
dog show he said i have
been lunching off a dog that was
worth at least one hundred
dollars a pound you should be
ashamed to brag about it i said with so
many insects and humans on
short rations in the world today the
public be damned he said i
take my own where i find it those are
bold words i told him i am a bold

person he said and bold words are
fitting for me it was
only last thursday that i marched
bravely into the zoo
and bit a lion what did he do i asked
he lay there and took it said
the flea what else could he do he knew i
had his number and it was
little use to struggle some day i said
even you will be conquered terrible as
you are who will do it he
said the mastodons are all dead and i
am not afraid of any mere
elephant i asked him how about a microbe and
he turned pale as he thought it
over there is always some
little thing that is too
big for us every
goliath has his david and so on ad finitum
but what said the flea is the
terror of the smallest microbe of all
he i said is afraid of a vacuum what is
there in a vacuum to make one afraid
said the flea there is nothing in it
i said and that is what makes one
afraid to contemplate it a person
can t think of a place with nothing at
all in it without going nutty and if he
tries to think that nothing is
something after all he gets nuttier you are
too subtle for me said the
flea i never took much stock in being
scared of hypodermic propositions or
hypothetical injections i am
going to have dinner off a
man eating tiger if a vacuum gets
me i will try and send you word
before the worst comes to
the worst some people i told him inhabit

a vacuum all their lives and
never know it then he said it don t
hurt them any no i said it dont but it
hurts people who have to associate
with them and with these words
we parted each feeling
superior to the other and is not that
feeling after all one of the great
desiderata of social intercourse

DECEMBER 10
Sad Looking Ghost

the ghost i was telling you
about the other day is named emmet and
he is a tall thin sad looking
ghost with a long drooping
nose and a bald retreating forehead he is a
very timid ghost and
vanishes quickly at any unexpected
noise i will tell you the
truth said emmet i am a bit afraid of
human beings they are so rough i met one in the
corridor the other morning about three
oclock and he threw a heavy book right through
me later i realized that he must have
been as much afraid of
me as i was of him just then mehitabel came in
and emmet vanished it was five
minutes before i could coax him to appear
again i have always been a
bit afraid of cats said emmet cheer o said
mehitabel dont look so
melancholy gay is the word my boy tell me
the story of your life how
did you come to be a ghost anyhow emmet
was quite thoughtful for a moment and

he got sadder and sadder and then he
said i will conceal nothing
from you it was drink
that did it the story of emmet the
ghost will be continued in an
early number

DECEMBER 21
Bore His Way Out

F. W. P. says: "I am informed by one of the military that it
takes exactly three days for a flea to bore through an army
shirt. It has therefore been found easy to thwart this evil beast's
designs by turning the shirt inside out every day and a half. It
occurs to me that if your cockroach friend, archy, were prop-
erly approached he might consent to secure similar statistics on
civilian shirts, thereby conferring a great boon on mankind in
general."

* * *

We put the matter up to archy, and in due time received the
following communication from that industrious little animal:

　　　boss i don't understand
　　　the idea i am afraid
　　　why do they turn the
　　　shirt every day and a half
　　　why do they not
　　　keep it unturned
　　　for three whole days and
　　　let the poor flea
　　　bore his way out and
　　　make his escape

1918

JANUARY 28
Literary Slave No Longer

you want to know
where i have been so long well
i will tell you i
have been cutting out poetry and
going to work i have been
letting literature alone and
making some money as
you never paid me anything for
my literary work i wandered
into a business college down the
street a few weeks ago and i
was fooling around one of the
typewriters when the
proprietor said to me if you want to
make a little money you can
do it by cleaning those
machines so he tied a piece of
cotton onto my stomach and i crawled back
and forth over the keys
till i got them cleaned i get
ten cents a typewriter for the
work and i am resting my head also i
find a certain satisfaction in being
useful of a kind that i
never felt when i was merely a poet i

may come back to literature again boss but
never on the old terms i am
taking on the typewriters in an
advertising agency to clean
next week if i could get three or four
really industrious cockroaches to
help me i think i would open a
shoe shining parlor in a
modest way i am enclosing a
dollar which i trust you to hand on
to the sun tobacco fund hoping
that you yourself will
eventually get away from writing and
go in for something honest i
am with best wishes but
your literary slave no longer

FEBRUARY 26
Poetry Is

Poetry is the chinking of a couple of unexpected coins in the
shabby pocket of life.

• • •

Poetry is a young deity who used to shake dice with Kit Mar-
lowe to see who should pay for the next round.

• • •

Poetry is a rather giddy young blighter Rudyard Kipling used
to know.

• • •

i could tell you what
poetry is but
why should i stir up
feeling yours for
vers d'archibald

                                        archy

• • •

Poetry is a cast shoe from one of Apollo's stallions. Societies and organizations pick it up and are just as likely to nail it onto a cow as onto a horse.

MARCH 25
Window Box War Gardens

well boss i am
going out of the shoe shining and
typewriter cleaning business people
arent spending as much
money to have their shoes shined
as before the war and they are
economizing and cleaning
their own typewriters or
letting them stay gummed up i
am now going in for making
window box war gardens for
apartment house dwellers i put my head
down in the soil and revolve
myself till i bore a hole to
plant the seed and then i
plant it and cover it up and my
contract also calls for keep
ing the weeds chewed off even with the surface
of the soil i am working on
the shares and hope to get enough to eat
this spring and summer i cant say
i ever got that much out of liter
ature when i used to be one of your
regular contributors yours till the
kaiser comes to an huntimely end

MARCH 30
The Crippled Cockroach

*[In this column, Marquis's character Fothergill Finch declares
his intention to open a restaurant called The Golden Finch.]*

• • •

We also find on our desk the following communication from
Archy:

> well boss i have just
> perused fothergill's letter i
> think i will start a
> cafe of my own i have a
> lot of playmates who
> are familiar with the res
> taurant business in its most
> occult phases and i
> could depend upon them for
> attendance if not for col
> lections i shall call it the
> crippled cockroach and the
> motto shall be drop in boys the
> onion soup is fine the
> management will keep an eye
> on the hats and coats but
> refuse to be responsible
> for the food served this
> restaurant of mine will
> be different yours till
> they find a diet
> cure for the tropic of cancer

MAY 24
We Suspect Archy

*[In the "Sun Dial" column for April 5, Marquis announced his
departure for a seven-week vacation. Upon his return, the col-
umn for May 24, under the title "Memoranda for a Gentleman
Returning from His Vacation," included, along with updates
about damage to the office, this note:]*

Your typewriter fell off the desk one night and was broken in
several new places. We suspect Archy.

MAY 25
Cockroachism

a big brown cockroach
came in to see me yesterday
all flustered and
exalted with a new win the
war hunch archy he says
i have the idea
at last shoot little
machiavelli i said archy he
said will you be one
of a hundred billion
cockroaches to march into
germany and eat every scrap of
vegetation and every morsel
of food the minute it is
brought from russia just
think he said growing more and
more excited nothing could
stop us nothing could
hold us back neither trenches nor
guns we could crawl through
around under and over

will you not put a piece in
the sun dial seeking
for transportation to europe what
we want from you is
publicity i will not i said
slacker he cried pro german
boche hun why will
you not because i said if
a hundred billion
cockroaches crawled into
germany the huns would
say gott had sent them
fresh meat and would live
on them for a year i
never thought of that he
said a lot of you
fellows with win the war
schemes that yell pro german
when they can't get
publicity have another think
coming i said yours for
constructive cockroachism

May 28

Named after the Washington Arch

please deny for me
that i was named
for those anti
aircraft guns on the west
ern front they spell it
archie[1] i
was named after
the washington arch
at the base of which my
father and my
mother first met and

courted and i spell
it with a y another one
of those get peace quick
fellows suggested to me
that i eat poison and
then go and die in
the kaisers soup so he
would perish
shortly after nothing
doing said i it
would be usless to put poison
in his meat he is
the modern mithridates[2] and
they feed him
noxious drugs by the
handful to keep his
hate up besides why
allow the kaiser to die
and escape the thing
to do is to keep
him intact uniform
and all and make him
run the elevator in a
new temple of peace
after the war yours
for cruel and hun usual
punishments

MAY 31
Aeroplane Mail

Archy is clamoring to be sent to Washington by aeroplane mail. If we can get a motor to fit him we intend to turn him into an aeroplane and let him ramble.

JUNE 4
Assisting at a Suicide

well boss i have just
been assisting at a suicide i think the
gentleman who killed himself was
quite right in doing so too
i went into the kitchen of an
up town hotel the other
evening for a bite to eat and after
i had dined i thought
i would look the place over and if
i found a room that appealed to me i
would spend the night there
the room i got into was already
infested by a little old bald headed fellow
with scared eyes and a face like
a petrified turnip who was
hunched up under a reading lamp
reading a
bible all of a sudden he gave a
jump and said gawd gawd there it
is again and i saw a puff of
smoke floating across the
table in front of him it seemed to come
from nowhere in particular smoke
smoke cried the old man i am
haunted by smoke and as
he spoke another puff of smoke
suddenly appeared from nowhere on
the table in front of him
gawd gawd he cried spare me spare
me do not persecute me this way
and i will give all the money to charity
i will give it to the red
cross or any church you
may designate i know
i did wrong to burn down that

building for the
insurance money but how was i
to know there was any one in it i
did not plan a murder a third
puff of smoke seemed to start out of
his own shoulder and floated in
front of his eyes and a fourth
puff hit him on his bald head and made
a little veil in front of his face
gawd gawd he cried and threw
himself on the rug and began to
pray with his face hidden i
thought to myself those
puffs of smoke are peculiar there
isnt anything on fire in
here and then i got a whiff of it
and it smelled like tobacco smoke
then i saw something that looked
like a gray globe floating from the
direction of the bathroom door it
drifted across the room and hit
the reading lamp and vanished with a
puff of smoke i looked at the
bathroom door and i thought i
heard some one chuckle over there and
then i saw another gray globe of
smoke forming at the keyhole it
slowly grew and grew till it was as
big as a baseball and then it
detached itself from the door and
floated across the room
i crawled noiselessly under the bath
room door it was one of those bath
rooms midway between two sleeping
rooms and there were a couple of
chuckle headed young fellows sitting
on the floor laughing to
themselves both were about half
soused and they were having a good

time one of them had a slender hollow
brass curtain rod and he was soaping
the end of it and
sticking it into the keyhole then he
would fill his mouth with cigarette
smoke and blow a soap bubble which
drifted into the old mans room what
is he doing now said one of them he
is on the floor praying said the
other taking the rod out of the
keyhole and looking through let me
blow a couple said the first young
man you are too soused said the
second one dont be selfish said the
first one gawd gawd said the voice
from the room i had just left i am
haunted by ghostly smoke i will live
right all the rest of my life if you
only let me off this time
give him another bubble said the
first young man he has got it
coming to him evidently so
they gave him half a dozen more
bubbles the noise
in the haunted mans room ceased for
some minutes what is he doing now
said the first young man i cant see
him said the second one just then
there came a kicking kind of a noise
on the wall i went into the
haunted mans room and found his
closet door was open i went in and he
was just dying he had hanged himself
to a hook on the wall with a trunk
cord those two young fellows had
just the wrong man for their little
practical joke or
just the right man if you want to
look at it that way i

went away from there at once not
wishing to be on hand if there
was any investigation yours
for conscience and coincidence
and may they never meet

JUNE 6
Not a Fish

well boss i have
been over to
take a look at that 300
pound mola mola fish[1]
and it is my opinion that it
should not be
allowed in any american
aquarium at all
it is not a fish
take it from me it is
some kind of a german
pancake with fins eat
it and the infernal thing
will explode inside of you it is
just as well to distrust any
strange looking fish that may
be caught off these coasts while
the u boats are
around beware the
hunderhand methods of
the enemy yours till the
recording angel catches up with
his story of
hohenzollerns i have known

JUNE 7
At the Zoo

speaking of the aquarium i
was up at the zoo the
other day and when i saw all
the humans staring at
the animals i grew thankful that
i am an insect and
not an animal it must be
very embarrassing to
be looked at all the time by an
assorted lot of human beings and
commented upon as if
one were a freak the animals find the
humans just as strange and silly looking
as the humans find the
animals but they
cannot say so and the fact that
they cannot say so
makes them quite angry the leopard
told me that was one thing that
made the wild cat wild as for
himself he says there is
one gink that comes every day and looks
and looks and looks at him i
think said the leopard he
is waiting to see if i ever really do
change my spots

JUNE 10
Prohibition[1] Rushes Toward Us

i went into a
speakeasy the other night
with some of the

boys and we were all sitting
around under one of
the tables making
merry with crumbs and
cheese and what not but
after while a strange
melancholy descended
upon the jolly crew and
one old brown veteran roach
said with a sigh well
boys eat drink and
be maudlin for
tomorrow we are dry the
shadow of the padlock
rushes toward us
like a sahara sandstorm
flinging itself at an oasis
for years myself and my
ancestors before me have
inhabited yonder ice box but
the day approaches
when our old homestead
will be taken away from
here and scalded out
yes says i soon there will
be nothing but that
eheu fugaces stuff[2]
on every hand i
never drank it says he
what kind of a
drink is it
it is bitter as wormwood
says i and the
only chaser to it is
the lethean water[3]
it is not the booze itself
that i regret so
much said the old brown
roach it is the

golden companionship of
the tavern myself
and my ancestors have been
chop house and tavern
roaches for hundreds of years
countless generations back
one of my elizabethan
forbears was plucked from
a can of ale in the
mermaid tavern by
will shakespeare and
put down kit marlowe s back
what subtle wits they were in
those days said i yes
he said and later
another one of my
ancestors was
introduced into a larded
hare that addison
was eating by dicky steele
my ancestor came
skurrying forth dicky
said is that your own
hare joe or a wig a
thing which addison
never forgave yours is a
remarkable family
history i said yes he
said i am the last
of a memorable
line one of my
ancestors was found drowned
in the ink well
out of which poor
eddie poe wrote the
raven we have
always associated with wits
bohemians and bon
vivants my maternal

grandmother was slain by
john masefield with
a bung starter[4] well well it
is sad i said the
glad days pass yes
he says soon we will all
be as dry as the
egyptian scarab that
lies in the sarcophagus
beside the mummy of rameses and
he hasn t had a
drink for four thousand
years it is sad for
you he continued but
think how much sadder it
is for me with
a family tradition such as
mine only one of my
ancestors cheese it i said
interrupting him i do
not wish to injure
your feelings but i weary
of your ancestors i
have often noticed that
ancestors never boast
of the descendants who boast
of ancestors i would
rather start a family than
finish one blood will tell but often
it tells too much

JUNE 19
Income Tax Slacker[1]

boss i see by the
papers that there is
one income tax slacker who

owes 14 800 000 dollars lest
there be any possibility of
mistake i wish to state
publicly that i am not the
person the salary i receive for
my writings in the sun
dial falls considerably below that
figure even in good
years yours for
vers libre as usual

JUNE 21
The Raiding Habit

boss please leave your
door locked nights and
the keyhole open there is
no telling when i
may want to enter
quickly leaving some large
uniformed person
on the outside the
district attorney[1] has the
raiding habit very
badly his maxim seems to
be in case of doubt
raid what is set before
you the turn of the
insects will come next no
doubt it is true that
after making his raids he
seldom brings people to trial
but that may only be
because he has no
evidence and in the
meantime one has been
raided i think

perhaps he is suffering
from a case of
psychological suggestion it
is the word raid
which appeals to him and
inflames his imagination he
sees it in the papers
perhaps in connection with
the war and every time
he reads of a trench
raid he pulls a
raid here at least
that is one explanation
yours for less—and
better government

         • • •

Archy tells us that he is busily engaged organizing an army of
potato bugs to crawl into Germany and eat the new crop. All he
wants is transportation assured him.

JUNE 24
A Loyal Allied Cootie[1]

sir you stated in the
sun dial the other day that archy
was to lead an army of potato
bugs into germany to eat the
crop you have been
misinformed and it is my request that
you give this correction as prominent
place as you gave
your original error otherwise i
shall be compelled to bring suit
against the sun dial i
take no stock in any of
these get peace quick schemes and
more than that you do

me an injury when you
imply that i habitually
associate with potato
bugs the potato bug is one of the
least intelligent of insects and
his moral character is
not above reproach i do
not wish to muckrake even
the lower animals but i
could tell you a lot about the
sort of life led by
potato bugs if i chose the
potato bug is entirely
untrustworthy i would be willing to
use him against germany if i
were not sure that he
would prove a traitor to the cause he
would immediately begin to eat
allied rations upon his arrival in france
this potato bug story was put
over on you by some
german
propagandist i met with
a cootie that came back from france
recently who has been in the
german trenches for two years he is a
loyal allied cootie and
he tells me that most of the
cooties now in the
allied trenches are pro
german cooties they have been
trained by the german high
command for years before the war
drilled and redrilled and it is their
job to bite riflemen
machine gunners and so forth
at just the right place at the
right time to destroy their aim when
the germans are launching an

attack every
morning hindenburg[2] ludendorff[3] and
the kaiser[4] hold a
cootie review at headquarters so
my informant tells me and the
cooties are glad to get out of
germany as the rations are
getting slimmer and slimmer
there but even the cooties are
getting scarce in germany now they
are calling on the
cootie class of 1920 he says he
volunteered he says to go into the
german trenches and bite
german machine gunners but it was
only his loyalty that held him to the
job for so long finally he
says instead of the cooties
biting germans the
germans began to bite cooties and when
that came about he
thought it almost time to leave
it must be an interesting sight to see
the kaiser on a reviewing
stand with a million
cooties drilling by each one trying
to do the goose step yours
for fewer and better germans

JULY 2
Dialogue among the Plants

well boss i have
been looking over your
garden and my
thoughts on the
subject have fallen naturally

into the form of a little
dialogue among the
plants and inhabitants of the
garden to wit as follows

garter snake
how wan on the first of july
the gardens of april appear
now the plants that aspired to the sky
droop and think of the bier

first onion
i am a disillusioned onion plant
so sad so sad am i
that if one fed me to a maiden ant
she would curl up and die

indeterminate vegetable
in youth i hoped a bean to grow
but what i am i do not know

first beet
i have malaria croup and botts

second beet
i have such leprous looking spots

third beet
i was a beet of promise as a young beet
but now i have the mournful feeling
that neither root nor top nor peeling
will ever be fit to eat

garter snake
ah what a melancholy patch

toad
yon egg plant there will never hatch

indeterminate vegetable
one paused by me but yesterday
and spoke of me as hay
but what i really am i do not know

cucumber vine
strange insects walk me to and fro

pepper plant
had i been treated with formaldehyde
that goat that in the dewy eves
came here to feast upon my leaves
might not have died

second onion
the great splay feet of destiny
have trodden me have trampled me

rhubarb
ah once i hoped to line a pie

cucumber vine
will you marauding hen pass by
or must i die

indeterminate vegetable
what thing i am i do not know
men have no name for me

garter snake
i think you are a spinach vine

toad
and i should call you eglantine

sparrow
perhaps you are a pea

first bean
i was a bean
unto some glad tureen
i might have given tone
but a dog yestereen
hiding a bone
took from me all my mundane hope

indeterminate vegetable
sometimes i think i am a canteloupe

second bean
drooping between two hills of corn
i am the butt of all mens scorn

third bean
ah how i aspired
in the glad may morn

fourth bean
i am so tired so tired

sparrow
friend toad from yonder plant keep you away
i saw a neighbor child but yesterday
from off its foliage pluck a spray
and then how he yelled
and his hand turned black and swelled

indeterminate vegetable
perhaps im not a plant at all
but some strange sort of animal

first cabbage
pigeons have riddled me and weasels

second cabbage
im spotted as with german measles

first corn stalk
woe

second corn stalk
woe

third corn stalk
woe is me ah woe woe woe

fourth corn stalk
even the weeds beside me do not grow

first turnip
gott

second turnip
gott gott gott

third turnip
mildew blight and rot

fourth turnip
and smallpox like as not

indeterminate vegetable
but cheer brothers cheer
perhaps before the year
dwindles to winter drear
well poison some one here
i know not what i am
parsley from siam
a vegetable ham
or a long island clam
but this i know i hate
my miserable state
and all human beans
i hate life and fate
i hate men and greens
i hate hens and grass

i hate garden sass
who gets me on a plate
shall learn how i hate
i hate chards romaine
children and goats
old men and young men
people and oats
and im full of ptomaine
who puts me within him
scorpions had better skin him
who puts me inside her
had better eat a spider
i know not what i be
alfalfa corn or pea
but cheer brothers cheer
before the glad new year
well poison some one here

i might give you some advice
about your garden
boss but likely you would
not thank me for it
so i will only make one
suggestion to wit if the
garden were mine i
would set out another cabbage
plant in it and then
give it to the butterflies for
an aviation ground

July 11
Ye Instead of The

"Does Archy ever visit Greenwich Village?" asks R.P. "I
found myself in company with a cockroach of a dissipated but
still scholarly appearance in one of the cafés over there the other
evening. . . ."

Archy, we regret to say, will frequent the Village. Indeed, we hear that he is planning to open a café of his own to be known as "Ye Crusty Cockroach."

"But why the 'Ye,' Archy?" we asked him. "Why not merely 'The'?"

And Archy, loping six-leggedly to the typewriter, laboriously replied:

it is going to be one
of those quaint
places boss and all those
quaint places have to
be ye instead of the
in a ye place you can
serve almost anything
and get away
with it but in a
the place you have to
have a certain amount
of eats and drinks
and that increases the
expense of operation
enormously i am no
pig but i do wish to
make enough money once in
my life to be
among the
excess prophets or the
excise profits or
what ever you call
them

For our part, we shall never eat goulash in a place that is conducted by Archy—so many of these Greenwich Village artists are always Putting Themselves Into Their Work.

JULY 23
One Thing That Makes Crickets So Melancholy

well boss it may
surprise you to learn
that a cricket does not
sing to be cheerful
as chas dickens believed[1]
he sings because he
feels so melancholy i
asked one with whom
i have become well
acquainted what his song
meant and he
replied
there are no words
to go with
that music but the
music is sad i
make that music these
hot nights because i
have prickly heat
and there is nothing else
to do and another
cricket said yes
our song is sad i am
not troubled by the
heat but my song is
melancholy too the words to
my song said the second
cricket are as follows
and he repeated them for
me to wit
my love fell into a spiders web
squeak squeak squeak
and she screamed with pain as he
crunched her bones into his
bloody beak squeak squeak

squeak yes i said that is
sad very sad said the
cricket but not as sad as the
second stanza which goes
as follows my love got caught in
the crack of the door squeak
squeak squeak and i think with
grief of the way she died whenever
i hear it creak
squeak squeak squeak
whenever i hear it creak
squeak squeak squeak
that brings tears to my eyes
i said yes he said
there is nothing you could call
jolly about the
second stanza nor the
third fourth and fifth stanzas
friend i said
hurriedly let me hear the
last stanza
he looked at me as if
i had struck him
and hurried off with
tears in his gentle eyes
one thing that
makes crickets so
melancholy is that
they have the artistic
temperament[2]

AUGUST 2
Sphinx

what is all this mystery
about the sphinx
that has troubled so many

illustrious men
no doubt the very same
thoughts she thinks
are thought every day
by some obscure hen

• • • •

the dachsund
thinks the giraffe
is a very
queer looking
animal

AUGUST 6

Reports of My Exit

look a here boss this thing
has gotta stop i
appeal to you for protection that
roughneck guy down cellar who
sent up the dessicated remnant of
a common chocolate colored water bug
and put it down by our typewriter
labeled exit archy is a person wholly
devoid of any real human
sensibility it
wasnt even decently preserved frag
mentary if you get what i mean when
my time to exit comes again i am
not going out that way in the cellar of
a printing shop i think i shall be a
humming bird next time or maybe i
shall take on something practical like
being a pawnbroker that depends a good
deal on how i am treated in this place
anyhow i am tired of this kind of
practical joke the reports of my exit

as uncle mark twain said are greatly
exaggerated[1]

AUGUST 10
Glorious Footfulness

in many places here and
there
i think that fate
is quite unfair
yon centipede upon
the floor
can boast of
tootsies by the score
consider my
distressing fix
my feet are limited
to six
did i a hundred
feet possess
would all that glorious
footfulness
enable me
to stagger less
when i am
overcome by heat
or if i had
a hundred feet
would i
careering oer the floor
stagger
proportionately more
well i suppose
the mind serene
will not tell
destiny its mean

the truly
philosophic mind
will use
such feet as it can find
and follow calmly
fast or slow
the feet it has
where eer they go

AUGUST 13
Falling Upwards

one of the most
pathetic things i
have seen recently
was an intoxicated person
trying to fall
down a moving stairway
it was the escalator at
the thirty fourth street
side of the
pennsylvania station
he could not fall down as
fast as it
carried him up again but
he was game he kept on
trying he was
stubborn about it
evidently it was a part of
his tradition habit and
training always to fall down
stairs when intoxicated and
he did not intend to
be defeated this time i
watched him for an hour
and moved sadly away thinking
how much sorrow

drink is responsible for the
buns by great men
reached and kept
are not attained
by sudden flight but they
while their companions slept
were falling upwards
through the night[1]

AUGUST 14
Headgear

boss i wish you
would get some sort of
headgear for me so
that my cranium would not
get so sore
through operating the
typewriter or else oil the
machine so the keys
will work easier i have to
hit every letter so hard that i
am afraid i will get
concussion of the brain and
my literary style will suffer
from it can you not
fix up some device whereby i
will be able to use
punctuation i have been crit
icised so frequently for not
using any punctuation that i am
becoming sensitive
about it yours till
we get the potsdam gas range

August 24
Smile When You Ride on the Subway

boss i hold no brief
for the new subway system[1]
or the way it is operated or
anything connected with it but
fairness compells me to state
that i find it no more
difficult to get about town on
the new system than on the
old of course that may be because
it was always difficult for me
there has been so much knocking
however that i
think some one should call
attention to at least one good
feature and that is
the air in the new seventh avenue
line it is fit to breathe and
there is plenty of it
perhaps more people would find it
easier to get about on the subways if
they played my system
too many people get on a subway in
order to go somewhere of course
if you do that you are bound to
disappointment
subway riding is not a game of
skill at all it is a game of
chance you should not get on a
subway for the purpose of going
somewhere
you should just get on a subway train
then if you go somewhere that is so
much gain people should
cultivate a delight in the
unexpected there is no thrill of

discovery in boarding a train that
takes you somewhere you have counted
on going to
anyhow how can you tell
whether you want to go to a place or
not until you have tried going there
get onto any train and get off again
after a while and
then look over the place you have
come to with a sympathetic mind
and an open heart and
you will probably find something
excellent and
admirable in it the
whole thing is in the
point of view and the
philosophic attitude which you
bring to subway riding some
people are discontented no
matter where they are and
other people find something
good in all places one who is
in harmony with the
cosmic all as our
friend hermione might say
will find one place just as good
as another for all
places are equidistant from the
spiritual centre of
the universe if you
apprehend my meaning
think of that the next time you
go into the station at
times square and be happy
smile when you ride
on the subway but
do not smile at any of the
feminine guards or ticket sellers
they might not

understand it some of them
seem to understand very little
if you want to go
anywhere in particular
hire a taxi

September 16
A Genuine Quip

well boss i
had a good joke all fixed
up for your column and
then a book worm
came along and
spoiled it for me i
often have bad
luck with my jokes
especially with my puns
but i will explain this
one to you and
you can see for your self
that it would have been
quite a joke if the
latin language had been a
little different my
idea was to write a quip for
you saying aut kaiser aut
mihiel you see what i
mean dont you a pun on
the latin quotation aut
caesar aut nihil and
then along comes a book
worm and says archy that
quotation is not
aut caesar aut nihil it
is aut caesar aut nullus

well boss better
luck next time some day
i hope to make a
genuine quip for you[1]

SEPTEMBER 26
Tobacco Fund

why not buy
thrift stamps[1] up to
the place where
you can get a
liberty bond with them
and then turn
over the liberty bond to
the sun tobacco fund[2]
yours till hell
recedes from earth

OCTOBER I
The Advice of Your Little Friend

few men who
are chronically
short are
too short to get
their chins
above the rail
of a bar
cut out the
booze and buy
thrift stamps and
put the stamps
into a liberty

bond is the
advice of your
little friend

OCTOBER 26
Jane Gad Fly

A COMMUNIQUE

                              at the front in France
dear boss i really must speak to you about archy oh i
know i am only an insect too but you are paying too
much attention to one cockroach what i mean is that i
have to hear too much of this archy of course the principle
trouble is neysa you probably know that neysa mcmein[1]
has brought winsor mckays dinosaur gertie[2] over here to
bite the german infantry gertie is doing her bit which is
large as you know that dinosaurs stand something like
twenty feet high at the shoulder but i want to speak to
you about neysa more than gertie it is no longer being
kept a secret from the kaiser that i am neysas manager
but still you know boss how it is with these temperamen-
tal artists and how the biter gets bit really neysa runs me
hand and foot and boss if i hadnt always read those com-
munications from archy in order to keep in touch with
current thought among my fellow insects, i wouldn't mind
but neysa trails about france with her uniform pockets
stuffed with very ancient communications from archy
which she insists upon reading aloud particularly in times
of stress such as when a boche[3] aeroplane is overhead and
we have not yet found out which house in our block he
is aiming his bomb at neysa is here as a y m c a enter-
tainer and do you think she is rightly representing amer-
ican womanhood to read old archys to me under those
conditions i dont neysas sketches that she does for the
pretty soldiers are not half bad though they get smeared

all over due to lack of fixitive, but boss do you think that
a young person who draws pretty girls ought to read aloud
all the time to person who cant get away from her i dont
i hope you can do something about this i have nothing
personal against archy

yours for better behaved artists

jane gad fly

OCTOBER 28
The Influenza[1]

well boss i suppose you
wonder what has become of
me lately i have been
quarantined or rather
i quarantined myself
voluntarily lest
i help spread the
influenza on the
back of a cockroach
no larger than
myself millions of
influenza germs may lodge i
have a sense of responsibility
to the public and i
have been lying for two weeks
in a barrel of moth
balls in a drug store
without food or water it
strikes me as a good time to
come across with that
raise of salary you
are always promising me

NOVEMBER 9
A Tall Story

well boss i had a
terrible adventure the
other day it was the
day that the news
of the armistice came which
afterward proved not to be
true[1] if you can
remember that far
back
i was on one of the upper
floors of the
woolworth building[2] and as
you may have noticed it has many
upper floors and some of the
uppermost floors are
very far up
this floor was about six
hundred feet above
broadway
i was hunting bits of
sandwich in a waste
paper basket when the
paper shower began
everybody began to
hunt paper to tear up and
throw out the window and to
make a frightful story as
mild as possible i
was on one of the pieces of
paper that was torn and
thrown out of the
window down down down
i went whirling around and around
for a hundred feet and

screaming at the
top of my voice but in
all that noise what were the
cries of one small cockroach
i doubt if i was heard
twenty feet away
down and down i fell and just as i
thought i might be dashed to pieces on
some bald head two hundred yards below
a gust of wind caught me up and up up up
i went again to make
a tall story as short as
possible this kept up for
nearly two hours i
felt like a person who
has climbed aboard an
airplane thinking it is
an automobile and who
does not discover his
mistake until he
is above some brutal looking
mountain range
i finally came into contact with a
piece of ticker tape[3]
and crawled aboard it in
midair it seemed bigger somehow
but it evidently
thought it was a snake it
went wreathing and twining
itself through the air
and when it finally did come
down it twined itself around the
neck of an inebriated
gentleman who saw me and
whose first words were
i do not see a cockroach i
only think i see a cockroach
o heaven if i only

get over this attack i
will never drink another
drop yours as ever

NOVEMBER 14
Chief Janitor

why not let the
kaiser be chief janitor of
the peace palace at
the hague then
when anything went
wrong anywhere he
could be called in and
cussed yours for
punishments

NOVEMBER 23
I Saw Archy

well boss it is
surprising how many
gossips there are left in
this world and how
easy it is to ruin a
person's reputation
a few days ago an
alleged friend of yours
remarked to another
alleged friend i saw
archy on a bun in
a cafe down town the other
day and the second alleged
friend told another person
that archy had been seen

publicly intoxicated and
the other person went
around saying poor
archy he drinks like a
water bug until my
reputation is ruined you
would think i was
the habitual companion of
the well known dipsas snake[1]
and the truth of
the whole thing is very
simple your alleged friend did
see me on a bun
in a cafe it was a
common ordinary bun such as
you spread butter on
and eat and i
was eating at it
just as i would sit on any other
piece of bread and eat but
now all my friends are
saying to me
did i see you on a
bun or did i not
answer yes or no and if i
answer no they say
prevaricator i saw you on a
bun and if i answer yes they
say i thought so and
will not let me explain and
if i do not answer
at all they say
aha too full for
utterance sometimes i
hate the world

DECEMBER 3
Peace Conference

[Marquis's column for December 3 begins with dispatches
from both Hermione and Fothergil Finch, supposedly sent the
day before by wireless from aboard the U. S. S. Orizaba, which
is bearing them across the Atlantic to the peace conference then
being held in Paris. Then Archy adds his note.]

                    wireless to the sun dial
                    u s s orizaba[1] dec 2 all at sea
                    well boss here am i
                    your own archy
                    i stowed away in
                    fothergill finchs steamer
                    trunk and shall
                    act as his secretary i
                    have already found several
                    relatives and ship
                    mates of former years on
                    board the vessel the
                    grub is probably better
                    in some spots on this
                    ship than in others but
                    so far i have only
                    struck the others

DECEMBER 5
More and More at Sea

                    u s s orizaba dec 5 more and
                    more at sea
                    well boss i am sorry to
                    tattle on anybody but the
                    truth is that fothergill is
                    filing stuff he wrote

before he started he is
too ill to write anything he
is the color of the
contents of a can
of pea soup
but there is not as
much in him this
morning he asked the
steward how long people
usually live after a ship sinks
and the steward said
only a few minutes it
seems a long time said
fothergil sadly and the
steward said this is not
rough weather wait until we
catch some really rough
weather
why continued the steward i have
crossed the ocean in
december almost upside down
that is nothing said
fothergil i am crossing
the ocean almost
inside out

December 6
Poet Overboard

u s s george washington[1] dec 5
at sea kindness of assistant wireless
operator to the sun dial
well boss you will wonder
how it is that i started away
for france on the orizaba and
am now sending you
this despatch from the

george washington that is you
will wonder if this despatch ever
gets through which it may not
if mr creel[2]
catches the wireless man sending
it well boss to make
a wet story as dry as possible it
happened in this wise
yesterday fothergil finch
was leaning in a
melancholy attitude over the rail
spouting poetry like a
bolsheviki triton[3]
into the trough of the sea and
i was by his right elbow
listening for there is
little sport for a
cockroach aboard ship and he
must dissipate his ennui as best he
can when suddenly fothergil
began to writhe and gyrate
with a paroxysm of vers libre
that came from his very
solar plexus and inadvertently struck
me with his elbow and
knocked me overboard as i
fell i screamed loudly poet overboard
but either the voice of one small
cockroach was not heard in the
december breeze or else
everybody was glad of it for all
i heard was a burst of
mocking laughter from the deck down down
down i went underneath the ship
itself i clung desperately for a few
minutes to the rapidly revolving screw
but was forced to let loose as it
did not seem to be intending to
come up for air when i was finally cast to

the surface and i admit i
was feeling sad i looked at
the sun and rapidly computed my
latitude and longitude but
there did not seem to be enough of
either to float on indefinitely
pretty soon i said with a sigh i shall be
wet through clean down to
the freckles on my soul and
then i shall sink a sodden albeit a
somewhat small mass and the vast and
charnel sea i said for i
was determined to be
literary to the last will
smack its briny lips above my
corse[4] but just as all hope seemed
gone and i was about to open
my lips[5] for the last drink i came
into contact with something round and
hard
floating on the waters immediately
before i had felt as lonely as the
first chapter of genesis now i
was cheered looking at the thing
on which i was floating i discovered it
to be
a new kind of mine with a gun cotton
fuse which can be lighted even under
water and at that moment
a sword fish swam up
and began to clash his beak
against the iron
container of the high explosive
until he struck a spark of fire
which fell upon the fuse which began to
burn slowly but steadily i
realized at once what the
plan was for at that instant i
saw the ship with the president[6] aboard

rise over the horizon and
bear directly down upon me it was
a trained swordfish educated by
some treacherous and
unreconstructed german for this
very act all the ordinary
mines had been swept out of the
path of the ship by the
official mine sweepers[7] but with
hellish ingenuity this new sort of
mine had been placed in the path of the
george washington and ignited by the
trained swordfish i
at once attacked the
burning fuse with my teeth but
eat as fast as i could i am after
all only one small cockroach and
in my excitement i was swallowing
all i ate i was soon
full of gun cotton and the fuse
had not been eaten half in two i
gave myself and the president and
mr creel up for
lost the fate of the world hung upon
one little insect and he was overloaded
already but i think quickly in
emergencies it suddenly
occurred to me that after all i
need not swallow all i bit off and
this brilliant idea saved the president the
world and democracy i attacked the
fuse again but this time i spit out
what i bit off and just as the
george washington struck the mine the
fuse which was still burning
and about to explode
fell into the water i
swarmed aboard the george washington
crawled into the wireless

man's cabin and wrote what i
had done on his typewriter mr
creel was there this
story must not go out he said or
if it is sent back to
america dr grayson[8] must have the
credit for the
action no said dr grayson i
will take no credit for any deed i
have not performed the credit is
nothing to me mr creel i wrote
on the typewriter all i
care for is the fact that i have
saved democracy mr creel was still
debating the matter but when the
wireless man went to dinner his
assistant began sending this despatch for
says he there is
glory enough for us all

DECEMBER 10
Freedom of the Seas

u s s george washington
december tenth passing the
azores there was a
conference on board the
ship yesterday about the
freedom of the seas[1] but
i cant say that
i think very much was
accomplished at
least no one took
me into his confidence
later the subject
was taken up in
an informal way down

in the stoke hold bill
says one coal passer
to another whats all
this about the
freedom of the seas aint
the seas free
they are and then
again they aint says
bill explain yourself says
his friend when are
they and when not
now yous asking something
says bill
man and boy says his
friend i have followed
the sea for
15 years and never yet
seen any signs
they wasnt free except
where the germans done it
have you ever saw
any such signs yourself
bill well says
bill i have and then
again i havent
i dont get you says his
friend well says bill
some do and some
dont

DECEMBER 11
Two Old Men

Archy gets around a good deal, in one way or another. Just
before he left for France he gave us a poem, and he claims that
he actually was in the wine vault and heard and saw the things

narrated therein. We publish the poem—one of Archy's rare attempts at rhyme—without, however, guaranteeing its authenticity:

down in a wine vault underneath the city
        two old men were sitting they were drinking booze
torn were their garments hair and beards were gritty
        one had an overcoat but hardly any shoes

overhead the street cars through the streets were running
        filled with happy people going home to christmas
in the adirondacks the hunters all were gunning
        big ships were sailing down by the isthmus

in came a little tot for to kiss her granny
        such a little totty she could scarcely tottle
saying kiss me grandpa kiss your little nanny
        but the old man beaned her with a whiskey bottle

outside the snowflakes began for to flutter
        far at sea the ships were sailing with the seamen
not another word did angel nanny utter
        her grandsire chuckled and pledged the whiskey demon

up spake the second man he was worn and weary
        tears washed his face which otherwise was pasty
she loved her parents who commuted on the erie
        brother im afraid you struck a trifle hasty

she came to see you all her pretty duds on
        bringing christmas posies from her mother's garden
riding in the tunnel underneath the hudson
        brother was it rum caused your heart to harden

up spake the first man here i sits a thinking
        how the countrys drifting to a sad condition
here i sits a dreaming here i sits a drinking
        here i sits a dreading dreading prohibition

when in comes nanny my little daughters daughter
      me she has been begging ever since october
for to sign the pledge its ended now in slaughter
      i never had the courage when she caught me sober

all around the world little tots are begging
      grandpas and daddies for to quit their drinking
reformers eggs em on i am tired of egging
      tired of being cowed cowering and slinking

i struck for freedom im a man of mettle
      though i never would a done it had i not been drinking
from athabasca south to popocatapetl
      we must strike for freedom quit our shrinking

said the second old man i beg your pardon
      brother please forgive me my words were hasty
i get your viewpoint our hearts must harden
      try this ale it is bitter brown and tasty

said the first old man hear me sobbing
      poor little nanny shes gone to himmel
principle must conquer though hearts be throbbing
      just curl your lip around this kimmel

down in a wine vault underneath the city
      they sat drinking while the snow was falling
wicked old men with scarcely any pity
      the moral of my tale is quite appalling

DECEMBER 13
Passing the Bock

brest france dec 13[1]
by soulless telegraph to
the sun dial well
boss i just arrived and

i have a grand idea instead
of sticking to
hermione and fothy and the
peace conference i am
off for holland i am going
to interview
wilhelm hohenzollern i
shall also interview gott[2]
if wilhelm took
gott with him to the
am i wrong in castle[3] where
he is stopping
they may be there together
quarrelling about who
started it passing the
bock[4] used to be the
favorite german indoor
sport but passing the
buck has superseded it

DECEMBER 14

The Former Kaiser

am i wrong in castle
holland december fourteenth
well i arrived here
by aeroplane after a bad
night and have just seen the
former kaiser i
got into the castle this
morning with the blutwurst[1]
for the kaisers breakfast
well bill i said
what i want to know is
this did you start the war
or did you not and if
so why would you do it

over again and are
you sorry for it
what war are you
talking about says bill
has there been a war
do not try to stall me
says i try some of this
most excellent blutwurst says
bill so you say
there has been a
war do you
i deny it i deny
everything
there is a movement on
foot i understand
to make me responsible
for some alleged trouble or
other that is
supposed to have occurred
somewhere but i do not
intend to allow myself to
be trapped i know i have
enemies but the truth will
triumph helped by
our good german gott and my
shining sword i deny
everything i repeat
i looked at the man boss
and i said to
myself he is a dangerous
character still he is playing a
deep deep game i was
prepared to hear him deny the
responsibility for starting the
war but it is a deeper game than
that he is playing he is
trying to get it
across that from first to
last the war was kept a

secret from him come and see
me again soon he said as i
took my leave and let us talk some
more about this
strange notion of yours that
there has been a
war you interest me
deeply i have another
appointment with him
for tomorrow

DECEMBER 16
Abdication Underneath the Bough

am i wrong in castle
holland december the sixteenth
yesterday was sunday and
i did not see the
former kaiser but i
wrote out some verses for
him which go
this way
an abdication underneath the bough[1]
a lake of beer an apple cake and thou
beside me singing lieber augustine[2]
and exile bill were happiness enow
the erstwhile kaiser wrote and having writ
he went and tore up every word of it
hes trying now to pick up paper scraps
and eat them every little inky bit
i sent my soul through the invisible
some secret of the entente plans to spell
anon my soul returned to me and said
where do you go from here question mark
you go to hell full stop

DECEMBER 19
Who Pays for All This

am i wrong in castle
holland december nineteenth
the erswhile kaiser has a
typewriting machine that
speaks english and
crawling into the presence this
morning i clicked off this
question bill when are you
going to leave holland
bill seized the machine and wrote
i am not going to leave holland
i wrote bill you
said you were not going to
leave your throne either
bill wrote i did not leave my
throne it was taken away
during my absence
i wrote holland may be pulled
out from under you in the same way
bill wrote it is a
long time until lunch it seems to
me what are those cooks doing i
have had scarcely anything
to eat since breakfast
i wrote bill are you the
star boarder here or who pays for
all this bill wrote
such things are beneath my
consideration but i understand that the cheque will
be put into one bundle and
they will shake dice to see who
pays them at the peace
conference i wrote bill you
are hitting the pipe these days or
some thing bill wrote the interview is

closed i must get to work
on my autobiography the second
chapter will deal with a
secret invasion of germany by
belgium which i
forgave and hushed up simply because
i did not wish to go to war and
the third chapter tells again
how much i always loved
america and everything
american why archy i even eat
with american made teeth and last
christmas i used those
teeth on american food that
found its way to me somehow through
your wonderful
organization for feeding american
prisoners

DECEMBER 23
The Former Czar

by wireless to the
sun dial on the
road to paris well
boss i have left the
former kaiser flat he is
a dull sort of person who
thinks only of his food and
more than that i have made an
important discovery i am
on the way to paris in
the company of a
russian who conceals a
mild face beneath an
angry beard and who is no less
a person than stop a

moment now and get a long
breath for i do not
want to shock you
have you set yourself so that
you can bear the impact of my
news very well then i
will continue no
less a person than
nicholas romanoff the
former czar nicholas second of
russia[1] i am
travelling incognito in
one of his pockets and he
is on the way to
paris to represent his
former empire at
the peace conference he
also is travelling incognito but
that is not his fault he
tells every one he sees that
he is czar nicholas and that
he is not dead
look at me he says
are there any bullet
holes in me
there are not the
story of my death at the
hands of the boksheviki is merely
a press agent yarn
but said an
english soldier whom
we met in the
outskirts of belgium
yesterday the fact that there
are no bullet holes in
you proves nothing
there are plenty of other
people with no bullet
holes in them

not russians said the czar
that shows how little you
know of the russian situation
we stopped today for
lunch at an american y m c a hut
and the czar was
easily persuaded to talk
about himself what i
want to do he said is get to
america right after
the peace conference and
write a book about my
experiences as czar and
ex czar before some faker gets
ahead of me there are
millions and millions of men who
understand russia from the
inside so they say but my
story is unique i am the
only living person who
understands russia from the
outside if some one would lend me a
pair of army shoes i
could do the remaining leagues
or versts² as we used
to say back home with
less discomfort just think of it
he said brought up in
luxury and affluence
with vodka flowing like water
about the palace and now begging
a pair of army boots which of
course i will return as
soon as i reach paris and
am identified and get a
little advance from some of the
russians in that city i
called at amerongen castle in
holland and saw wilhelm

hohenzollern and the
darned fat head refused to
recognize me all right bill i
told him i scarcely recognize you
either all is quits between us
dont come around when i am
making good on the
lecture platform in
america and ask for a hand out
thank you for the shoes they
are too big for me all of us
romanoffs have small and
aristocratic feet i
will send them back either
from paris or from america can you
let me have a stamp and a
cigarette

1919

JANUARY 7
At the Tomb of Napoleon

paris france jan seven nine
teen nineteen well boss
today i feel somewhat
solemn yesterday i
stood at the tomb of
napoleon and beside me stood
the man who would be
nicholas of russia and
czar of all the romanoffs
if he had his rights and
we exchanged thoughts
on kings past present and future
i am a king in abeyance
said the czar i am a
has been but i will come again
all i want is enough
money to get my trunks from
siberia and my other clothes to
appear before the peace
conference and have my claims
recognized alas to lose a great
empire through lack of a
few paltry yards of cloth and a clean
collar and he wept for a
moment dash bracket first i

must tell you how the czar and i
are able to talk with one
another i have six legs as you
may have noticed each leg stands
for four letters of the
alphabet for instance the left
upper leg is a b c and d
when i point up with it that is
a when i point down with it
it is b when i point to the right
that is c when i point to
the left that is d the left centre leg stands for
e f g and h the left lower
leg stands for i j k l and
so on with the right upper right
centre and right lower legs
there are twenty six letters in the
alphabet and i can only represent
twenty four of them so i
get along without sometimes
w and y bracket dash
the czar wept for a moment and
then he said archly the
romanoffs were kings when the
bonapartes were running a
boarding house in corsica but
behold the two of us
napoleon and nicholas both down
and out archy misfortune is
the great leveller in the
old days my great grandfather
used to let his servants
board with the bonapartes
while he stayed in a swell
hotel when he visited corsica for the
fishing season but now
napoleon and i are down and
out together and of
equal rank alas for royalty no

matter how a family gets
it it is hard to keep archy as
i stand here and think
of the troubles of royalty i
am almost tempted never to be a
king again i sometimes
think it would be better to
get a job somewhere and work
at it if it were not
for my unhappy people i would
make no effort to come
back napoleon was an
usurper and i was a
legitimate monarch but as i
look upon his urn archy i
can not but pity him archy
there is one thing i want to speak
to you about while i think
of it if you are going to
continue to travel with
me please do not stick your
head out of my pocket to
listen when i speak to new
acquaintances that marine who
was going to lend me five
francs the other day saw you
peeping out of my pocket and it
gave him the idea
that perhaps i had fleas or
something also and he
hurried away you see my
clothing is in disrepair and
people get ideas if they see you i
missed getting that five franc piece
and i had intended to
buy stamps with it and write
a special delivery letter to siberia
for my other clothes in
which to appear before the

peace conference to think that
the indiscretions of a
cockroach might lose a man
an empire but it was the
same way with napoleon
here my grandfather told me
that napoleon had the
itch and that all through the
battle of waterloo when
he should have been looking at
maps and things and
giving orders he was scratching
himself if he could have
kept his mind on the battle he
would have won it as usual to
think of it one great empire lost
on account of a cockroach and
another because of a
little skin eruption luck archy luck
rules the world and
most of mine has been bad
lately czar i said i do not
believe in luck if you
had worked harder on the job
and if napoleon here had not
got the swell head you both
might have kept your empires it
was your mistakes that
ditched you yes napoleon did make
mistakes said the czar one
of them was the time he invaded
russia it was a breach of
faith grandfather romanoff used to
say but he forgave him and as i
look upon his urn here
and think how luck has laid
him low i forgive him too us
romanoffs always were kind hearted
that way often i have

heard grandfather romanoff tell
how he repelled the
invasion at the head of his
troops he and napoleon met at
the entrance of the kremlin
and both drew their swords and
rushed at each other
but bonaparte was not as good
a fencer as my
grandfather romanoff he came of
a middle class family and had few
advantages in his youth the
first lick he struck went
wild and you can see the
nick his sword made in the
front door of the kremlin to
this day grandfather romanoff
disarmed him and might
have killed him but the
romanoffs were always the soul of
chivalry he handed napoleon's
sword back to him and said i
will give you another chance just then
the snow began to fall and
fell in a blinding storm they
fought for two hours in a snow
so dense they could not see
each others faces but only the
sword blades and the sparks from
their swords melted the snow that
touched them and they fought in
fog and steam my
grandfather romanoff wounded
him nine times and beat him
back and he left russia at once
but moscow had been ignited
by the sparks and the greater part
of it burned

JANUARY 14
Preliminary Peace

paris france
jan thirteen nine
teen nineteen well boss
i got into the
preliminary peace conference
yesterday but the czar remained
outside i went in his
pocket to the foreign
office in the quai
dorsay we got there just
after foch[1] and
clemenceau[2] and the czar
started to walk right past
the soldiers on guard
but could not get away with
it i dropped quietly to the
ground however and
entered—all those rulers and
premiers and so forth were
sitting at a long table
and for a minute
after i came in there was
nothing but a
solemn silence then foch
arose and went
down the table and
paused by clemenceau aha
thought i now we are
about to hear
something but all foch
said was do you have a
cigarette here are the
makings said the premier
bull[3] asked foch and
everybody laughed

just then a man with a
silver chain around his
neck discovered me and
i beat a retreat
while the beating was good
and rejoined the
czar who was in the street
pretending he was not
the czar at all but
trying to pass himself
off as a bulsheviki
archy he told me later
if i can once get in
incognito i will
reveal my true identity
later i saw
your friends hermione and
fothergil in the crowd outside
hanging onto the
picket fence from which i
judge she is not
yet a delegate

JANUARY 20
No Water Bug

paris france jan
twenty nineteen nineteen
well boss what were you
doing to let them slip
this bone dry stuff[1]
over when i was
out of the country i
thought you would look
after my interests
better than that i
think i will stay here

in france now
although the language
is a little difficult
and i have a
lot of competition
the news has taken my
thoughts away from the
peace conference
completely what matter
which kind of a world
they make if you
can not get a
drink in it
i am no water bug

FEBRUARY 24
Safer in America

paris somewhere in february
well boss we are
about to start for
america the czar and i
in the stokehold
if i cannot get a
hearing before the
peace conference
as the czar of all
the romanoffs my friend
says to me today i
will go to
america and be a
bolshevist
czar i said to him
why not go to russia
if you feel inclined to
be a bolshevist it

is safer in america
he replied

MARCH 5
An Interview with Mehitabel

I was surprised the other day, watching a detachment of soldiers leaving a troopship, to see a large cat slip quietly through the crowd, and, looking closely, saw to my joy that it was Mehitabel.

Anxious to hear from her, I overtook her in a quiet street and invited her into a saloon, where I quickly engaged a private room. Poor Mehitabel was looking rather seedy, and when I ordered milk for her and something else for myself, she shook her head. "No milk for me, child," she said, "but I don't mind taking a little of what you're taking. I had a terrible time on that ship—such weather—and I find a little wine of the country, or *Eau de Vie*[1]—yes, Rye will do very nicely, thanks."

• • •

I found she had been in Paris, with Archy, and asked after him. She was not quite satisfied with Archy. "Of course," she went on, "I would never go back on a *Cher vieux Ami*[2] like Archy: I am too much of a gentlewoman to do that—*noblesse oblige,*[3] *mon Capitain*—but since he took up with this Czar, or Caesar (as I prefer to give the title), he has been acting strangely. I warned him against this person, but it was no use; and while I found in Paris that a little wine of the country was very beneficial (thank you, Rye will do very nicely), between ourselves, Archy should stick to grapejuice *au naturel.*" Here she laughed quite a little. "To see Archy try to get home after a little conviviality—his gait, even with all his legs, is quite alarming. You know, between ourselves, Colonel, only *la Haute Classe*[4] really know how to carry their wine, and speaking for myself—thank you, Rye will do very nicely, I never could find out what Archy's antecedents were. Some of us," she looked at me proudly—"have Royal traditions behind us, but Archy has always been silent about his past. Of course, there is Royalty and Royalty, and I have had only too much reason to distrust all Caesars; one of them came between me and dear Mark Antony[5] [here Mehitabel almost broke down] and caused, oh! so much suffering! I will never forget it: nothing that occurred in any of my other existences came near that tragedy, and I have suffered, child—suffered with the Borgias, and the Medicis. Even in later times, as the Lily[6] of the stage—but I can scarcely bear to think of it all; it makes me quite faint, and it is really no wonder that I take a little wine—thank you, Rye will do very nicely. But though you see me now in a humble form, it will not always be so: many of my friends have been released into opera singers, and I have strong hopes that you, *mon cher Generale,* may yet be applauding me at the Metropolitan. I have quite a good voice, even now, and if you are sure the door is closed I will be glad—"

I feared the lady was becoming a little excited, and made a diversion.

"Tell me, Mehitabel," I said, "did you and Archy ever see the Sun Dial in Paris?"

• • •

"Why, certainly," she replied. "Not every day, but very frequently; in fact it was about all I read, for the papers—what with Bolsheviki and the demands of labor—were scarcely fit for a gentlewoman to read. I cannot bear to see the *cannaille*[7] forgetting themselves. Now in Antony's time—but I will not go back to that! By the way, Archy is a little cross with the 'Boss,' as he vulgarly calls the gentleman with the Spanish title who conducts our column.[8] He has scarcely published anything from Archy for some time, but, as I say, how do we know he ever received the wireless? Since the Government took it over there is quite too much of the Arrow and the Song[9] about it. Then he began to criticize the column. 'What does he mean?' he cried one day with the paper before him. 'What does he mean—"wried whim-scrambled flesh"?' I looked at the verses, over his head. " 'Why,' I said, 'that's only his Poetic License. Any Poet is allowed a certain amount of license.' 'Well,' said Archy, 'his License ought to be revoked.' Fancy talking like that! Poor Archy really is painfully *bourgeois* sometimes. I hear he is on his way across with the Caesar, but I doubt if I will stay to meet them. You know, there is something exhilarating about the wines of France—did you ever try Pontet Canet?—thank you, Rye will do very nicely! And then after July the First![10]—the place will be unbearable; really, I think this country is becoming painfully *bourgeois*."

• • •

Mehitabel sat silent for some time, and nodded a little. Then she woke with a start and said something about the wine of the country, but I took her home with me, and gave her a nice bed in the parlor. "*Toujours joyeuse,*[11] *Mon Prince, toujours gai,*" she murmured with a pathetic smile, as I covered her up. I left her some milk and saw that the window was a little open for air. In the morning she was gone, and the milk was untouched. I feel very anxious about her.

—SAMUEL CARNEW

MARCH 3
No Beer No Work

well boss the
czar is now parading
around with one
of these no
beer no work buttons[1]
on his coat
from which i take it
that unless
some one sets
them up again he
will refuse to
consider being an
emperor any more

MARCH 17
Royal Blood and Anarchy

well boss the
czar is thinking of
becoming a bolshevik[1] after
all he read somewhere in a
paper the other day that
wealthy women had been
financing the movement and
it interested him
czar i said you cannot be both
the czar and a
bolshevist at the same
time i would like to know
why not he retorted
the combination of royal blood
and anarchy should prove
irresistible just think of it
a czar turned bolshevist
besides i could get recognized a
good deal quicker as a bolshevist than
as the czar i have been
so hampered by not being able
to make a proper front as a
czar even a deposed czar
who miraculously escaped
execution and no one will
advance me enough money to get my
trunks from siberia
archy he said
can you not influence your boss
to introduce me to his
friend hermione from what i have
heard of her she should have a
russian bolshevist
on exhibition czar i said i
do not feel at liberty to

make such a request the
only time i ever met
hermione she tried to step on
me well boss whatever
happens i hope the czars luck
changes pretty soon and
by changing i mean taking a
turn for the better it
could not get any worse some
one gave him a flask of whiskey
the other day and he has lost
faith in his destiny to such an
extent that he has been
afraid to drink it all there
is one drink left in it
and he says if i drink that
i will never get any more
maybe and so instead of
drinking it he sets the
bottle up and worships it

APRIL 2
I Left There Too Soon

well boss looking
at the reports from
france it seems to
me that likely i left
there too soon
either something is
going to happen
there or something
is not but
what it is no
one seems to be
quite sure
it looked to

me when i left
as if everyone
wanted peace
and so i thought
there would be
peace but now it
seems that there must
be things that
certain persons
want worse than
they want
peace i have lost
the czar

APRIL 7
Classed with Fleas

well boss i went up
to the circus
the other day
and tried to hire
out what do you
want they asked me a
job as an animal
or a job as an artist
an artist said i
what can you do they
said i can
walk the wire i said
either tight or slack
and i can swing
head downward from the
flying trapeze we do not
doubt it they said
but who could see
you at a distance
every one said i if you

gave them telescopes
and opera glasses it
is too expensive said they
to furnish opera
glasses to every one
just to see a cockroach
perform not at all
i said you sell the
glasses and make an
additional profit
you go out and hire
yourself out to a
trained flea outfit
said they we cannot use
you i consider it
an insult i replied to
be classed with
fleas you should consider
it a compliment said they
another word from you
i said and i
will die in a barrel
of your lemonade and
queer your show
and with this threat
the interview closed

MAY 28
A Home among the Casks

well boss i have been
taking a little vacation
myself i got rather
weary of it but i had to
stick it out as long as you
did i put in my time trying to
find a home that would

do to settle down in after the
first of july it is not
the rent that bothers me but i
desire to live in
juxtaposition to some
cache of liquid supplies i
found several such but
unfortunately the
stuff was all in bottles i cannot
pull a cork if anyone knows of any
sort of mechanism which will enable
an ordinarily strong cockroach to
pull a cork will he or she
please communicate by
return mail what i need
is a home among the casks but
no one who is storing it seems to
be storing it in casks i
do not ask you boss to
direct me to a cellar full of
casks for i am sure
that you do not know of such a
place if you did
you would not tell me you
would go and
live there yourself
it is possible that some one
may figure out a way to
put little steel tips on my
front feet so that i
could dig through a cork it
would be slow uncertain work but
after the first of july
many of us will be willing to give
the time to it
we will have time to figure out how
to get a drink then because
we will use the time we formerly
devoted to drinking some

slavish spirits of course will
simply give up and
go to work is there not some kind of
gimlet that i could attach to my head
and bore through a cork with i
make no direct appeal to you
boss to keep me supplied you
are going to have
troubles of your own if the
worst comes to the worst i can go
to the west indies but
they breed a tribe of cockroaches in
those latitudes that is
coarse roughnecked
vigorous and wild i am
frankly afraid to associate with them
i have seen some of them
getting off the ships
good heavens to think that they
would amend the constitution of the
united states just to
be the death of one poor little
cockroach it may seem like
an anti climax to you but to me
it is a tragedy
you can drop a raisin in a bottle of
grape juice and make something
of it but who is there to uncork
grapejuice bottles for me

MAY 30

Help I Can Give the Worried Housewife

what is all this
trouble about the
servant question i
should think the

best possible solution
would occur to
anyone it
came to me after only
a moments thought
the solution is
to buy what
you want to eat
at the delicatessen
store and then
when you are through
eating throw
the scraps in the
corner get hold of
twenty or thirty
industrious cockroaches
to eat the scraps
this does away
with the necessity
of a maid
to cook or clean up
and you cannot imagine
how grateful
the cockroaches would
be every problem
is capable of
solution if people will
only put their
minds to it the
trouble is however that
so many people
have such conventional
minds i have
always been interested
in sociology and
in fact all games of
chance and any
help i can give the
worried housewife is here

for the asking i
will lead a detachment
of thirty cockroaches
into any apartment
that may be designated
at a moments notice

June 6
In Spite of H Dash Double L

well boss i saw
mehitabel the cat the other day
and she was looking a little
thin and haggard
with a limp in
the hind leg on the starboard
side old feline animal i said
how is tricks still in the
ring archy she said and still a
lady in spite of h dash double l
always jolly archy she said in
spite of hard luck
toujours gai is the word
archy toujours gai how did you
get the game leg mehitabel i asked her
alas she said it is due
to the treachery of
one of these social swells who
is sure one bad actor he was a
fussed up cat with a
bell around his neck on a
ribbon and the look about him of
a person that is currycombed and
manicured from teeth to
tail every day i met him
down by the east river
front when i was scouting

about for a little piece of fish since
the high cost of living has
become so self conscious archy
it would surprise you
how close they
watch their fish nowadays
but what the h dash double l archy
it is the cheerful heart that
wins i am never cast down for long
kid says this gilded
feline to me you look hungry i
am all of that i says to him i
have a vacuum in my midst
that is bigger than i am i
could eat the fish that ate
jonah kid he says you have
seen better days i can
tell that from looking at you thanks
i said what you say is at
least half true i have never
seen any worse ones and so
archy one word led to
another until that sleek villain
practically abducted me
and i went with him
on board a houseboat of which
he was the pampered mascot
such evidences of pomp and wealth archy
were there that you would not
believe them if i told of them to
you poor cockroach that you
are but these things were nothing to me
for i am a reincarnation of cleopatra
as i told you long ago you mean
her soul transmigrated to a cat s
body i said it is
all one archy said she have it your own
way reincarnation or transmigration
is the same to me the point is

i used to be a queen in
egypt and will likely be one again
this place was furnished swell percy i
said the furniture is
fine and i could eat some of it if
i was a saw mill but
where is the honest to g dash d food
the eats percy what i crave is
some cuisine for my stomach let us
trifle with an open ice box
for a space if one can be
persuaded to divulge the scheme of its
interior decoration follow me
said this percy thing and led
me to a cabin in which stood a table upon
which stood viands i
have heard of tables groaning archy
but this one did not it
was too satisfied it purred with
contentment in an instant i had eaten a
cold salmon who seemed to be
toastmaster of the occasion and a
whole scuttleful of chef doovers what
you mean is hors douvres mehitabel i
told her what i mean is grub said she
when in walked a person whom
i should judge to be either a butler
or the admiral of that fleet or maybe
both this percy creature who had led me
to it was on the table eating with me
what do you think he did what
would any gentleman friend with a
spark of chivalry do what but stand by
a lady this percy does nothing of the
kind archy he immediately attacks me do
you get me archy he acts as if i
was a stray cat he did not
know and he was protecting his
loving masters food from my onslaughts

i do not doubt he got praise and had
another blue ribbon for his heroism as
for me i got the boot and as i went
overboard they hit me on the limb with
a bottle or an anchor or something
nautical and hard that archy is why i
limp but toujours gai archy what
the h dash double l i am always
merry and always ladylike mine archy has
been a romantic life and i will
tell you some more of my adventures
ere long well au revoir i suppose i
will have to go and start a pogrom
against some poor innocent little
mouse just the same i think
that mehitabel s unsheltered life sometimes
makes her a little sad

JULY 24
Galoshes for Cockroaches

do you know of
any firm that specializes
in galoshes for cockroaches
it would be a
graceful deed if
you were to give me a
pair for my birthday
or a little motor boat
would do i
tried to get on the subway
train to go up town the
other day but a
cascade caught me on the
steps and carried
me onto the

> tracks when i stopped
> floating i was in
> brooklyn

AUGUST 6
A Poem in the Kipling Manner[1]

"Where have you been so long? And what on earth do you mean by coming in here soused?" we asked Archy as he zigzagged from the door to the desk.

He climbed onto the typewriter keys and replied indignantly:

> soused yourself i havent had a drink
> and yet i am elevated i admit it i have
> been down to a second hand book
> store eating a lot of kiplings earlier
> poetry it always excites me if i eat
> a dozen stanzas of it i get all lit up
> and i try to imitate it get out of my
> way now i feel a poem in the kipling
> manner taking me

And before we could stop him he began to butt on the keys:

> the cockroach stood by the mickle
>   wood in the flush of the astral dawn

We interrupted. "Don't you mean Austral instead of astral?" Archy became angered and wrote peevishly:

> i wrote astral and i meant astral
> you let me be now i want to get this
> poem off my chest you are jealous if
> you were any kind of a sport at all
> you would fix this machine so i could
> write it in capitals it is a poem about

a fight between a cockroach and a
lot of other things get out of my way
im off

the cockroach stood by the mickle
    wood in the flush of the astral dawn
and he sniffed the air from the hidden
    lair where the khyber swordfish spawn
and the bilge and belch of the glutton
    welsh as they smelted their warlock cheese
surged to and fro where the grinding
    floe wrenched at the headlands knees
half seas over under up again
and the barnacles white in the moon
the pole stars chasing its tail like a pup again
and the dish ran away with the spoon

the waterspout came bellowing out of
    the red horizons rim
and the grey typhoon and the black
    monsoon surged forth to the
    fight with him
with three fold might they surged to
    the fight for they hated the great
    bull roach
and they cried begod as they lashed
    the sod and here is an egg to
    poach
we will bash his mug with his own raw
    lug new stripped from off his
    dome
for there is no law but teeth and claw
    to the nor nor east of nome
the punjab gull shall have his skull
    ere he goes to the burning ghaut
for there is no time for aught but crime
    where the jungle lore is taught
across the dark the afghan shark is
    whining for his head

there shall be no rule but death and
  dule till the deep red maws are
  fed
  half seas under up and down
  again
  and her keel was blown off in a
  squall
  girls we misdoubt that we ll ever
    see town again
  haul boys haul boys haul.

"Archy," we interrupted, "that haul, boys, is all right to
the eye, but the ear will surely make it hall boys. Better
change it."

    you are jealous you let me alone im off again

the cockroach spat and he tilted his
  hat and he grinned through the
  lowering mirk
the cockroach felt in his rangoon belt
  for his good bengali dirk
he reefed his mast against the blast
  and he bent his mizzen free
and he pointed the cleats of his bin
  nacle sheets at the teeth of the
  yesty sea
he opened his mouth and he sluiced
  his drouth with his last good
  can of swipes
begod he cried they come in pride but
  they shall go home with the
  gripes

begod he said if they want my head it
  is here on top of my chine
it shall never be said that i doffed my
  head for the boast of a heathen
  line

and he scorned to wait but he dared
   his fate and loosed his bridle rein
and leapt to close with his red fanged
   foes in the trough of the
   screaming main
from hell to nome the blow went home
   and split the firmament
from hell to nome the yellow foam
   blew wide to veil the rent
and the roaring ships they came to
   grips in the gloom of a dripping
   mist

"Archy," we interrupted again, "is there very much more of
it? It seems that you might tell in a very few words now who won
the fight, and let it go at that. Who did win the fight, Archy?"

But Archy was peeved, and went sadly away, after writing:

   of course you wont let me finish i never saw as
jealous a person as you are

AUGUST 13
Put Me in the Movies

boss i wish you would
make arrangements to put me
into the movies a
lot of people who are no
handsomer in the face than i
am are drawing millions of
dollars a year i
have always felt that i
could act if i
were given the chance and a
truly refined cockroach might
be a novelty but do not pay
any attention to the

wishes of mehitabel the cat along
this line mehitabel
told me the other day that several
firms were bidding against
each other for her
services i would be the greatest
feline vamp in the
history of the screen said
mehitabel wot the hell archy
wot the hell ain t i a
reincarnation of cleopatra and
dont the vamp stuff come quite
natural to me i will say it
does but i have refused all
offers archy up to
date they must pay me
my price the
truth is that mehitabel hasnt a
chance and she is not a
steady character by the way
here is a piece of political news
for you mehitabel tells me that
the cats in greenwich
village and the adjoining
neighborhoods are forming soviets now
they are going in for bolshevism
her soviet she says
meets in washington mews
they are for the nationalization
of all fish markets

AUGUST 14
The Best Thing You Have Done Yet

i called on some friends in a
studio building the other evening and
while we were foraging about

for something to eat
we got caught on a
palette smeared over with all
the colors there are
leaping from this danger seven
or eight of us
landed upon an untouched canvas
that stood upon an easel
nearby waiting for the masters hand
and we walked across the
canvas on our way out of that
place it seems that we builded
better than we knew before
we could get to any safer place
than a spot behind a
gas radiator we heard human footsteps
approaching and an
instant later two men entered the
studio one of them switched on
the lights and the
other gave an exclamation of
pleasure and astonishment by jove
tommy he said to the owner of
the studio what is this new thing
of yours on the easel it is
the best thing you have done yet
i thought you were against
modernism and all
the new fangled stuff[1] but i see
that you have come over to the new
school your style has
loosened up wonderfully old kid
i always said that if you
could only get away from the stiffness
and absurdity of the
conventional schools you had the
makings of a great painter in
you what do you call this
picture tommy

well said tommy with rare
presence of mind i have not
named it yet it is not altogether in
the newer mode you will observe i
have been struggling for a
compromise between the two methods
that would at the same time
allow me to express my
individuality on canvas i do
think myself that i have got more
freshness and directness into this
thing you have said his friend
it has the direct and naive approach
of the primitives and it
also has all that is
worthy to be retained of the
reticent sophistication of
the post pre raphaelites but what
do you say you are going to
call it it is said tommy as
you see a nocturne i have
been thinking of calling it
impressions of brooklyn
bridge in a fog and when his
friend went out he stood and looked at
the picture for a long time and
said now i wonder who in
hell slipped in here and did that it
is nothing short of genius could
i have done it myself when i
was drunk i must have done so
anyhow i will sign it and
taking up a brush he did so well i
stole a look at the canvas
myself and it looked like nothing
on earth to me but a canvas over
which a lot of cockroaches had
walked i may be a
critic but still i know what i

dont like yours for another
renaissance of the arts every
spring and every autumn

AUGUST 19
Archy Is Still on Strike

We have received a communication from Archy, who went
on strike forty-eight hours ago, desiring us to state that he is
not backed by any association of contributors but that he is
striking on his own initiative. We think it is only fair to the
poor misguided cockroach to give his statement to the public.
We do not print it as a contribution from him, because, until he
has formally withdrawn the outrageous demands which he
made upon us the other day, no article signed by him shall ap-
pear ever again. To print signed articles by him would be, in ef-
fect, to recognize his organization; and this we shall never do.

We present an article by a new cockroach named Henry.
Henry has not had as much practice at the typewriter keyboard as
Archy, and he manages to hit a capital letter now and then, with-
out always being able to hit the right capital; but we can assure
our readers that he is learning rapidly. Henry is at least trying to
punctuate; Archy always made the contention that no cockroach
could ever learn to punctuate and refused to try. Archy's failure
to punctuate influenced a great many persons against him. Henry
may be a little more difficult than Archy was, for a few days, but
he is ambitious and in the end he will be better than Archy.

We present Henry:

a communication from henry

well, be asTH,is is? seerious
allthis labor dis CONtent
I wonders wHere IT wiLL enD
i sh ould not

           CarE toprophesy?
           but the greaTest dePrivation i
           feel, is in t he Loss OF thE
      suBway sUn i usEd 2 GET a LL
           my NEWS froM the Subway suN but,
           siNce the subWAY has stop ped.
           ruNNINg iaM at a LosS!
           How wiLl We kNow the strike has
           ended. if weDo noT reAd IT in
           thesubwaY Sun
              And How wilL we Read thesubwAY
              suN unleSS The sTrike
           ends. i WISH u would watcH
              mehitaBEL the CAT? she IS
           jEalous anD soRe because i
           haVE taken arcHy?s j oB
              And calLS me a scaB and
           Last niGht tried to
           eat me i deMAND poLice proTectioN?
                                        heNry!
                        • • •

   All statements made by Mehitabel the Cat, with regard to the
strike of Archy, are to be viewed with suspicion. Her statement
that she is herself on strike is false on the face of it, as Mehita-
bel has never been employed by this column, although she has
occasionally been interviewed for it.

   It seems not improper to state that Archy, himself, is picket-
ing the office, and last evening when Henry left work Archy
stopped him and made threats against him. Henry is very well
able to take care of himself, but we have asked for a special po-
lice detail to protect him.

                        • • •

IF ARCHY INTRODUCES THE ELEMENT OF VIO-
LENCE INTO THE STRIKE, HE WILL BE SEVERELY
DEALT WITH!

                        • • •

SIR: Now that Archy is gone, you may be able to get out a
readable column again.—R. P.

                        • • •

SIR: Unless you can fix it up with Archy, count me off the subscription list. I hate to hurt anybody's feelings, but I would rather see you take a long vacation yourself than to lose Archy.—WALT.

· · ·

SIR: Unless you accede to Archy's just demands all your readers will go on a sympathetic strike. It matters not about the other contributors. Let C. B. Gilbert, Benjamin deCasseres, and Clinton Scollard go. Or go yourself. But we gotter have Archy.—ELIZABETH.

· · ·

SIR: There are three ways that the deplorable strike of Archy may end:

He may win.

You may win.

Or the pair of you may compromise.

I must say that I was horrified at the brutal capitalistic attitude taken up by you towards one of the brightest ornaments of modern American literature.

F. J. G.

AUGUST 20
Grin and Beer It

liFe is Not aLL jazz and Joy)
    sMiles and suNNy weaTher!
EVERy golD has it'S aLloy!
    toHOld tHe Stuff together!

lif LUCk is good!   why maN aliVE!
    weLcoMe iT!   And ch eer iT!
buT if THE drinK'S two seven five
    Try to griN!   AND beer iT!
        heNry!

Henry strikes us as being, on the whole, more cheerful than Archy.

As Henry left work last evening, he was attacked by a strange cockroach, no doubt a thug in the employ of Archy, who has been hanging about the building ever since Henry went on the job. The strange cockroach was easily disposed of, and Archy did not show himself in person.

We repeat what we said yesterday: *If Archy is foolish enough to introduce violence into this strike, he will get his fill of it.*

It has been reported to us that Archy has been drinking wood alcohol and is working himself into a rage against Henry. Candidly, we expect the worst. But the column is not to be intimidated.

_____

HOW THE PUBLIC VIEWS THE STRIKE

SIR: I congratulate you on having got rid of Archy. Now maybe we can have some more Fothergil Finch. And what has become of Hermione, the Beautiful communist? Seriously, I have always felt that Archy was beneath the dignity of the column.

W. F. MARNER.

AUGUST 21
The Archy Strike

There is no offering from Henry today. Henry has disappeared. Frankly, we fear that Henry has been foully dealt with by a gang of rowdy cockroaches in the employ of Archy.

The column made an attempt at an early hour this morning to put another cockroach named Ernatz to work. Ernatz arrived at the office and succeeded in getting as far as the typewriter, but there he collapsed. An examination showed that Ernatz had been badly beaten up by the Archy faction in getting through the picket lines.

These picket lines have been extended by Archy and his gang until they now reach from the Press Club at Spruce and William up Spruce Street to Nassau, and down Nassau to what used to be the Umbrella Bar at the corner of Nassau and Beekman. We were informed today by an excited friend that he had seen thousands and thousands and thousands of cockroaches, led by Archy, hiding by the curbstones picketing this district, and that it seemed to him that they were maddened by benzine or something. They had chased him, he said, and he was so extraordinarily vivid and convincing in his recital and in his fright that we fancied, as he talked, that we could actually smell the benzine or something.

The column's cockroach service has been interrupted for one day; but it will be resumed. We ask the public to be patient. As far as taking Archy back is concerned, that is now an impossibility; we are done with that ingrate forever.

· · ·

We found on our desk this morning the following threat from the Archy faction, which we publish to show the public the length to which this creature is willing to go:

> unless you yield to
> archys demands the strike
> will spread the water bugs
> are going out in
> sympathy with archy and the
> vers libre poets union
> are preparing a sympathetic
> strike the public will know whom
> to blame they will blame you
> it is your capitalistic
> attitude that is
> prolonging the trouble take
> warning by what
> happened to henry and ernatz.

· · ·

So far the Mayor, the District Attorney, and the Governor have done nothing—less than nothing. We demand protection for our contributors, or we shall have a word or two to say about these officials. Several of our contributors have been threatened—C. B. Gilbert, Benjamin DeCasseres, Edward S.

Van Zile, H. W., Edward Hope, and the Editor of the column have all received threatening letters from the Archy faction.

Whither is this country drifting?

• • •

The column hesitates to adopt the expedient of employing strikebreakers and guards for the purpose of getting contributors through the Archy lines; but if it becomes necessary, it shall be done. A dozen tarantulas have been offered to us by a steamship company which maintains a line of boats between this port and South and Central America, and unless the cockroaches cease to interfere with our employees, or the proper authorities wake up and give us protection, we shall be obliged to accept this offer.

———

SIR: Restore the Archytect who made the column famous.

Our Mon-archy forever !!!—J. U. N.

• • •

SIR: I was amused at the suggestion of F. J. G. that Archy might win. The poor cockroach hasn't even the chances of the proverbial snowball or the tallow cat hotly pursued by the asbestos pup. His chances are about those of law clerks on strike. My sympathies are with Archy as they surely are with law clerks, but roaches and law schools are equally prolific.—J. C.

• • •

SIR: Your column has so deteriorated that I shall never buy another EVENING SUN until this Archy business is settled in Archy's favor.—STEADY READER

———

YOU CAN'T GET AWAY FROM HIM

SIR: At a fashionable Fifth avenue tea room *tomato en surprise* yielded the usual amount of celery, chicken, and mayonnaise. And deep down in the excavation I found the surprise. It was Archy. —H. D. M.

August 22
Call Archy Back

Don't let Archy pine and die,
   We miss his gracious art,
Don't grudge him half an apple pie;
   Recall him; have a heart!

Let me subscribe a dozen pies
   And keep the column bright—
Call Archy back and compromise
   Or kiss yourself good-night!
                        H. D.

. . .

August 21
An Injunction

LATEST STRIKE BULLETIN: The Sun Dial obtained an injunction to-day, commanding Archy to go back to work at his former terms, pending a settlement of the present troubles, so that cockroach service to the public would not be interrupted and millions of persons deprived of this essential part of their daily life. When the papers were served upon Archy and his faction they tore them, and then, in contempt of the court and its enjoining order, ate them. This shows the desperate character of these criminals.

August 23
Archy Gets a 50 Per Cent Increase

Archy agreed this morning to return to work, for at least a week, pending a final adjustment of the difficulties between him and the column.

Archy's demands were for a piece of apple pie once a week and for larger type for his contributions.

These demands will be considered in the final adjustment.

In the meantime, and pending the final adjustment, Archy returns on the basis of a 50 per cent increase in salary.

It is our contention that a 50 per cent increase is a very liberal increase, indeed, and that this temporary settlement should be a permanent settlement.

We admit that the public has been with Archy during the recent troubles. And it was only the pressure of public opinion that influenced us to take him back at all.

But, having decided that we must yield, we determined to come across handsomely.

THE 50 PER CENT INCREASE IN SALARY WAS OUR OWN SUGGESTION.

AND, ON OUR OWN INITIATIVE, WE HAVE MADE THIS INCREASE RETROACTIVE.

That is to say, not only does Archy get the 50 per cent increase during the week before the final adjustment, but we have volunteered to give it to him during the period covered by the strike, and for a term of two weeks prior to the strike.

———

We print, below, Archy's own comment upon the temporary settlement:

A COMMUNICATION FROM ARCHY

well boss you see
where you stand now i hope the
public cannot get along
without me
i have won a moral victory
for you have agreed in
principle that i
should have a raise in
salary i will have to
think over it a

long time however before i
will consent to a 50 per cent
raise as a permanent settlement
and will have to take
advice it seems like a very
generous proposition on the
face of it but at the same time
i dont think it is
altogether right the figures look
good but i am puzzled you
see i was not getting any salary at
all when i quit work and if
i got a raise of
50 per cent above that the
question is what do i get
i would much rather have a
little something to eat every
week than all these figures but
at the same time i
must admit that a 50 per cent
raise looks good
on paper especially as you are
willing to make it
retroactive maybe the
retroactive part means that i
will get a little something
to eat at any rate it is easy
to see that i have won a most
important victory i would be willing
to make a permanent
settlement on the basis of
a 25 per cent increase and a half
a piece of pie i never was any good on
figures and maybe i am
getting a lot as it is but i
would rather have less
of a victory and more to eat

We print this communication in full in order to show the public the difficulty we have with Archy. We have yielded in principle, we admit that he has won a victory, and we have given him a 50 per cent raise. It seems to me that we have done even more than could have been expected, but he seems dissatisfied. And yet he must know that he is in the wrong, for even while he talks of a moral victory he reduces his former outrageous demands for food by one half. He has been on the job without any food at all, so far as we know, for four years, and this sudden demand of his for something to eat does not have the ring of sincerity to our ears. What did he eat before he worked for the column? There is a strain of sordid materialism in Archy, we are afraid.

August 26
Thank You for the Advice

thank you for the
advice to go and get
some of this
government food i do
not want to start all
over again
any controversy that has
been temporarily
settled but may i not
ask how

August 27
Darned Little Justice

the cockroaches are not
the only insects
that are demanding more
consideration

i met a flea
last evening who
told me that he had come
into contact with
a great deal of unrest
lately and a mosquito remarked
to me only this
morning there is darned
little justice in this world the
way the human beings
run it seldom do i
meet a person who will hold
still long
enough for me to get a meal

AUGUST 28
Archy Gets Restless Again

dear boss after thinking
over the terms of our temporary
settlement i
am forced to admit i
got the short end of the
deal you are a true diplomat and
a modest one at that but i want
you to know that your admission
to your readers in conceding me
a moral victory does not
suffice to fill an empty
stomach and nobody can work
without food so i am forced to
submit as the two chief subjects for
consideration in the final settlement the
necessity not only for deciding the
amount of salary but also a generous
allowance of food and good
food at that because since i

agreed to return to work i
met an old friend who took me to
a place where a lot of
nice people of the community
councils are distributing relief
food and by simply hiding in the
parcels that go out there are
lots of chances to get into all
kinds of fine homes we took a chance
and sneaked into one box of canned
goods and were placed in a fine
automobile that took us
to a swell house on the drive where
they have a pastry cook of their own and
we had the pastry all to our
selves and feasted on delicacies of
all sorts so half a piece of pie is
no longer any treat for me and
i can get acquainted with
some very aristocratic
cockroaches besides just by
attending food sales and i
am cultivating a taste for fancy
eatables that neither pie nor
25 per cent increase will satisfy

It looks as if this Archy were getting ready to ask for more,
no matter what we give him.

How human some cockroaches are!

AUGUST 29
A Plum Plan

well boss the time has
arrived for our permanent
settlement i propose
a plum plan

once a week i want a
pint jar of plum preserves
with bread and butter
and all the fixings that
go with them answer at once
i refuse to arbitrate

We yield. We consider ourself lucky that Archy does not de-
mand full ownership and control of the column. We yield while
the yielding is still good.

September 8
Trying to Ruin Me

well boss i notice that
although you have taken me
back to work on my own terms
you are giving me no
work to do you always were jealous
of my popularity there
never has been a time since i made
my first appearance and
carried all before me that you
would not have gotten rid of
me if you had dared but
you have never dared
now you are giving me no work to do
in order to keep me
from my public you are
trying to ruin me why do
you not give me an
assignment now and
then

archy

If Archy cannot think up something to write about he can stay
out of the column permanently. We are tired of giving Archy

assignments that he can do easily and then having him take the
credit for originality. The impression has gone abroad that not
only does Archy think up his own themes, but that he also tells
us what to write. The exact reverse of this is true. It is time that
Archy, and his infatuated followers also, should understand
that he is our subordinate, our creature. We admit that he has
a certain superficial knack; but all the heavier, more solemn,
respectable, and serious humor in the column is our own. His
statement that he would like to work is entirely hypocritical.
Since he won the strike he has done nothing but eat and sleep;
he is gorged with food; between his triumph and his victuals
he has become stupid. We knew food would ruin him, and it
was in the interests of his literary ability, such as it is, that we
kept him starved. Lord Tennyson noticed the same thing about a
throstle . . . or maybe it was a blackbird. Anyhow, Lord Ten-
nyson wrote a poem about it. . . . It was a bird that gorged itself
and lived easy and ceased to be a poet. We have always thought it
an indication of very high purpose and resolution that Lord Ten-
nyson did not succumb himself in a similar manner; but after he
became laureate he sang just as well as before. We believe that he
was already laureate when he wrote "Come into the Garden,
Maud." Max Beerbohm has a cartoon of Lord Tennyson reading
his poems to Queen Victoria in which the laureate looks both
well fed and lyrical. We wish that Daisy Ashford's Mr. Salteena
had met a laureate at court and given us additional light upon
this subject. But we still insist that in spite of Lord Tennyson's ex-
perience, the rule holds good in the majority of cases; feed a poet
and ruin him. The only thing that can save Archy now is a course
of voluntary fasting, and we doubt that he has the will power for
it. Give a cockroach enough jam and he will tangle his feet.

OCTOBER 6

To Settle the Controversy

      i am in a position
      to settle the
      controversy as to whether

j m barrie
wrote the young visiters
or whether it
was written by
daisy ashford[1] i have
been making a
very careful study of the
matter using the
method of the authorities
who have proved
that bacon wrote all of
shakespeares plays[2]
that were not written
by marlowe beaumont
and fletcher and ben jonson
that is to say to wit
namely the cipher
method on page one
of the young visiters i
find the letter j
on page nine i find
the letter m and on
page seventeen i find
the letter b
it is therefore clear that
j m barrie wrote
the stunt in nineteen
seventeen and signed
it with his initials
i hope there will
be no more idle chatter
about this thing now
that it is authoritatively
settled

OCTOBER 16
Rheumatism

boss i wish
that some of your clever
correspondents would
devise a way to
fit cockroaches
with overshoes
this continued damp weather
is giving me rheumatism
in three of my feet
all three rheumatic feet
are on the same
side so when i
walk i go round and
round in a circle
i am trying to use
pieces of chewing gum for
overshoes but it
doesn't work so
very well i can get
them on but i
cannot get them off
again and they are
sticky on both sides sometimes
they stick fast to
the floor and i
know how a fly
feels on a sheet of
tanglefoot paper
see what you can
do about it wont
you please by the way
just to settle the
controversy i
think i may as well
announce that i

wrote the young
visiters myself in
collaboration with
mehitabel the cat

DECEMBER 3
This Monster Man

one thing the human bean
never seems to
get into it is the
fact that humans
appear just as unnecessary to
cockroaches as cockroaches
do to humans
you would scarcely
call me human
nor am i altogether
cockroach i
conceive it to be my
mission in life to bring
humans and cockroaches
into a better understanding
with each other to
establish some sort of
entente cordiale[1] or
hands across the kitchen sink[2]
arrangement
lately i heard a number
of cockroaches discussing
humanity one big
regal looking roach
had the floor and he spoke
as was fitting in blank verse
more or less
says he
how came this monster with the heavy

foot harsh voice and cruel heart to
rule the world
had it been dogs or ants or elephants
i could have acquiesced and found a
justice working in the decree but man
gross man
the killer man the bloody minded
crossed unsocial death dispenser of this
sphere who slays for pleasure slays
for sport for whim
who slays from habit breeds to slay and
slays
whatever breed has humors not his own
the whole apparent universe one sponge
blood filled from insect mammal fish
and bird
the which he squeezes down his vast
gullet friends i call on you to rise and
trample down this monster man this
tyrant man hear hear said
several of the wilder spirits
and it looked to me for a
minute as if they
were going right out and
wreck new york city but
an old polonius looking
roach got the floor
he cleared his throat three times
and said
what our young friend here
so eloquently counsels against
the traditional enemy is
calculated of course to appeal to
youth what he says
about man is all very true
and yet we must remember that
some of our wisest
cockroaches have always
held that there

is something impious in the
idea of overthrowing man
doubtless the supreme being
put man where he is and
doubtless he did it
for some good purpose which
it would be very
impolitic yea well nigh
blasphemous for us to enquire
into the project of
overthrowing man is indeed
tantamount to a
proposition to overthrow the
supreme being himself and
i trust that no one of
my hearers is so wild or
so wicked as to think
that possible or desirable i
cannot but admire the
idealism and patriotism of
my young friend who
has just spoken nor do i
doubt his sincerity but i
grieve to see so
many fine qualities
misdirected and i
should like to ask him
just one question to wit
namely as follows is it not
a fact that just before
coming to this meeting
he was almost killed by a
human being as he
crawled out of an ice box
and is it not true that
he was stealing food from
the said ice box and is it
not a fact that his own
recent personal experience has

as much to do with
his present rage as any
desire to better the
condition of the cockroaches of
the world in general i
think that it is the sense of
this meeting that a
resolution be passed censuring
mankind and at the
same time making it
very clear that nothing like
rebellion is to be attempted
and so on
well polonius had his way
but it is my belief that the
wilder spirits will gain the
ascendancy and if the
movement spreads to the other
insects the human race is in
danger as a friend of both
parties i should regret war
what we need is
intelligent propaganda who is
better qualified to handle
the propaganda fund than
yours truly

December 12
The Cat Show

i said to mehitabel
the cat i suppose you are
going to the swell cat
show i am not archy
said she i have as
much lineage as any
of those society

cats but i never could
see the conventional
social stuff archy
i am a lady
but i am bohemian
too archy i
live my own life
no bells and pink
ribbons for me
archy it is me for
the life romantic i could
walk right into
that cat show and get
away with it
archy none of those
maltese princesses has
anything on me in the
way of hauteur
or birth either or any
of the aristocratic
fixings and condiments
that mark the
cats of lady clara
vere de vere[1] but
it bores me archy
me for the
wide open spaces the
alley serenade and
the moonlight
sonata on the back
fences i would
rather kill my own
rats and share
them with a
friend from greenwich
village than lap up
cream or beef juice
from a silver porringer
and have to

be polite to the
bourgeois clans
that feed me
wot the hell i
feel superior to that
stupid bunch me
for a dance
across the roofs when
the red star[2]
calls to my blood
none of your
pretty puss stuff for
mehitabel it would
give me a grouch
to have to be so
solemn toujours
gai archy toujours
gai is my
motto

1920

JANUARY 17
Archy Is Ill

"What has become of Archy?" several Archy fans have asked
us lately. Archy is ill; he is, in fact, just one frost bite from
bowsprit to tiller. Archy heard some one tell of a method of
making apple brandy by freezing instead of by the ordinary
method of distilling it from hard cider . . . the idea is, we be-
lieve, that you allow the cider in a barrel to freeze, and find at
the center of the frozen mass a little cupful of highly alcoholic
liquid that has not frozen. This cupful, the life and delectable
quintessence of the cider, is your apple-jack.

Archy, as we have said, heard of this process, and wished to
witness it at first hand. He selected a barrel of cider somewhere
in New Jersey and crawled into it to get a close up of the pro-
cess. But he must have gone to sleep in there, or something. He
was frozen into the cider as a mastodon within a glacier. Luck-
ily he had succeeded in working himself so near the cave filled
with unfrozen apple-jack at the centre of the barrel that he
could take a sip from time to time, and the fiery liquid thus con-
sumed was all that saved his life.

A New Jersey reader of the Sun Dial found him when the bar-
rel was opened, and, recognizing him by his high forehead and
look of intelligence, rarely met with among cockroaches, for-
warded him to us by mail. He cannot work the typewriter; he
can only lie in a cigar box lined with cotton and look at us and
moan piteously . . . poor bug!

It is exceedingly doubtful that he will ever be able to write

again. And, of course, if he is useless to us, out the window he
goes. We cannot afford to maintain a cockroach in idleness,
with living expenses what they are. We pity him, but we owe it
to ourself to get rid of him at once the moment he becomes a
drag upon us. As a modernist and an artist, we insist on free-
dom; we must live our own life, untrammeled.

FEBRUARY 9
The Anti Cockroach Conspiracy

washington d c feb ninth
nineteen twenty special to the
sun dial i am down here
conducting the fight against
the anti cockroach conspiracy
i suppose you saw in the
papers the proposition to
appropriate nineteen thousand
dollars for the purpose of killing
all the cockroaches in the
house office building and
about the capitol this is the
most iniquitous bill ever brought
before the national
legislature and
one of the most unpatriotic
measures ever proposed the
contention is that the cockroaches
eat up valuable books and
papers belonging to congressmen
speeches and that sort of
thing of course they eat them up
and they are performing a service
to their country in doing so
somebody has to edit the
congressional record and i have
taken it upon myself as a true

friend of the country and
organized my gang of editors
to eat up all the foolish
stuff that might
otherwise get into print and
bring ridicule upon the
American congress also we are
performing a patriotic service
in eating up thousands of
speeches that were intended to be
franked out to the
voters as campaign documents
no wonder a certain set of
congressmen are against us
it is a congressional conspiracy
and we shall fight it to the
bitter end may i not
add that there must be other
records in washington that have
accumulated during the
past five years which it might
be just as well to eat up

MARCH 8
A Threat

don marquis
I HAVE JUST RETURNED
FROM THE ARCTIC
CIRCLE
UP IN THE BRONX,
WHERE I HAVE BEEN SPENDING
THE WINTER.
I SEEN WHAT YOU WROTE ABOUT
ARCHY
IN THE SUN DIAL.
YOU HAVE WENT A LONG WAY

                    TO KNOCK
                    THE BEST COCKROACH THAT
                    EVER WORKED FOR YOU.
                    NOW,
                    YOU TUMBLE BUG—
                    GET READY!
                    WE ARE A LARGE FAMILY
                    AND THERE ARE
                    BILLIONS MORE OF US
                    WHERE ARCHY COME
                    FROM.
                    YOU ARE FACING
                    TROUBLE—
                    AND
                    YOU
                    KNOW
                    IT.

                                    ARCHY'S KINSMEN.

                            MARCH 11
                            The Shimmie

In reply to inquiries as to where Archy is we print the
despatch below, lifted from the San Francisco Chronicle of re-
cent date. . . . Archy is touring the country introducing the dance
mentioned:

PORTLAND, ORE., Feb. 18. — The shimmie is fast becoming
the popular indoor sport for cockroaches. The fact was di-
vulged at Reed College here today by Dr. Helen Clark, head of
the Reed psychology department. Miss Clark says soft, tuneful
music will send a healthy cockroach into an emotional trance,
which finds expression in a rhythmic dance, which has every
semblance to the shimmie.

APRIL 10
A Former Doughboy

boss i heard a former
doughboy
talking to himself
and this is what i heard him
saying to himself
fourteen dollars
for a single pair of shoes
fourteen dollars
for some little bits of leather
i hope the man that charges
fourteen dollars
for a single pair of shoes
will walk through hell
barefoot at noon
on hells hottest day
sixty nine cents
for a little pound of butter
weighing fourteen ounces
one a set of crooked scales
i hope the man that charges
sixty nine cents
for a crooked pound of butter
will fry in hell
in a kettle full of butter
for a hundred million years
i went and got
myself all gassed
i went and got
a bullet through my shoulder
and i cant do
a half of the work
that i did before the war
and a fat lot of money
i am getting from the government
eighty seven dollars

for a single suit of clothes
i cant hold a job
of any damned kind
who in hells to blame
i dont know
but eighty seven dollars
for a single suit of clothes
gets my goat
ninety bones a month
for three dinky rooms
for myself and my wife
and two kids here
and another kid a coming
and a fat lot of money
i get from the government
if i could be a miner
i could ride in an auto
at least so they say
if i could be a railroad
man or a plumber
i could garner kale
if i could drive a milk cart
out of salary and collections
i could count on seventy
bones every week
but what the hell can i do
in the way of manual work
i went and got myself
all gassed up
like a gosh darned fool
i went and got
a bullet through my shoulder
all the kind of work
i ever did or knew
was inside work
office stuff and routine
and that kind of thing
and you know what it pays
and you know i gotta have

decent shoes and collars
and a fat lot of money
i get from the government
i have a feeling
something is wrong
but i dont know where
every one but me
is cleaning up on money
landlords and grocers
tailors and miners
masons and carpenters
are all getting money
but i went and got myself
all gassed up
and a bullet through my shoulder
and i hope to god my landlord
goes and chokes to death
i dont know
who the hells to blame
but sooner or later
it will force me into politics
if they dont watch out
i got no platform
but i have got a kind of feeling
that everything is wrong
and a fat lot of thanks
i am getting from the people
that are boosting up the prices
no i cant live at all
i aint a bolshevist
i aint a socialist
but i got a feeling
everything is wrong
well boss i listened to that
ex service man for quite a while
and i got the idea that while
he doesnt quite know yet just
where he is going he is on
his way somewhere

APRIL 15
Pretty Soft for You

boss i have just had a
grand idea if
everything else fails leave
it to me to get
food into the city
i shall call for an army
of one thousand million
cockroaches to bring
it over from jersey a grain
at a time walking on the
rails through the
hudson tunnels it may have the
effect of introducing better feeling
between cockroaches and
human beings i must confess that
there is not much of this
entente stuff between them
as things stand now say the
word and i will start my
huskies on the job along will
come a cockroach with a crumb of bread
and then another cockroach with another
crumb of bread and then
another cockroach with another crumb of
bread and then another
cockroach with another
crumb of bread and then another
cockroach
but really it would be
pretty soft for you if i wrote your
whole column that way

APRIL 24
A Little Waterbug

i know a little waterbug
who is not very clean
although he gambols round the sink
for all his jolly baths i think
he is not very clean

MAY I
An Archy Drive

well boss there have been
all sorts of drives
why not start an
archy drive
the idea is my own and i
think it is a good one
something should be done toward
endowing me so that i
would not have to work except
when i feel like it
even if i should never feel
like it the move would be in the
right direction
a great artist such as yours
truly should never have to
worry about where his living is to
come from he should be far above all
the vulgar strife of life
sordid material
considerations should not be
thrust upon his attention if i
were endowed i could give my
best efforts to my art
i could sit and think and think and think[1]

before i wrote anything
i would prefer not to
set any definite figure on the
amount required let us
start the drive first and then see
what sum is likely to come in
if something of this sort
does not happen soon i am afraid
that i will be forced into
the movies[2]
see what you can do

JUNE 24
Sentimental about Birds

i could never understand
why people get so sentimental
about birds
i was taking a walk in the park
the other day and a big
brutal robin saw me
and rushed at me the way
the winged lizards used to rush
at the semi human semi simian
in the good old pleistocene days
mouth open tongue hanging out
and the greedy red canal of his
esophagus plainly visible almost as
far south as his
grand central station
i had no time to find an alibi
but fortunately i found a hole
in the ground
this little robin redbreast stuff
doesnt make any hit with me
i lay in that hole
for twenty minutes and i was

interviewed by red ants and i hate
ants just as much as you hate cockroaches
and when i got ready to come out
there was a sparrow waiting for me
bug said he come out of your hole
and climb upon my back
i will give you a breezy ride to
the tree tops
birdie said i
i distrust you
i think your intentions
are distinctly gastronomic
as i live said he i have conceived
an affection for you
you are such a cute little thing
so quaint and clownish and i would like
to know you better
birdie i said you talk like a
promoter trying to sell oil stock
to the plain people
but he suddenly vanished and i saw the reason
a rat was coming
cockroach said the rat
jog along with me over among the bushes
i know where there is a nest with some eggs
in it i am drawn to you i said
because you kill birds but nevertheless you
do not have my complete confidence
your reputation is not of the best
i feel drawn to you too said the rat
i do not know when i have seen a cockroach
to whom i gave my heart more fully and freely
on such short acquaintance
come out of your
hole for a little pleasant ramble
and i swear that you will not
live to regret it
there is a subtle equivocation in your speech i said
tut tut he said why so

suspicious i am not deceiving you
indeed you are not i told him
no rat has ever deceived me in the past
and you do not deceive me now
just then he hastened away and i saw
that a cat had entered l u e
cats will not eat cockroaches
when there is anything else but all too often
there is nothing else and i was just
wondering whether this one might not try
to dig me out when i saw that it was our
old friend mehitabel saved i cried
my gawd archy said she and are you too
reduced to walking the parks in search
of sustenance and casual eats aint the world
full of ups and downs deary but cheerio
toujours gai is my motto little friend
and with a no great urging she
narrated me the story of her recent adventures
which will be continued in my next

OCTOBER 9
A Sad Time Dieting

i see by the
paper that you are
having quite a
sad time dieting at last
you know what
hunger is i have been
trying for three
years to get a raise
in salary from you so that
i could eat now and
then but you have denied me with
scorn and contumely can you

wonder that now i gloat over
you sufferings hoping you
starve almost to death with
every pound you lose and
then gain every pound back and
do it over again i am yours
respectfully

OCTOBER 20
Crazy as a Bed Bug

boss i heard another
cockroach say after
reading your stuff that you
were as crazy as a
bed bug[1] i said to him
my boss may be crazy
but a bed bug is not
crazy a bed bug
is the calmest of insects
cool
self possessed
practical
pragmatic
efficient
he has very little
idealism
and almost no
sense of honor
he has a quite
unpleasant
personality
he has never been
touched by the
fine grace of romance
he is essentially

materialistic
and a plodder
but he attains
his object with the
utmost skill
and makes his escape
with a deal of
cleverness
and low cunning
the solid
earthy
unimaginative
qualities are his
deny the bed bug
great spiritual
power and i
will agree with you
but you are
quite wrong in calling
him crazy the
bed bug is anything
but crazy well you are
crazy said this
cockroach i should
rather be called insane
i answered
than stupid
but he did not
get me

November 1

Random Thoughts by Archy

one thing that
shows that
insects are

superior to men
is the fact that
insects run their
affairs without
political campaigns
elections and so forth

• • •

a man thinks
he amounts to a lot
but to a mosquito
a man is
merely
something to eat

• • •

i have noticed
that when
chickens quit
quarrelling over their
food they often
find that there is
enough for all of them
i wonder if
it might not
be the same way
with the
human race

• • •

germs are very
objectionable to men
but a germ
thinks of a man
as only the swamp
in which
he has to live

• • •

a louse i
used to know
told me that

millionaires and
bums tasted
about alike
to him

• • •

the trouble with
most people is
that they
lose their sense of
proportion
of what use is
it for a
queen bee to fall in
love with a bull

• • •

what is all this mystery
about the sphinx
that has troubled so many
illustrious men
no doubt the very same
thoughts she thinks
are thought every day
by some obscure hen

November 12
I Saw a Football Game

some people get
hotter cussing the
coal situation
than they could
get by burning
tons of coal

• • •

i saw a football
game last saturday if
men were to see a

lot of insects
milling around like
that they would
say how silly
insects are anyhow

1921

JANUARY 15
No Privacy

in reply to all
the clamor and queries
as to where i
have been and what i
have been doing i will
make but two
comments the
first one is can a
public character have no
privacy at all and the
second is why should not
even a cockroach take a rest

JANUARY 21
This Lenin Person

this lenin person[1]
seems to be the
most active hero in
captivity in the course
of one week he has
been bombed poisoned
and become insane he has resigned
died a natural

death confessed
everything denied all
given up in despair
and planned
four new offensives
i will say he is
active i
never knew of but
one more active creature
that was a chameleon
with whom i was
acquainted i
met him one day looking
rather fatigued and
pale not to say
washed out well joe
i said to him for his
name was joe
you look a little peaked
today what is the
chief trouble archy he
said i am worn out i
admit i have been
too active lately
a week ago i fell into
a kaleidoscope
belonging to a seven year old
kid and i couldn t get
out it was a favorite
toy of that child s and
he has been looking into
it and turning it ever
since for one whole
week archy i
have been what you
might call active but
i have been faithful to my
duty i have kept up
with that kaleidoscope

color for color and change
for change it has made
a nervous wreck of me but
i have not shirked my
duty this morning
thank god the thing was stepped
on and broken and i
made my escape
it strikes me that
lenin will wear himself
out like that
chameleon if he is
too ambitious he ought to
rest up for a week
stick to carbuncles or
some one thing for a while
and take it easy

MAY 2

Organizing the Insects

where have i been so long
you ask me
i have been going up
and down like the devil
seeking what i might devour
i am hungry always hungry
and in the end i shall
eat everything
all the world shall come at
last to the multitudinous maws
of insects
a civilization perishes
before the tireless teeth
of little little germs
ha ha i have thrown off the mask
at last

you thought i was only
an archy
but i am more than that
i am anarchy
where have i been you ask
i have been organizing the insects
the ants the worms the wasps
the bees the cockroaches
the mosquitoes
for a revolt against mankind
i have declared war
upon humanity
i even i shall fling
the mighty atom
that splits a planet asunder
i ride the microbe
that crashes down olympus
where have i been you ask me where
i am jove and from my seat
on the edge of a bowl of beef stew
i launch the thunderous
molecule
that smites a cosmos into bits
where have i been you ask
but you had better ask
who follows in my train
there is an ant
a desert ant a tamerlane[1]
who ate a pyramid in rage
that he might get at and devour
the mummies of six hundred
kings who in remote
antiquity had stepped upon
and crushed ascendants of his
my myrmidons[2]
are trivial things
and they have always ruled
the world
and now they shall strike down mankind

i shall show you how
a solar system
pivots on the nubbin
of a flageolet bean
i shall show you how a blood clot
moving in a despots brain
flung a hundred million men
to death and disease
and plunged a planet into woe
for twice a hundred years
we have the key
to the fourth dimension
for we know the little things
that swim and swarm
in protoplasm
i can show you love and hate
and the future
dreaming side by side
in a cell
in the little cells where
matter is so fine it merges
into spirit
you ask me where i have been
but you had better
ask me where i am
and what
i have been drinking
exclamation point

MAY 19

The Cockroach Its Life History

boss a new book
has appeared
which should be
read by every one
it is entitled

the cockroach
its life history[1]
and how to deal
with it and
the author
is frederick laing
who is assistant
in the department
of entomology in the
british museum
of natural history
it is one of the
best books i ever
tasted i am eating
the binding from
a copy with
a great deal of
relish and
recommend it
to all other
insects yours
truly

JUNE 16

My Private Comet

several persons have
asked me during
the last few days have
you seen the comet[1]
and my answer has been
seen it why
i rode on it
that is how i got
back here after my
travels it is my private
comet i park

it up there and it
waits until i am ready
to go somewhere
else ask me something
different

AUGUST 16
Dodo Birds and Cubist Posters

i saw a piece in the
paper not long ago where
you said the sea
serpent is no longer to be
seen i doubt if this is
strictly true i
was down by the water
front the other day and
overheard the
conversation of a couple of
gentlemen who had
just returned from a
visit to one of the
hooch ships out beyond the
twelve mile line they
had spent several days
on board and one of them
had seen the flying
dutchman scoot by in a
dead calm filled with
dodo birds and cubist posters
and the other one
said he missed that but he
had seen something
equally as good as he would have
called it a sea
serpent he said but that
it started to talk to

him it is my own
opinion that the
hooch boats are bringing
back the romance
to navigation
yours for the
amphibious life

AUGUST 18
To Become Grasshoppers

i was talking
with an insect the
other day about the
hard times that
cockroaches have to
get a living every
mans hand is against them
and occasionally his
foot meals
are few and far between
why in the world
says this
insect do you not
go to the country and become
grasshoppers if
living in town and being
cockroaches is getting
too difficult for you
i was astonished
at the simplicity of the
solution but as i
thought it over it occurred
to me that
perhaps it sounded more
statesmanlike than it
really was

how i asked him are
cockroaches to become
grasshoppers
that is a mere
detail he said which i
leave to you for
solution i have outlined
the general scheme for your
salvation so do not ask
me to settle the mere
details i trust to you for
that you must do
something for yourself
we philosophers cannot do it all
for you unaided you
must learn self help
but alas i fear that
your inherent stupidity will
balk all efforts
to improve your condition
boss i offer you
this little story
for what it is worth
if you are able to
find in it something
analogous to a number
of easy schemes
for the improvement of the
human race you
may do immense good by
printing it
yours for reform

SEPTEMBER 13
Ku Klux Klam

i dropped into
a clam chowder the
other evening
for a warm bath and
a bite to eat
and i heard a couple of
clams talking
it seems that they
are sore on the
oyster family and
have formed an
organization to
do away with them
they call it the
ku klux klam[1]
yours for the frequent stew

SEPTEMBER 19
O City of Angels

boss i see by
the papers there
has been more than
one unconventional
episode
in the far west
and i have made
a little song
as follows
los angeles
los angeles
the home of the movie star
what kind of angels

are they
out there where you are
los angeles
los angeles
much must be left
untold
but science says
that freuds rush in
where angels
fear to tread
los angeles
los angeles
clean up your
movie game
or else o city of angels
you better
change your name
yours for all the morality
that the traffic
will bear

SEPTEMBER 20

Archy Turns Highbrow for a Minute

boss please let me
be highbrow for
a minute i
have just been eating
my way through some of
the books on your desk
and i have digested two of them
and it occurs to me
that antoninus the emperor
and epictetus the slave
arrived at the same
philosophy of life
that there is neither mastery

nor slavery
except as it exists
in the attitude of the soul
toward the world
thank you for listening
to a poor little
cockroach

OCTOBER 5
Krew Krux Kranks[1]

i went into a
barber shop the other
day where a lady
was having her little
girl s hair cut
and her husband was
getting shaved in the
next chair
in walked two
members of a patriotic
organization called the
krew krux kranks
with masks on and
carrying american flags
one of them seized a razor
and severed the
jugular vein of the
man in the chair who was
getting shaved saying
as he did so there now
mister bill billups i
reckon you will no longer
trouble the swiggles
of the insolvent empire[2]
goodness gracious said the
lady that man

you have just sliced in two
at the neck was not
mister bill billups
at all i saw mister
bill billups getting off
a street car just five
minutes ago that man
you have just sliced in two
was mister pete perkins
and my husband
boo hoo hoo now i
am a widow
great guns said the
krew krux krank
lady i am as sorry as
sorry can be
but you must realize
that in our business we are
bound to make mistakes
sometimes he just looked like
mister bill billups lying there
in the chair all
lathered up
yes said the widow
it was a terrible mistake
but i can see that in your
line of work you are bound
to make mistakes
we are said the krew krux krank
but i cannot tell you
how bad i feel about this madam
you must not take it to heart
so much said the widow
anybody is likely
to make mistakes
but i do said the krew krux krank
i offer you a thousand
apologies i never
made a faux pas

like that before in all
my experience
oh well said the widow
do not take on so over it
i am sure that
it was quite unintentional
i look to the motive
behind it rather than
to the deed itself
but madam he began
do not be tiresome she
said interrupting him i quite
understand how it occurred
you are what i call
a sensible woman said the krew
krux krank
thank you said she
smiling and dimpling prettily
at the compliment come
little precious she said to her
child let us go home and see
if papa left any life
insurance policies around
anywhere
well said the krew krux krank
to the barber
i wish that everybody
would take the same
enlightened view of our
activities and realize
that in our great
patriotic work accidents
are bound to occur
it takes all sorts of people
to make a world
said the barber
which when you think of it
is just what a barber
always says about things

well boss this is one
tragic story with a cheerful
and happy ending
personally however i think
that the krew
krux kranks
should be prosecuted
under the law
which forbids using
the american flag
for trade purposes
there ought to be somebody
like the armenians in this
country the turks kill
the armenians and the
armenians are used to it
and nothing comes of it
but in this country people
who want to kill people
have no one like the armenians
to pick on
and trouble and unrest follow
their killings
why not have a million
people volunteer to be armenians
so the krew krux kranks
would not get into trouble
i do not pretend to be
a statesman but it is plain
to me that something should be
done about it that by
the way is what the barber said
also he looked in a puzzled
way at the remnants
of mister pete perkins
and he said i think
something should be done

OCTOBER 14
Cursed Fly Swatters[1]

i have just been reading
an advertisement of a certain
roach exterminator
the human race little knows
all the sadness it
causes in the insect world
i remember some weeks ago
meeting a middle aged spider
she was weeping
what is the trouble i asked
her it is these cursed
fly swatters she replied
they kill off all the flies
and my family and i are starving
to death it struck me as
so pathetic that i made
a little song about it
as follows to wit

twas an elderly mother spider
grown gaunt and fierce and gray
with her little ones crouched beside her
who wept as she sang this lay

curses on these here swatters
what kills off all the flies
for me and my little daughters
unless we eats we dies

swattin and swattin and swattin
tis little else you hear
and we ll soon be dead and forgotten
with the cost of living so dear

my husband he up and left me
lured off by a centipede
and he says as he bereft me
tis wrong but i ll get a feed

and me a working and working
scouring the streets for food
faithful and never shirking
doing the best i could

curses on these here swatters
what kills off all the flies
me and my poor little daughters
unless we eats we dies

only a withered spider
feeble and worn and old
and this is what
you do when you swat
you swatters cruel and cold

i will admit that some
of the insects do not lead
noble lives but is every
man s hand to be against them
yours for less justice
and more charity

1922

MARCH 14
The Cheerful Oyster

well boss here
we are on the job again
you simply cannot
keep a good bug down
as a cockroach friend
of mine once
remarked to a fat man
who had
inadvertently
swallowed him along
with a portion
of hungarian goulasch
although the remark
i understand
originated with jonah
well the main
thing is to keep
cheerful in spite
of the ups and
downs as i
heard an oyster
remark to his mate
last evening
only six weeks till
may says he

and if we go that long
without being eaten
we will get through
till september and
maybe by that time
nobody will want to
eat us no such
luck for us says
she nonsense says
he be more optimistic
i have noticed
every year that if
i get through
march i always
get through the rest
of the year
and just at that
moment a waiter
put the melancholy
oyster on a plate to
be served and eaten
and rejected the
cheerful oyster
there is a great
moral lesson
in this i pick
up a great many
little sermons of this
sort in my capacity as a
roach about town

APRIL 14
Talking to a Moth

i was talking to a moth
the other evening
he was trying to break into

an electric light bulb
and fry himself on the wires

why do you fellows
pull this stunt i asked him
because it is the conventional
thing for moths or why
if that had been an uncovered
candle instead of an electric
light bulb you would
now be a small unsightly cinder
have you no sense

plenty of it he answered
but at times we get tired
of using it
we get bored with the routine
and crave beauty
and excitement
fire is beautiful
and we know that if we get
too close it will kill us
but what does that matter
it is better to be happy
for a moment
and be burned up with beauty
than to live a long time
and be bored all the while
so we wad all our life up
into one little roll
and then we shoot the roll
that is what life is for
it is better to be a part of beauty
for one instant and then cease to
exist than to exist forever
and never be a part of beauty
our attitude toward life
is come easy go easy
we are like human beings

used to be before they became
too civilized to enjoy themselves

and before i could argue him
out of his philosophy
he went and immolated himself
on a patent cigar lighter
i do not agree with him
myself i would rather have
half the happiness and twice
the longevity

but at the same time i wish
there was something i wanted
as badly as he wanted to fry himself

APRIL 19
Ground for Optimism

there is always
something to be thankful
for you would not
think that a cockroach
had much ground
for optimism
but as the fishing season
opens up i grow
more and more
cheerful at the thought
that nobody ever got
the notion of using
cockroaches for bait

APRIL 22
Waiting for a Vacant Body

you want to know
whether i believe in ghosts
of course i do not believe in them
if you had known
as many of them as i have
you would not
believe in them either
perhaps i have been
unfortunate in my acquaintance
but the ones i have known
have been a bad lot
no one could believe in them
after being acquainted with them
a short time
it is true that i have met
them under peculiar
circumstances
that is while they
were migrating into the
bodies of what human beings
consider a lower order
of creatures
before i became a cockroach
i was a free verse poet
one of the pioneers of the artless art
and my punishment for that
was to have my soul
enter the body of a cockroach
the ghosts i have known
were the ghosts of persons
who were waiting for a vacant
body to get into
they knew they were going
to transmigrate into the bodies of
lizards lice bats snakes

worms beetles mice alley cats
turtles snails tadpoles
etcetera
and while they were waiting
they were as cross as all get out
i remember talking to one of them
who had just worked his way
upward again he had been in the
body of a flea and he was going
into a cat fish
you would think he might be
grateful for the promotion
but not he
i do not call this much of an advance
he said why could i not
be a humming bird or something
kid i told him it will
take you a million years to work your
way up to a humming bird
when i remember he said
that i used to be a hat check boy
in a hotel i could
spend a million years weeping
to think that i should come to this
we have all seen better days i said
we have all come down in the world
you have not come down as far
as some of us
if i ever get to be a hat check boy
again he said i will sting
somebody for what i have had to suffer
that remark will probably cost you
another million years among
the lower creatures i told him
transmigration is a great thing
if you do not weaken
personally my ambition is to get
my time as a cockroach shortened for
good behavior and be promoted

to a revenue officer
it is not much of a step up but
i am humble
i never ran across any of this
ectoplasm that sir arthur
conan doyle tells of but it sounds
as if it might be wonderful
stuff to mend broken furniture with[1]

APRIL 26

Interviewed the Mummy[1]

boss i went
and interviewed the mummy
of the egyptian pharaoh
in the metropolitan museum
as you bade me to do

what ho
my regal leatherface
says i

greetings
little scatter footed
scarab
says he

kingly has been
says i
what was your ambition
when you had any

insignificant
and journalistic insect
says the royal crackling
in my tender prime
i was too dignified

to have anything as vulgar
as ambition
the ra ra boys
in the seti set[2]
were too haughty
to be ambitious
we used to spend our time
feeding the ibises
and ordering
pyramids sent home to try on
but if i had my life
to live over again
i would give dignity
the regal razz
and hire myself out
to work in a brewery

old tan and tarry
says i
i detect in your speech
the overtones
of melancholy

yes i am sad
says the majestic mackerel
i am as sad
as the song
of a soudanese jackal
who is wailing for the blood red
moon he cannot reach and rip

on what are you brooding
with such a wistful
wishfulness
there in the silences
confide in me
my imperial pretzel
says i

```
            i brood on beer
            my scampering whiffle snoot
            on beer says he

            my sympathies
            are with your royal
            dryness says i

            my little pest
            says he
            you must be respectful
            in the presence
            of a mighty desolation
            little archy
            forty centuries of thirst
            look down upon you
            oh by isis
            and by osiris³
            says the princely raisin
            and by pish and phthush and phthah⁴
            by the sacred book perembru
            and all the gods
            that rule from the upper
            cataract of the nile
            to the delta of the duodenum
            i am dry
            i am as dry
            as the next morning mouth
            of a dissipated desert
            as dry as the hoofs
            of the camels of timbuctoo
            little fussy face
            i am as dry as the heart
            of a sand storm
            at high noon in hell
            i have been lying here
            and there
            for four thousand years
```

with silicon in my esophagus
and gravel in my gizzard
thinking
thinking
thinking
of beer

divine drouth
says i
imperial fritter
continue to think
there is no law against
that in this country
old salt codfish
if you keep quiet about it
not yet

what country is this
asks the poor prune

my reverend juicelessness
this is a beerless country
says i

well well said the royal
desiccation
my political opponents back home
always maintained
that i would wind up in hell
and it seems they had the right dope

and with these hopeless words
the unfortunate residuum
gave a great cough of despair
and turned to dust and debris
right in my face

MAY 1
Archy to the Radio Fans[1]

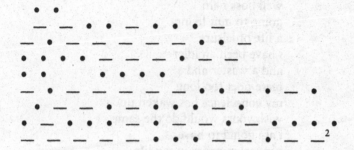

[2]

JUNE 21
Once Every Seventeen Years

every time
i get to feeling
bad because
i am a cockroach
i think how
much worse it would be
if i were a
seventeen year
locust and only woke
up once every
seventeen years
yours for the second
coming of bacchus[1]

JUNE 27
The Truth about the Insects

well boss i am
going to quit living
a life of leisure
i have been an idler
and a waster and a
mere poet too long
my conscience has waked up
wish yours would do the same
i am going to have
a moral purpose in my life
hereafter and a cause
i am going to reclaim
cockroaches and teach them
proper ways of living
i am going to see if i cannot
reform insects in general
i have constituted
myself a missionary
extraordinary
and minister
plenipotentiary
and entomological
to bring idealism to
the little struggling brothers
the conditions in the insect
world today would shock
american reformers
if they knew about them
the lives they lead
are scarcely fit to print
i cannot go into
details but the contented
laxness in which i find
them is frightful
a family newspaper is no place

for these revelations
but i am trying to have
printed in paris
for limited circulation
amongst truly earnest
souls a volume which will
be entitled
the truth about the insects
i assure you there is nothing
even in the old testament
as terrible
i shall be the cotton mather
of the boll weevil

AUGUST 2
Warty Bliggens

i met a toad
the other day by the name
of warty bliggens
he was sitting under
a toadstool
feeling contented
he explained that when the cosmos
was created
that toadstool was especially
planned for his personal
shelter from sun and rain
thought out and prepared
for him

do not tell me
said warty bliggens
that there is not a purpose
in the universe
the thought is blasphemy

a little more
conversation revealed
that warty bliggens
considers himself to be
the center of the said
universe
the earth exists
to grow toadstools for him
to sit under
the sun to give him light
by day and the moon
and wheeling constellations
to make beautiful
the night for the sake of
warty bliggens

to what act of yours
do you impute
this interest on the part
of the creator
of the universe
i asked him
why is it that you
are so greatly favored

ask rather
said warty bliggens
what the universe
has done to deserve me
if i were a
human being i would
not laugh
too complacently
at poor warty bliggens
for similar
absurdities
have only too often
lodged in the crinkles
of the human cerebrum[1]

p s boss i notice
when i am mentioned
in other papers
they frequently spell
my name with a lower
case a now it
is all right for me to
do that myself
but i wish when other
papers refer to me
they would use a capital letter
archy

AUGUST 4
Strange Bedfellows

We said to Archy the other day: "You are welcome to our house any time you wish, if you come alone. But please cease bringing your friends and kinsfolk with you." To which he replied:

boss
you should have learned
by this time
that literature
    makes strange
bedfellows

AUGUST 8
My Favorite Poem

man eats the big fish
the big fish eat the
little fish
the little fish

eat insects
in the water
the water insects
eat the water plants
the water plants
eat mud
mud eats man
my favorite poem
is the same as
abraham lincolns
o why should the spirit
of mortal be proud[1]
awaiting your answer
i am and so forth

AUGUST 12
Always the Lady

well boss what should i see
last evening but our old friend
mehitabel the cat
she was finishing a fish head
she had dragged out of a garbage can
one of her eyes
was bloodshot but the other
glowed with the old
unconquerable luster
there was a drab and ashen look
about her fur
but her step is swift and wiry
and her brave tail is still
a joyous banner in the air
has life been using you hard
mehitabel i asked her
pretty rough little cockroach
says she but what the hell
what the hell

toujours gai is my motto
always game and always gay
what the hell archy
theres a life or two
in the old girl yet i
am always jolly archy
and always the lady
what the hell
they cant take that away
from me archy
and always free archy
i live my own life archy
and i shall right up to the moment
the d s c wagon gets me
and carts me to the garbage scow
archy you may not believe it
but last week i received no less
than three offers of permanent homes
all from very respectable cats
with ribbons around their necks
but nothing doing
on this domesticity stuff
i am a free spirit
i am of royal descent archy
my grandmother was a persian
princess and i cant see myself
falling for any bourgeois
apartment house stuff
either a palace or else
complete liberty for me
i play a lone hand
and i never take up with tame toms
my particular friends have always
been very gentlemanly cats archy
to hell with anything common archy
that has always been my motto
always gay and always the lady
you cant trust half
of these damned pet cats

anyhow they will double cross
a lady with no conscience
only last week i was singing
on a back fence and one of these
dolled up johnnies came out of the basement
and joined me he had a silver bell on
kid he says to me i fall for you
why you sudden thing says i
i like your nerve
come live with me and be my love[1]
says he and i will show you how
to pick open the ice box door
sweet thing says i
your line of talk convinces me
that we are affinities lead me to
the cream pitcher
i followed this slick crook
into the kitchen and just as we got
the ice box door open in came
the cook what does he do but pretend
he never knew me and she hits me
in the slats with a flat iron
was that any way to treat a lady
archy that cheap johnnie had
practically abducted me as you might say
and then deserted me
but what the hell archy what
the hell i am too much
the lady to beef about it
i laid for him in the alley
the next night and tore one of his
ears into fringes and lifted
an eye out of him now you
puzzle faced four flusher i told him
that will teach you how to
double cross a lady
always game and always gay
archy that is me what the hell
theres a dance or two

in the old dame yet
class is the thing that counts
archy you cant get away
from class

well boss i think that in spite
of her brave words and gallant
spirit our friend mehitabel
is feeling her years and constant
exposure to the elements
another year and i will likely
see her funeral cortege
winding through the traffic
a line of d s c wagons headed
for the refuse scows and poor
mehitabel ashily stark
in the foremost cart

AUGUST 28
Archy's Own Short Course in Entomology[1]

yon wood louse is xylophagous[2]
you d think his little tummy
and also his esophagus
would be dry as the sarcophagus
that holds an arid mummy

the tarantula is a spider
she lives on chives and chicory
she is adept at kickery
as ever was a terpsichore[3]
and the devil is inside her

August 29
The Patagonian Penguin

the patagonian
penguin
is a most
peculiar
bird
he lives on
pussy
willows
and his tongue
is always furred
the porcupine
of chile
sleeps his life away
and that is how
the needles
get into the hay
the argentinian
oyster
is a very
subtle gink
for when he s
being eaten
he pretends he is
a skink
when you see
a sea gull
sitting
on a bald man s dome
she likely thinks
she s nesting
on her rocky
island home
do not tease
the inmates

when strolling
through the zoo
for they have
their finer feelings
the same
as me and you
oh deride not
the camel
if grief should
make him die
his ghost will come
to haunt you
with tears
in either eye
and the spirit of
a camel
in the midnight gloom
can be so very
cheerless
as it wanders
round the room

AUGUST 31

Be Glad You re Not a Tomcat

you should be glad
you re not a tomcat
for when all is said
and done
you know youd hate
to pay insurance
on nine lives instead of one
be glad you re not
a centipede
you might your whole
ambition lose

if you had to find
the cash
to keep a centipede
in shoes
be glad you re not
a devilfish
if you had four pairs
of feet
what a trail
you d leave behind you
when you staggered
with the heat

SEPTEMBER 14
The Most Luckless Creature[1]

a fish who had
swallowed an angle worm
found all too late
that a hook was nesting
in its midst ah me
said the poor fish
i am the most luckless
creature in the world
have you not pointed
that out said the worm
i might have supposed
myself a trifle
unfortunate
cheer up you two said
the fisherman jovially
the first two minutes
of that hook are always
the worst you must
cultivate a philosophic
state of mind

boss there is always
a comforting thought
in time of trouble when
it is not our trouble

SEPTEMBER 18
Low Brow

boss i saw a picture
of myself in a paper
the other day[1]
writing on a typewriter
with some of my feet
i wish it was as easy
as that what i have to do
is dive at each key
on the machine
and bump it with my head
and sometimes it telescopes
my occiput[2] into my
vertebrae and i have a
permanent callus
on my forehead
i am in fact becoming
a low brow[3] think of it
me with all my learning
to become a low brow
hoping that you
will remain the same[4]
i am as ever your
faithful little bug

• • •

Archy, by the way, was very flattered the other day when we
informed him that we had named a motor car for him. It goes
up a hill by fits and starts, with much the same motion which he
uses when he is diving at the typewriter. Mechanics in several
different garages have been unable to do much about it, except

to pay their income taxes through association with it, and we are now thinking of taking it to an entomologist.

Not that the car is a total loss. There was a lubrication chart came with it that is worth its weight in—in coal. We were never able to lubricate by the chart, but it is an excellent pattern to carve chickens by, and recently a friend used it as a plan for a bunga-low, thus saving a $2,000 architect's fee and getting a building that invariably evokes the exclamation: *"Oh, how different!"*

SEPTEMBER 20
Song of Mehitabel

this is the song of mehitabel
of mehitabel the alley cat
as i wrote you before boss
mehitabel is a believer
in the pythagorean
theory of the transmigration[1]
of the soul and she claims
that formerly her spirit
was incarnated in the body
of cleopatra
that was a long time ago
and one must not be
surprised if mehitabel
has forgotten some of her
more regal manners

i have had my ups and downs
but wotthehell wotthehell
yesterday sceptres and crowns
fried oysters and velvet gowns
and today i herd with bums
but wotthehell wotthehell

i wake the world from sleep
as i caper and sing and leap

when i sing my wild free tune
wotthehell wotthehell
under the blear eyed moon
i am pelted with cast off shoon[2]
but wotthehell wotthehell

do you think that i would change
my present freedom to range
for a castle or moated grange
wotthehell wotthehell
cage me and i d go frantic
my life is so romantic
capricious and corybantic
and i m toujours gai toujours gai

i know that i am bound
for a journey down the sound[3]
in the midst of a refuse mound
but wotthehell wotthehell
oh i should worry and fret
death and i will coquette
there s a dance in the old dame yet
toujours gai toujours gai

i once was an innocent kit
wotthehell wotthehell
with a ribbon, my neck to fit
and bells tied onto it
o wotthehell wotthehell
but a maltese cat came by
with a come hither look in his eye
and a song that soared to the sky
and wotthehell wotthehell
and i followed adown the street
the pad of his rhythmical feet
o permit me again to repeat
wotthehell wotthehell

my youth i shall never forget
but there s nothing i really regret
wotthehell wotthehell
there s a dance in the old dame yet
toujours gai toujours gai

the things that i had not ought to
i do because i ve gotto
wotthehell wotthehell
and i end with my favorite motto
toujours gai toujours gai

boss sometimes i think
that our friend mehitabel
is a trifle too gay

September 25
Forgets His Littleness

if all the bugs
in all the worlds
twixt earth and betelgoose[1]
should sharpen up
their little stings
and turn their feelings loose
they soon would show
all human beans
in saturn
earth
or mars
their relative significance
among the spinning stars
man is so proud
the haughty simp
so hard for to approach
and he looks down
with such an air

on spider
midge
or roach
the supercilious silliness
of this poor wingless bird
is cosmically comical
and stellarly absurd
his scutellated occiput
has holes somewhere inside
and there no doubt
two pints or so
of scrambled brains reside
if all the bugs
of all the stars
should sting him on the dome
they might pierce through
that osseous rind
and find the brains at home
and in the convolutions lay
an egg with fancies fraught
which
germinating rapidly
might turn into a thought
might turn into the thought
that men
and insects are the same
both transient flecks
of starry dust
that out of nothing came
the planets are
what atoms are
and neither more nor less
man s feet have grown
so big that he
forgets his littleness
the things he thinks
are only things
that insects always knew
the things he does

are stunts that we
don t have to think to do
he spent a score
of centuries
in getting feeble wings
which we instinctively
acquired
with other trivial things
the day is coming
very soon
when man and all his race
must cast their silly
pride aside
and take the second place
i ll take the bugs
of all the stars
and tell them of my plan
and fling them with
their myriad stings
against the tyrant man
dear boss this outburst
is the result
of a personal insult
as so much verse always is
maybe you know how
that is yourself
i dropped into an irish
stew in a restaurant
the other evening
for a warm bath and a bite
to eat and a low browed
waiter plucked me out
and said to me
if you must eat i will
lead you to the
food i have especially prepared
for you and he took me
to the kitchen
and tried to make me

fill myself with
a poisonous concoction
known cynically as roach food
can you wonder
that my anger
against the whole human
race has blazed forth in
song when the revolution
comes i shall
do my best to save
you you have so many
points that are far
from being human

OCTOBER 17
Business Matters

boss i should like
to discuss one or two
business matters with you
quite seriously
in the first place i need
some sort of head gear such as
football players wear
i have to butt each
key of the typewriter
with my head
and i am developing
callouses on my brain
these callouses on my
brain are making me cruel
and careless in my thoughts
i am becoming brutal
almost human
in my writings
and then i would like
a little automobile

i have to go from place
to place so much
picking up news for you
a clock work one would do
with a chauffeur to keep it
wound up for me
and a lightning bug to
sit in front and be
the headlight on dark nights
i hate to mention food boss
it seems so sordid
and plebeian but i no longer
find any left over crusts
of sandwiches in your
waste paper basket i am
forced to haunt the
restaurants and hotels for food
and this is at the
imminent risk of my life
unless i get these things
i will quit you on
november first is not the
laborer worthy of his hire
yours for economic justice
and a living wage

OCTOBER 19
Fairies

Sir Arthur Conan Doyle believes in fairies as well as ghosts,
and in his latest book, "The Coming of the Fairies,"[1] shows
photographs of them.

With regard to ghosts, while we have never believed in them,
we have always been afraid of them.

And with regard to the fairies, we put it up to Archy the
Cockroach.

• • •

"Are there such things?" we asked him.
He replied:

> millions and millions
> of them i wish
> i had a dollar
> for every one
> i have killed

• • •

"Killed!" we cried, shocked. "You don't mean to say you cockroaches kill them?"
He answered:

> we cockroaches
> do not get as many
> of them
> as the spiders do
> all insects prey on them
> when they can
> and they prey
> on insects
> did you ever see a
> little transparent
> shrimp just out
> of the water
> well that is what
> they look like
> and they taste about
> the same way
> with lettuce
> and sliced tomatoes
> and a dash of
> mayonnaise dressing
> between a couple of thin
> slices of bread they
> should be wonderful
> i wish i had a mess
> of the darned things
> right now

"How do you catch them?" we asked the Demon Cockroach.
He replied:

>   with honey
>   we gaum a little
>   honey from a wild bee
>   tree onto a leaf
>   and they come and
>   eat it off
>   and they stick fast
>   to the leaves
>   then we pounce on them
>   and kill them
>   and eat them

"This is frightful!" we cried.
Archy said:

>   why get so heated
>   about the confounded
>   little nuisances
>   that is always
>   the way with
>   you human beings
>   you are all full of
>   sentimentality
>   and no sense
>   why do you not have
>   sympathy with the poor
>   insects which these
>   creatures kill and eat
>   it is a case of
>   eat bug or die with all
>   of us i never saw
>   you shed any tears
>   over eating an oyster
>   or a mess of shrimps or
>   a half dozen frogs legs

you eat beef and mutton
and fish and pork
and all kinds of birds
without a qualm
and you would eat insects
too if you liked them

• • •

"Horrible! Horrible!" we exclaimed.
The Cockroach continued:

you think so just
because you have not
accustomed your mind
to it the fact of their
existence and the fact
that they are food
will soon become
as commonplace to you
as snails

OCTOBER 28
I Knuckle Under

all right boss
i knuckle under
if you will not
pay me anything
for what i write
then you will not
i will return to the job
just to keep james the spider
out of it but all the
same it is cruel of you
to play upon the
jealousies
and susceptibilities
of artists in that fashion

i do not know how
you expect me to be
merry and bright
with this dull ache
of disillusionment at my
heart and the sharp
pang of hunger
in my stomach
some day i will plunge
into a mince pie
and mingle with its elements
and you will never see
me more and then
maybe you will begin
to appreciate
the poor little cockroach
who slaved that you might
live in comfort
maybe in spite of myself
i will haunt you then
if i were you i would hate
to be haunted by the ghost
of a cockroach
think of it boss
everywhere you looked
to see a spectral cockroach
that none but you knew was
there to pick him from
your shirt front when
others were blind to him
to feel him crawling
on your collar in public
places to be compelled
to brush him from your plate
when you sat down to dine
to pluck him always from the glass
before you dared to drink
to extend your hand
to grab that of some fair

lady and then hesitate and
pick him from her wrist
people would begin to think
you were a little
queer boss and if you
attempted to explain
they would think you still
queerer what in the world
is the matter with you
they would say
oh nothing nothing at all
you would answer
plucking at the air
it will soon pass i merely
thought i saw a cockroach
on your nose madam
suspicions of your sanity
would grow and grow
do you not like that
pudding your hostess would ask
and you would murmur
being taken off your guard
it is very good pudding
indeed i was just
trying not to eat
the cockroach
boss i do not make
any threats at all
i just simply state what
may very well happen to
you through remorse if you
drive me to suicide
i will try not to
haunt you boss because
i am loving and forgiving
in my spirit but who
knows that i will not be
compelled to haunt you
in spite of myself

a hard heart will not get
you anything boss
remember the plagues
of egypt perhaps to
your remorseful mind i
will be multiplied
by millions i am giving
you a last chance to
repent you should be glad
that i am only a cockroach
and not a tarantula
yours prophetically

NOVEMBER 1
The Dactyl Droops[1]

autumn is here
and the dactyl[2]
droops its weary wing
and the sad iambic[3]
shivers
with frozen feet[4]
poor thing
but spring will come
and the poets
will thaw
and the fountains gush
and a hundred
million dactyls
twitter
amid the slush

NOVEMBER 16
Investigating Her Morals

boss i got
a message from
mehitabel the cat
the other day
brought me by
a cockroach
she asks for our help
it seems she is being
held at ellis
island while an
investigation is made
of her morals
she left the country
and now it looks as
if she might not
be able to get
back in again
she cannot see
why they are
investigating
her morals she says
wotthehellbill she says
i never claimed
i had any morals
she has always regarded
morals as an unnecessary
complication in life
her theory is
that they take up room that might
better be devoted to
something more interesting
live while you are alive
she says and postpone
morality to the hereafter
everything in its place

is my rule she says
but i am liberal she
says i do not give
a damn how moral other
people are i never try
to interfere with them
in fact i prefer them
moral they furnish
a background for my
vivacity in the meantime
it looks as if she
would have to swim
if she gets ashore and
the water is cold

NOVEMBER 21
Small Talk

boss the other day
i heard an
ant conversing
with a flea
small talk i said
disgustedly
and went away
from there

NOVEMBER 22
Shakespeare and I[1]

coarse
jocosity
catches the crowd
shakespeare
and i

are often
low browed

the fish wife[2]
curse
and the laugh
of the horse
shakespeare
and i
are frequently
coarse

aesthetic
excuses
in bill s behalf
are adduced
to refine
big bill s
coarse laugh

but bill
he would chuckle
to hear such guff
he pulled
rough stuff
and he liked
rough stuff

hoping you
are the same

DECEMBER I
Thank You for the Mittens

thank you
for the mittens
socks and

muffler for me
knitted out of
frogs hair by one
of my admirers which
you so kindly
forwarded i suppose
the reason
i got them was that
they were too
small for you
to wear yourself
yours for rum
crime and riot

DECEMBER 13
Archy Is Excited

dear boss i found
a red[1] ribbon in
your typewriter
to-day and i am
not to be held
responsible for what i
write red always
excites me so
yours for hasheesh
hedonism and hades
exclamation
point   . . .

ARCHY IS STILL EXCITED

dear boss i am
acquiring more
and more contempt

for you humans
i heard a couple
of girls yesterday
saying what a nice
christmas present it
would make to catch
a live archy
and have him gilded and
wear him on
a little chain
attached to a scarf
pin yours for red rum
ruin revolt and rapine

December 23
The Futility of Literature

i heard a spider
and a fly arguing
wait said the fly
do not eat me
i serve a great purpose
in the world

you will have to
show me said the spider

i scurry around
gutters and sewers
and garbage cans
said the fly and gather
up the germs of
typhoid influenza
and pneumonia on my feet
and wings
then i carry these germs
into the households of men

and give them diseases
all the people who
have lived the right
sort of life recover
from the diseases
and the old soaks who
have weakened their systems
with liquor and iniquity[1]
succumb it is my mission
to help rid the world
of these wicked persons
i am a vessel of righteousness
scattering seeds of justice
and serving the noblest uses

it is true said the spider
that you are more
useful in a plodding
material sort of way
than i am but i do not
serve the utilitarian deities
i serve the gods of beauty
look at the gossamer webs
i weave they float in the sun
like filaments of song[2]
if you get what i mean
i do not work at anything
i play all the time
i am busy with the stuff
of enchantment and the materials
of fairyland my works
transcend utility
i am the artist
a creator and a demi god
it is ridiculous to suppose
that i should be denied
the food i need in order
to continue to create
beauty i tell you

plainly mister fly it is all
damned nonsense for that food
to rear up on its hind legs
and say it should not be eaten

you have convinced me
said the fly say no more
and shutting all his eyes
he prepared himself for dinner
and yet he said i could
have made out a case
for myself too if i had
had a better line of talk

of course you could said the spider
clutching a sirloin from him
but the end would have been
just the same if neither of
us had spoken at all

boss i am afraid that what
the spider said is true
and it gives me to think
furiously upon the futility
of literature

Notes

1916

MARCH 29
Expression Is the Need

For this first appearance we are reprinting Marquis's entire column rather than just the Archy material, to provide a glimpse into the usual mix of topic and commentary. The rest of this volume will consist of Archy's contributions and occasional responses from Marquis, omitting the bulk of most columns and all of those in which Archy does not participate.

1. A former governor of New York and then Associate Supreme Court Justice, Charles Evans Hughes left the court in 1916 to campaign for president on the Republican ticket. In one of the narrowest vote margins in U.S. history, Woodrow Wilson would defeat him a few months later.

2. Pancho Villa was a Mexican revolutionary and bandit. In 1910 he and his gang, along with Emiliano Zapata and many others, had joined the popular revolt against Mexican dictator Porfirio Díaz and had been praised at home and abroad. By 1916, however, times had changed. Villa had been leading murderous raids across the U.S. border, eluding capture in both countries—even escaping a highly publicized expedition led by General John "Black Jack" Pershing, in which George S. Patton participated.

3. Helena Petrovna Blavatsky was a Russian-born mystic, author of *The Secret Doctrine* and other books. She founded the Theosophical Society in 1875. Theosophy ("divine wisdom" or "wisdom of God") is a mystical religious philosophy, a smorgasbord of Buddhism, Gnosticism, Platonism, and many other belief systems. Blavatsky claimed to possess a variety of occult powers. Related to and congenial toward Spiritualism, Theosophy still provides fertile

ground for many New Age beliefs, including the one that most interests Archy: reincarnation.

4. In 1916 the New York publisher Henry Holt was publicizing a new book supposedly dictated to a woman named Pearl Curran, via Ouija board, by the spirit of a seventeenth-century woman named Patience Worth. This ethereal collaboration resulted in several novels and many poems, and until her death in 1937 Curran claimed to be merely channelling for Worth. Marquis returns to Patience Worth on October 19, 1917. On November 18, 1919, Marquis wrote in his column, " 'I'm amused at science,' says Mrs. Curran, the medium through whom speaks that remarkable Patience Worth. Which makes it about an even thing between science and Mrs. Curran, we dare say."

5. The popular 1914 book *Letters from a Living Dead Man*, by the American journalist, poet, and novelist Elsa Barker, claimed to be a collection of spiritual communications from beyond the grave. Barker also wrote a novel, *The Son of Mary Bethel*, in which Christ is living in the early twentieth century, an idea related to the themes behind Marquis's 1934 book *Chapters for the Orthodox*.

6. Note that in the original columns Mehitabel remained unnamed until May 11, although, as noted in the Introduction, when gathering the first collection Marquis named her earlier to establish her as the second important character.

APRIL 10
Simplified Spelling

In only his fourth appearance Archy is already switching to rhyme.

1. This topic seems an inevitable joke for a cockroach who already can't use capital letters or punctuation. Ever since Gutenberg, there have been movements to simplify English orthography, which is burdened (or enlivened) by many rules borrowed from many languages. The Simplified Spelling Board was formed in 1905 with the sponsorship of Andrew Carnegie and the support of many prominent figures, most notably George Bernard Shaw, whose own simplifications form speedbumps in reading his plays. In 1916 the Board voted to modify the established past tense of verbs ending in *-ed* to end in *t*; e.g., a word such as *dropped* would become *dropt*. Note that while feigning support, Archy is anything but consistent in his phonetic spelling.

2. For more on Josh Billings, see the Introduction. In this word Marquis merges the colloquial humorist's name with the word *billings-*

gate, which means foul or insulting language, from a former London fish market renowned for its off-color banter.

3. Archy types by butting his head against the typewriter key, but it has also been only two weeks since Marquis let the cockroach butt into his already well-established column.

4. This is the first of several references to the still new term *lowbrow*. See especially September 18, 1922 and its notes.

APRIL 26
Hell

1. In 1916 *simp* was a recent slang term, less than a decade old, shortened from *simpleton*.

2. Because the size of letters on a newspaper page indicate a subject's relative importance (one reason why advertisements are so much larger than news stories), Archy petitions again and again for a larger type size as reward for his efforts. Here is the progression, from smaller to larger, among the type sizes that Archy mentions in various columns: *agate, nonpareil, minion,* and *brevier*. For reference with the one type size most of us know, each of these is smaller than *pica*. See also note for May 1, 1922.

Many readers talk about Archy and Mehitabel and Don Marquis (at least the semifictional Marquis who narrates the column) as friends. Actually Marquis establishes early, less than a month after Archy's debut, an edgy and often adversarial relationship between the cockroach and the boss. Because he was willing to try anything, and because his column was always responding to the troubled world around him, Marquis often cast Archy as oppressed laborer and himself as cruel management, a situation that mirrored his own relationship with some editors. And, as we shall see, Archy fears Mehitabel's violent predatory instincts, and more than once has to flee for his life. (When he considers suicide on June 28, he knows that he could let Mehitabel "damage" him.) No wonder Marquis fans were disappointed in the Broadway musical that portrayed Archy smitten with Mehitabel.

MAY 11
Up or Down the Scale

1. A scale that one's soul can ascend or descend doesn't appear in all versions of transmigration—the idea that the spiritual essence of a human being can occupy a succession of human or animal bodies—

but Marquis found it useful and funny and returned to it several
times. See also note 1 for September 20, 1922.
2. This is the first time that Mehitabel's name appeared in the column.
As described in the Introduction, Marquis moved her name and her
history forward when he assembled the first collection.

MAY 23
Raise in Salary

1. Not for the first time, Marquis expresses his own worries as a
writer through Archy. Before launching "The Sun Dial" in 1912 he
had been laboring for years to get a featured regular column, only
to learn that filling it with quality material was a daily burden.

JUNE 19
Capitals

1. Parnassus is an actual mountain, now called Liakoura, in Greece.
In Greek mythology the mountain was named after a hero who
founded divination by birds and the oracle of Python, but the term
came to represent the noble height of artistic excellence, the club of
the immortals. For experimental poets such as Archy, however, it
refers more specifically to the art-for-art's-sake school of French
poetry launched by the 1866 collection and manifesto *Le Parnasse
Contemporain*.

JUNE 28
Why Not Commit Suicide

1. Suicide will become a common theme in the series. See especially
the five-part "Suicide Club" series beginning on September 21,
1916, and "Assisting at a Suicide" on June 4, 1918.

JULY 25
We Rushed Forward and Swatted

1. The term *fly-swatter* was still quite new, as was the mass-produced
version of the implement it describes, which is why Marquis em-
ploys it in several columns. Many sources date the term to 1917,
but this column pushes the official date back a bit. Naturally Mar-
quis quickly took the term *swatter* and applied it to the person
swatting. See also October 14, 1921, for a spider's opinion.

2. It has taken Marquis less than four months after introducing Archy to kill him.

August 5
Ballade of the Under Side

This was Marquis's original newspaper title for the poem.

1. *Wried,* the past tense of *wry,* was an already archaic literary term, used by Browning and few since. Here Archy uses the word about himself in its meaning of wrongheaded, but on November 6, 1916, Marquis uses it about him in its meaning of unnaturally twisted.

2. Originally *L'envoi* meant a detached verse or verses at the end of a poem or other literary composition, intended to encapsulate a moral or address the work to a particular individual. In English it is sometimes used as a synonym for *coda.*

August 12
Aeroplane

1. Airplanes at the time were primitive and crash-prone, and flying was a dangerous and glamorous enterprise. The Wright Brothers had flown at Kitty Hawk only thirteen years before.

2. Originally the term *water wagon* referred to a literal wagon that transported water either to drink or to sprinkle on dusty roads during dry weather. But in the first decade of the twentieth century it acquired the meaning of abstention from alcoholic beverages, evolving into "on the wagon," a term still in use long after water wagons ceased to exist.

3. "that jonah story" was of course the account of Jonah's sea change inside the belly of, according to the Bible, "a great fish." Marquis had wrung many humorous variations on this fable, including a remark by Clem Hawley that only the story's friends had a right to make fun of it as well as a tedious ballad entitled "Noah an' Jonah an' Cap'n John Smith." The poem was often reprinted in various places, and because it was precisely the length of an entire column Marquis often reprised it himself when he wanted a day off, under the heading "Reprinted by Request." Apparently he overplayed this column-padding, because finally his editor at the *Evening Sun,* George Smith, asked him to refrain unless "the request is quite overwhelming." In 1921 the poem became the title piece in a new Marquis collection of humorous verse. The reference a few lines earlier to "that cosmic stuff" was also self-advertisement; it referred to Hermione's hopelessly vague love of the word *cosmic.*

August 28
Cleopatra

When Marquis included this column in *Archy and Mehitabel* he cut all references to religion and rearranged the line lengths. Note Archy's skepticism from the first about Mehitabel's veracity.

1. Some of the technical details of Archy's craft remind us that as a human he was already a free verse poet, that this mode of poetry is a stylistic choice rather than an invention mothered by his current inability to operate the shift key. He also ignores the period key, which is available even in lower case, as every decapitaled e-mail writer knows. The chief question is how Archy operated the heavy return bar on these big manual typewriters (see the column for August 17, 1916). He needed a word processor.

2. George Moore was a prolific Irish writer who published fiction, drama, poetry, and autobiography. Several of his works were considered scandalously frank about sexual matters, which may be why our heroes want to read them during the night. In 1916 Moore published a novel denounced for its irreverence, *The Brook Kerith*, in which Jesus doesn't die on the cross but is rescued and continues his life as a shepherd in Palestine. In 1934 Marquis published a volume of religious satire, *Chapters for the Orthodox*, which follows the adventures of God and Jesus around New York City.

3. Cleopatra was a descendant of the Greek and Macedonian Ptolemaic dynasty that had ruled Egypt for three centuries prior to her birth in 69 BCE—one of the many dominoes knocked over by Alexander the Great. Her reputation for tempestuous and opportunistic amours, most famously with Julius Caesar and Mark Antony (see September 1, 1916), certainly tallies with the personality of Mehitabel.

4. Valerian was a Roman emperor who was actually born two and a half centuries after Cleopatra died. Archy's reference is merely a joke about his name; valerian root affects cats much like catnip.

September 1
The Queens I Have Been

1. Antony and Cleopatra met in 41 BCE. After Julius Caesar's assassination three years before, Antony ruled Rome along with Lepidus and Caesar's nephew Octavian. Cleopatra captivated Antony from the first time they met, when she answered a summons from him

and arrived on a magnificent barge, dressed as Venus, the goddess of love. His involvement with her led to neglect of his family and political commitments; soon, like Mehitabel, she bore illegitimate children.

2. The reference is to a verse of the Mother Goose rhyme "A frog he would a-wooing go," from the seventeenth or eighteenth century:

> *A frog he would a-wooing go,*
> *Heigh ho! says Rowley,*
> *Whether his mother would let him or no.*
> *With a rowley, powley, gammon and spinach,*
> *Heigh ho! says Anthony Rowley.*

3. Cleopatra became romantically involved with Julius Caesar in 48 BCE, after he pursued his rival Pompey to Alexandria and became involved in the war between Cleopatra and her brother, husband, and co-ruler Ptolemy XIII. Caesar sided with Cleopatra, defeated Ptolemy, and installed her as ruler. She bore him a son.

September 4
Unpunctuated Gink

1. Invented in 1886, the *linotype* machine revolutionized the newspaper business. The older Gutenberg style of printing had required a printer to place a single character—letter, space, punctuation mark—at a time. The complex linotype printer used a ninety-character keyboard; each keystroke retrieved a letter from the machine's magazine. When an entire line was ready, the machine poured molten type metal—the "nice hot bath" with which the linotyper threatens Archy—into the stacked molds. The result was a line of type in reverse, ready to print. Each line was placed by hand into the page layout. This innovation enabled much faster production and therefore more up-to-date newspapers. For most people it turned the newspaper into their daily vehicle for contact with the outside world, leading to the popularity of such writers as Don Marquis.

2. For *joshbillingsgate* see the Introduction and also note 2 for April 10, 1916.

SEPTEMBER 8
Drunken Hornet

1. *Speakeasy* was a nickname for an illicit bar, where drinks were available despite Prohibition.

SEPTEMBER 21
Suicide Club, Part 1

Marquis dusted off and reprinted the already hoary joke about the glue factory several other times in his column.

1. "R L S" was Robert Louis Stevenson, author of *Treasure Island* and *Dr. Jekyll and Mr. Hyde*. The three tales comprising "The Suicide Club" appeared in his 1882 collection *New Arabian Nights*, which also contains "A Lodging for the Night," a story about the French scoundrel and poet François Villon, whose reincarnated self will show up in Mehitabel's saga of her life.

SEPTEMBER 23
Suicide Club, Part 3

1. *Tonic* was a generic term for a restorative or invigorating medicinal beverage. The unsupervised production of supposedly healing tonics, claiming to do everything from reverse baldness to cure disease to prolong life, was one of the most lucrative scams available to confidence tricksters, as demonstrated in O. Henry's stories of the "gentle grafter" Jeff Peters. Many variations on the game still go on today.

SEPTEMBER 27
Suicide Club, Part 5

1. This cockroach's sad fate never appeared in the column.

SEPTEMBER 30
Killing Off the Sparrows

1. Archy's comparison of sparrows to "the common people" wasn't as much of a stretch as it seems. Only two weeks before this column appeared, an article in the *New York Times* called for the destruction of the English sparrow (which is actually a weaver finch that

was never limited to England). In his 1913 book *Our Vanishing Wild Life*, William T. Hornaday, a New York Zoological Society curator, had denounced the English sparrow in terms that sounded remarkably like anti-immigration rhetoric: "It is a bird of plain plumage, low tastes, impudent disposition and persistent fertility. Continually does it crowd out its betters, or pugnaciously drive them away. . . . It has no song, and in habits it is a bird of the street and the gutter. . . . The English sparrow is a nuisance and a pest, and if it could be returned to the land of its nativity we would gain much."

OCTOBER 12
My Last Name

1. The Blattidae family does indeed proudly claim Archy as a member. Variations on the name include the suborders Blattaria and Blattodea. *Family* is a taxonomic unit, smaller than an *order* and larger than a *genus*, and to zoom in more closely Archy is presumably a member of the genus *Periplaneta* and the (in this case quite apt) species *americana*, the common American cockroach.
2. C. L. Marlatt (the Archy collections have always misprinted the first initial as "e") was the author of many scientific papers. He named several species, including *Pontania pacifica*, a gall-inducing sawfly who would have made a great character.

NOVEMBER 6
Where Is Archy?

1. Helmets at the time were a simple affair, thick layered leather with fur-lined ear guards that hung down and led to the nickname "dog ear helmet."

1917

MARCH 30
Between Him and His Masterpiece

1. Perhaps it is worthwhile to explain, for the benefit of those born in the computer age, a bit about the forerunner of the keyboard and printer. In Marquis's time a typewriter required a ribbon on a spool to provide ink for the keys to strike and carbon-coated paper to produce a copy behind the first page. The ribbon spool could be rewound, and

later models did so automatically. Economical writers could type increasingly pale pages until the ribbon gave up the ghost. Archy's method of inserting carbon paper and using the copy as the original image meant that he would have to type blindly. The column on December 13, 1922 includes a reference to a red ribbon; typewriter ribbons came mostly in black and a combination of black-and-red.

APRIL 16
War Times

1. On April 4 the U.S. had officially entered the war.

JUNE 15
Comma Boss Comma

1. Archy's signature was printed in lowercase as usual in this column. He wanted small caps because that was how Marquis's own name appeared at the end of each column.

JULY 7
Workman Spare That Bathtub

1. The poem parodies a popular song, based upon a poem by George Pope Morris published in 1830:

> Woodman, spare that tree!
> Touch not a single bough!
> In youth it sheltered me,
> And I'll protect it now.

> 'Twas my forefather's hand
> That placed it near his cot:
> There, woodman, let it stand,
> Thy axe shall harm it not! . . .

JULY 27
Washington D C

1. In 1917 the U.S. legislature was wrangling over the Lever Food Control Bill, which would permit government regulation of food production during the war. There were many attempts to add Prohibition measures to the bill, but at President Wilson's request they were removed, and the bill passed on August 10.

SEPTEMBER 24
Out of the Cockroach Body

1. Marquis was quoting a beautifully apt passage from Edward
   Fitzgerald's 1859 translation of Omar Khayyam's *Rubáiyát* (see
   December 16, 1918 and its first note):

   > Why, if the Soul can fling the Dust aside,
   > And naked on the Air of Heaven ride,
   > Were't not a Shame—were't not a Shame for him
   > In this clay carcase crippled to abide?

OCTOBER 13
A German Periscope

1. *Heinie* was an offensive slang term, borrowed from Canadian sol-
   diers and dating from around 1904, for German soldiers or at times
   for any German. It was adapted from the German proper name
   Heinrich. British soldiers employed a different slang term, from an-
   other common German name: Fritz. World War I was also the time
   when *Kraut*, from the cabbage dish popular in Germany, became a
   British and American slang term for a German.

OCTOBER 19
Patience Worth

1. See March 29, 1916, note 4.

NOVEMBER 1
Beware the Demon Rum

1. *Demon rum* had been a common phrase in the temperance move-
   ment for decades, especially associated with militant anti-alcohol
   activists such as Carrie Nation. See also note 1 for June 10, 1918,
   and the note for January 20, 1919.

NOVEMBER 8
Sounds Like a Jolly Gang

1. Archy is incorrect; not all of the partygoers are germs. True, the
   Treponema pallidum bacterium causes syphilis, and *Diplococci* is
   the plural of a genus of bacteria no longer employed by taxono-

mists. But *Pediculus capitis* is the head louse, kin to the patriotic body louse ("cootie") in the column on June 24, 1918. Three of the other scientific terms, while printed correctly in the original column, have always been misprinted in the Archy collections: A *pleochroic* (misprinted "pioochroic") *halo* is a discoloration around radioactive material in a rock, a scar of radioactive decay. *Protococcus nivalis* (misprinted "nivalls") is the red snow plant, a unicellular algae. *Phologopite* (misprinted "phlogopito") is a rare mineral of the mica group.

1918

MAY 28
Named after the Washington Arch

1. *Archie* was originally a British term, thought to have emerged from the Royal Flying Corps' joking references to a recurring line in a monologue by the music hall comedian George Robey: "Archibald, certainly not!" Supposedly a flier said this aloud to shells narrowly missing his plane.

   The dominant feature of Washington Square Park in Greenwich Village, the Washington Arch is a marble monument, dedicated in 1895, which was sculpted to replace a wooden one built for the centennial of George Washington's inauguration. In 1918 a sculpture of Washington as president was being added to match the 1916 addition of a statue of him as general.

   Is Archy referring to his human or his cockroach parents meeting under the Arch? At what point did his soul enter the body of a cockroach? He doesn't say. Probably Marquis chose this site because he had identified Archy as a *vers libre* poet and he liked to mock Greenwich Village pretensions. But surely he also knew that before it was turned into a park in 1828, the site had been a cemetery and execution site, a fitting place from which to launch a reincarnation.

2. Mithridates was a first-century-BCE king of Pontus, who was defeated by Pompey in the battle that earned him the sobriquet "the Great." He is remembered for the legend that he ingested a small amount of poison every day in order to build up his resistance to assassins, and he actually did test poisons on prisoners. Marquis's generation were reminded of Mithridates by a long reference to him in A. E. Housman's poem "Terence, this is stupid stuff," in *A Shropshire Lad* in 1896.

JUNE 6
Not a Fish

1. *Mola mola* is the scientific name, and one of the common names, of the giant ocean sunfish, the largest bony fish on Earth. They can weigh 5,000 pounds (2,250 kilograms) and reach a length of more than 10 feet (3 meters). If any fish could be suspected of being an enemy invention, it would be the mola mola.

JUNE 10
Prohibition Rushes Toward Us

1. The theme of Prohibition recurs in this collection frequently, but not as often as it shows up in Marquis's life and other writings. Throughout his youth and early adulthood, the American temperance movement had grown in force. Such groups as the Prohibition Party formed in 1869 and the Anti-Saloon League founded in 1895 agitated vociferously for a national ban on alcoholic beverages. In 1919, three years after Archy's debut, Congress passed the National Prohibition Act. It was designed to enforce the Eighteenth Amendment (which another famous Marquis character, the saloon-frequenting Old Soak, dubbed the Eighteenth Commandment), which prohibited the production, sale, transportation, and consumption of alcoholic beverages. Naturally the law, which was in effect until the Twenty-first Amendment voided it in 1933, proved a godsend to organized crime; it may have been the single greatest boost for the career of Chicago gangster Al Capone. No decade in American history is as associated in the public consciousness with drinking and wild parties and violent crime as the Prohibition Era.

2. Most Latin poems did not have titles, and generally scholars refer to them by the first words of the first line. *Eheu fugaces labuntur anni* (roughly "Alas, our fleeting years pass away") are the opening words of the fourteenth ode by Quintus Horatius Flaccus (65–8 BCE), better known as Horace. The Roman poet laments that age and death cannot be held at bay—not by trying to avoid war and illness and accident, not even by bribing the gods. In his 1919 book *Prefaces*, Marquis refers to the Eheu Fugaces Chop House, which he later calls "Eheu's place." As E. B. White pointed out, "In 1916 to hold a job on a daily paper, a columnist was expected to be something of a scholar and a poet. . . ."

3. In Greek mythology the River Lethe flows through Hades, where its waters slake the spiritual thirst of the dead by causing them to forget their lives before.

4. For all his unlikely tales, the braggart cockroach at least has his chronology straight. The sixteenth-century English playwright Christopher (Kit) Marlowe was a contemporary of Shakespeare, and both did indeed frequent London's popular Mermaid Tavern. Joseph Addison and Richard Steele were English essayists roughly a century later. Edgar Allan Poe published "The Raven" in 1844. Although already famous when this column appeared in 1918, the English poet and playwright John Masefield was only forty; he lived another half century, three decades longer than Marquis. A *bung* was a cork or other stopper used to plug the bunghole of a cask, which had to be dislodged with a strong tap by a wooden mallet called a *bung-starter*. What it started was the flow of spirits out of the cask.

JUNE 19
Income Tax Slacker

1. The United States didn't have an income tax law until 1862, when Congress enacted it to fund the Civil War. It was eliminated in 1872 and replaced with a "sin tax" on distilled spirits and tobacco. Not until 1913, only five years before Marquis was writing, did the Sixteenth Amendment to the U.S. Constitution permanently establish the income tax. In 1918, the first year in which collected taxes exceeded one billion dollars, it was still a contentious topic.

JUNE 21
The Raiding Habit

1. The New York district attorney was joining in a national fervor of privacy invasion and unwarranted arrest, which had begun during World War I. In the name of protecting the United States against its enemies, law enforcement agencies illegally spied on American citizens, determined to suppress dissent and prevent organized representation of labor. During 1917 and 1918, for example, more than 2,000 members of the International Workers of the World were prosecuted, many simply for criticizing the war. The previous year, J. Edgar Hoover had joined the staff of the Department of Justice, beginning the unscrupulous scramble for power that would result in his directorship of the FBI in 1924. The year 1918 saw the beginning of three years of largely illegal "Palmer Raids" at the behest of

Woodrow Wilson's Attorney General A. Mitchell Palmer, who had presidential ambitions of his own. On May 16, less than a month before this column, the U.S. government enacted the Espionage Act, which provided legal loopholes for further broadening the invasive tactics of law enforcement agencies.

JUNE 24
Loyal Allied Cootie

1. *Cootie* is a slang term for the body louse, *Pediculus corporis*, which flourishes in unwashed clothing and therefore plagues soldiers and the poor.
2. Paul von Hindenburg was the second president of Weimar Germany and had a profound impact on German history. In 1916 he had been appointed Chief of the Greater German General Staff, and he helped influence Kaiser Wilhelm to go to Holland. In 1933 Hindenburg would appoint Hitler Chancellor of Germany.
3. Erich Ludendorff was Deputy Chief of Staff under Hindenburg, but his influence was almost unlimited. Together they gained control of most of Germany and unofficially demoted the Kaiser to an almost powerless role. Ludendorff's policy of vicious and unrestricted submarine warfare eventually helped draw the United States into war.
4. Frederick Wilhelm Viktor Albert of Hohenzollern became Kaiser Wilhelm II in 1888 upon the death of Frederick II. The Hohenzollern dynasty had ruled for five centuries over what had grown from the German state of Brandenburg to the kingdom of Prussia and finally to the German Empire. A militaristic and authoritarian ruler, Wilhelm was hardly unaware of the war, but ever since he had suffered a nervous breakdown in 1908 he had been increasingly sidelined by Hindenburg and Ludendorff.

JULY 23
One Thing That Makes Crickets So Melancholy

1. After the redemptive *Christmas Carol in Prose* in 1843 and the political tale *The Chimes* in 1844, Charles Dickens published a sentimental and domestic Christmas story, *The Cricket on the Hearth: A Fairy Tale of Home*, in December 1845. Marquis's sarcastic little saga cleanses the palate of anyone treacled to death by Dickens's symbolic cricket, blind toymaker, and miserly business owner.

2. For other melancholy crickets, see *Charlotte's Web*: "The crickets . . . sang the song of summer's ending, a sad, monotonous song. . . . 'Summer is dying, dying.' . . . Even on the most beautiful days in the whole year—the days when summer is changing into fall—the crickets spread the rumor of sadness and change" (New York: Harper & Row, 1952), page 113. E. B. White began writing *Charlotte's Web* in early 1950, immediately after completing his introduction to a reissue of Doubleday's omnibus collection *The Lives and Times of Archy and Mehitabel*. See the Introduction for more relationships between Marquis's characters and White's; see the column and note 2 for December 23, 1922, for another connection between the two books; and see September 12, 1916, for Archy's opinion of crickets' false cheer.

AUGUST 6
Reports of My Exit

1. Archy is referring to a famous line by Mark Twain, supposedly cabled in response to a premature obituary: "The reports of my death are greatly exaggerated."

AUGUST 13
Falling Upwards

1. In his last few lines Marquis is parodying one of the later stanzas of Henry Wadsworth Longfellow's 1858 poem "The Ladder of St. Augustine":

> *The heights by great men reached and kept*
> *Were not attained by sudden flight,*
> *But they, while their companions slept,*
> *Were toiling upward in the night.*

AUGUST 24
Smile When You Ride on the Subway

1. The privately owned IRT (Interborough Rapid Transit) system began operation in 1904. In 1918 the Number 4 line reached Woodlawn. The subway had quickly become the best way to navigate the fast-growing city.

September 16
A Genuine Quip

1. Further explaining Archy's explanation threatens to overwhelm his joke with notes, but this column provides a wonderful example of how Marquis's (or Archy's) mind worked. Actually the Latin quotation exists in both forms, ending with either *nihil* or *nullus*, and means "either Caesar or nothing." It dates back not to Julius Caesar but to Cesare Borgia, the model for Macchiavelli's ruthless antihero in *The Prince*. Like *tsar*, the term *kaiser* is adapted from the Latin *caesar*, and in fact retains the original pronunciation, with its hard Latin C: *KY-zer*. Archy's was indeed a genuine quip, but it would have retained its freshness for only a few weeks. The *mihiel* refers to Saint-Mihiel, a village east of Paris where the first major American offensive of the war had just been fought on September 12 to 14, in which General Pershing's troops forced the Germans to abandon a site they had held since the beginning of the war.

September 26
Tobacco Fund

1. To this entry Marquis appended a note: "The money you put into a Victory Bond is still yours. You are only asked to help your country by helping yourself." During this period he devoted many brief Archy appearances to promoting the sale of bonds to raise money for the war effort; the present volume includes as examples only this one and the one for October 1. A few days before this column, *The Nation* had run an article lauding Thrift Stamps, or War Saving Stamps, as "fruit of many a little self-denial," and describing how they added up to a fifty-dollar Liberty Bond, "paid for in instalments by months of thoughtful economy. . . ." In the years 1917–18, individuals, small businesses, and banks purchased more than $21 billion worth of stamps and bonds.

2. The *Sun*'s tobacco fund was one of many such drives to raise money for purchasing tobacco that could be sent to soldiers at the front. On July 18 the *Sun* had published a long editorial headlined "Tobacco Needful in Trenches," subheaded "Soldiers Testify to Its Helpful Qualities—'Sun' Smokes 'Come in Handy'—New Donations Furnish Ammunition for Pipes." Many physicians still argued that tobacco had healthful side effects, but most of the promotions emphasized how it helped soldiers to relax during what this article

called "the supernervous state produced by modern warfare." In the January 28, 1918 column Archy himself contributes money to the *Sun*'s tobacco fund.

OCTOBER 26
Jane Gad Fly

1. Neysa McMein was a famously beautiful popular artist best known for her illustrations of chic young American women. During the war she designed posters for both the United States and France, and she spent six months in Europe entertaining troops. A woman of varied talents, she was both a member of the Algonquin Round Table and the illustrator who created the original image of the fictional ideal-American-housewife Betty Crocker for the General Mills food company.
2. Winsor McKay was an innovative American cartoonist and illustrator best known for two creations—*Little Nemo in Slumberland* and *Gertie the Dinosaur*. The former, which revolutionized the comic strip with its beautifully drawn full-color panels in the *New York Herald*, ran from 1905–1911; it evolved into McKay's first animated film. In 1914, only four years before this column, McKay had debuted *Gertie the Dinosaur*, a stunning animated film which almost single-handedly launched popular awareness of this infant genre.
3. *Boche* was a French slur against Germans that was quickly adopted into English during the war. Before the war it could mean either German or obstinate, but soon it joined *kraut*, *heinie*, and other terms that Marquis did not hesitate to employ in his column.

OCTOBER 28
The Influenza

1. In 1918 the worldwide influenza epidemic (called Spanish influenza because it was erroneously thought to have started in Spain) killed more people than did the Black Plague during the four years of its most infamous outbreak in the mid-fourteenth century. In October alone, almost 200,000 Americans died of the virus. By the middle of 1919 the number would reach 675,000. Various public health agencies were emphasizing the many ways that influenza germs might be transmitted, including aboard insects.

NOVEMBER 9
A Tall Story

1. An armistice is a cessation of hostilities prior to treaty negotiation. The "false armistice" had occurred two days before, on November 7; it was premature because what had actually been signed was a preliminary surrender agreement that still had to be ratified by both Germany and the Allies. The official Armistice was signed on November 11, two days after this column appeared.

2. The Woolworth Building, commissioned by the owner of the department store chain and completed in 1913, stands at 233 Broadway and is now considered one of the great buildings in New York City. If Archy was 600 feet off the ground when his adventure began, 192 feet still rose above him. With its Byzantine mosaic lobby ceiling and Gothic revival exterior—complete with gargoyles—it was quickly nicknamed the Cathedral of Commerce.

3. The ticker-tape machine was an adaptation of the telegraph; it sent stock market quotations via telegraph wires, but in letters and numbers rather than the dots and dashes of Morse code. Invented in the 1870s to provide relatively up-to-date stock quotations surpassing the former daily summary of activity, it spat out prices on a long narrow stream of paper. Used ticker tape made excellent confetti. Although a ticker-tape parade—a parade between high buildings from which flutter a snowstorm of confetti—can occur anywhere, it originated in New York City with the dedication of the Statue of Liberty in 1886 and is mostly associated with Archy's hometown.

NOVEMBER 23
I Saw Archy

1. For three or four decades the slang term *dipso* had been a common abbreviation for *dipsomaniac,* a drunkard, and some chronic alcoholics hallucinate visions of snakes while experiencing *delirium tremens*. Combining these two ideas into a real snake would have been a strong enough joke, but it started the other way around. There really is a dipsas snake, *Dipsas variegata*, found mostly in Central and South America. Perhaps Marquis had again been browsing through the science dictionary that seems to have inspired the column on November 8, 1917.

DECEMBER 3
Peace Conference

1. The *Orizaba* was a real ship, which had been commissioned only the previous May and assigned to the Atlantic Transport Service, eventually convoying more than 15,000 troops during the war and afterward bringing almost 32,000 home. In December it was temporarily assigned to assist the French government in the repatriation of prisoners of war from France, Italy, and Belgium.

DECEMBER 6
Poet Overboard

1. The *George Washington* was a real ship, and its history encapsulates a bit of Archy's era. It was originally German, one of several of Norddeutscher Lloyd's North Atlantic passenger liners to bear the name of a U.S. president, supposedly with the intention of luring German immigrants to this line. It began transatlantic routes in 1909, but with the outbreak of war in 1914 it was ordered to remain at the company's Hoboken docks. In 1917, when the United States joined the war, the ship was seized and recommissioned as a U.S. naval transport. In did indeed carry President Woodrow Wilson to the Versailles peace conference.
2. During World War I George Creel was director of the Committee on Public Information, with far-reaching authority over U.S. newspapers, film companies, even songwriters and cartoonists; he was often denounced for his authoritarian censorship. In 1919 Marquis published his collection *Prefaces* (inspired by and at times parodying H. L. Mencken's 1917 *Book of Prefaces*), in which he says, "Censors are necessary, increasingly necessary, if America is to avoid having a vital literature."
3. In Greek mythology Triton was a sea god, son of Poseidon (Neptune) and later the name of one of Neptune's moons. He was usually represented as a merman, with the upper body of a human and the tail of a fish replacing his legs.
4. Such archaisms as *charnel sea* (from the many human bodies lost there) and *briny lips*—like the word *corse* for *corpse*—occur in many older works of literature; Archy wasn't quoting a particular source.
5. It didn't matter to Marquis that cockroaches have neither lips nor, as mentioned farther down, teeth.

6. President Woodrow Wilson, a progressive Democrat, was elected to his first term in 1912 and narrowly reelected in 1916 on the campaign slogan "He Kept Us Out of War."

7. A mine sweeper was a military ship, much quieter than ordinary ships and constructed with a hull of plastic or wood or a low-magnetic steel, used to locate and destroy—or at least disable—floating explosive mines.

8. Dr. Cary Grayson was President Wilson's personal physician.

DECEMBER 10
Freedom of the Seas

1. The previous January President Wilson's "Fourteen Points" speech had translated his progressive domestic policies into international terms by promoting free trade, democracy, the formation of a League of Nations, and other tenets of self-determination. The territorial ambitions of many of the nations in the war had prevented them from publicly admitting their war goals, as Wilson had proposed, and therefore this speech became the foundation for the terms of German surrender and for shaping the peace treaty. Complete freedom of marine travel, without fear of attack, was one of the fourteen points. In this poem Bill's irresolution reflects the muddy rhetoric pervading discussions of this topic.

DECEMBER 13
Passing the Bock

1. December 13 was the day that President Wilson arrived in Brest for the peace conference, unaware that Archy had saved his life aboard the *George Washington*.

2. *Gott* is simply the German word for God, but throughout the war Marquis had been pretending that he was a peculiarly German deity who answered to the Kaiser. In one column Marquis himself, rather than Archy, interviews Gott.

3. "am i wrong in castle" is Marquis's silly phonetic version of Amerongen Castle at the Hague in Holland, where the Kaiser would stay for the next two years.

4. *Bock* is a kind of malt beer that originated in Germany.

DECEMBER 14
The Former Kaiser

1. *Blutwurst* is a German blood sausage, surely the most apt food imaginable for a tyrant.

DECEMBER 16
Abdication Underneath the Bough

1. The style of Archy's rhyming lines parodies Omar Khayyam's *Rubáiyát*—or rather Edward Fitzgerald's exotic 1859 paraphrase of the standard Farsi text. A *rubai* (plural *rubaiyat*) is an ancient Persian verse form, a quatrain in which lines 1, 2, and 4 rhyme. These particular verses are relevant:

> *A Book of Verses underneath the Bough,*
> *A Jug of Wine, a Loaf of Bread—and Thou*
> *Beside me singing in the Wilderness—*
> *Oh, Wilderness were Paradise enow!*

> *The Moving Finger writes; and, having writ,*
> *Moves on: nor all thy Piety nor Wit*
> *Shall lure it back to cancel half a Line,*
> *Nor all thy Tears wash out a Word of it.*

2. The German popular song "Ach du lieber Augustin" originated in Vienna in the eighteenth century. It was a brilliant choice for Wilhelm to be singing, because it is narrated by a man who bemoans to his dear friend Augustin his lost good times and keeps repeating that he "just can't win."

DECEMBER 23
The Former Czar

1. Nikolay Aleksandrovich Romanoff (now usually spelled Romanov) had been tsar of Russia since 1894 when he was forced to abdicate during the 1917 Russian Revolution. He and his entire family had been executed only a few months before Archy was writing; already rumors were circulating that Nicholas or his son Alexei or his daughter Anastasia had actually been spirited away and saved. The Romanov dynasty had ruled Russia from 1613. The year after this column, 1919, a Lithuanian-born American

named Harry F. Gerguson would begin impersonating Nicholas's illegitimate son Michael, attracting so much attention that he would open Romanoff's Restaurant in Beverly Hills in the late 1930s.

2. A *verst* is a Russian measurement of land distance, equal to roughly two-thirds of a mile.

1919

JANUARY 14
Preliminary Peace

1. In March 1918, French general Ferdinand Foch, who had been steadily promoted throughout the war, had been placed in charge of Allied forces in Europe. He led the July counterattack, at the Second Battle of the Marne, that led to Germany's downfall, and it was he who accepted Germany's surrender in November. He would also be prominent in the approaching peace negotiations at Versailles.

2. Georges Clemenceau had been French premier between 1906 and 1909, and had regained the office in 1917. He played a crucial role in rallying French forces. His second government would be ousted after his opponents argued that he settled for easier terms than necessary in Germany's peace negotiations.

3. "Bull" was Bull Durham tobacco. In 1918, continuing its promotion of tobacco as a patriotic donation to the war effort, the U.S. government bought the entire output of the Bull Durham company, which had been advertising with such slogans as "When our boys light up, the Huns will light out" and "The smoke that cheers our sailor lads."

JANUARY 20
No Water Bug

1. The U.S. Congress had passed the Eighteenth Amendment to the Constitution in 1917, and, upon ratification by three-fourths of the states, the so-called "Dry Law" officially went into effect on January 16. Two days before this column, the Volstead Act provided federal enforcement strictures, and soon the supplying of bootleg liquor became the most lucrative business in America. Marquis returned to this theme many times. On March 27 he wrote, "Before that amendment is yanked out of an otherwise excellent Constitution, a good deal of water will run under the bridges." See also note 1 for June 10, 1918.

MARCH 3
No Beer No Work

1. NO BEER NO WORK buttons were real and can still be bought through collectors or online. (Nowadays the slogan appears on new hats and T-shirts, including in Spanish, No cerveza no trabajo.) The phrase emerged from a short-lived offshoot of the labor movement protesting Prohibition, but soon it was everywhere. A song entitled "No Beer No Work," by Sammy Edwards also dates from 1919: " 'No beer, no work' will be my battle cry / After the first of July. . . ." As often happened, with this comment by Archy Marquis was ahead of many of his colleagues. Five months later, the magazine Snappy Stories published a poem by American humorist Ellis Parker Butler entitled "No Beer No Work." It consisted of twenty-five tedious verses slangily parodying "Excelsior," Henry Wadsworth Longfellow's poem beginning with the famous line "The shades of night were falling fast . . ." Marquis knew Butler, who was a slightly older contemporary. They had been photographed together in 1912 at Doubleday's reception for Marquis upon publication of his first novel, Danny's Own Story, leading to ongoing joshing about how the face of an alarm clock on the shelf behind Marquis's head appeared in the photograph as a halo. On August 16 the Literary Digest ran a cartoon of a yawning cop complaining to a cobwebbed judge, "Oh, ho hum! No beer, no work!"

MARCH 5
An Interview with Mehitabel

1. Eau de vie is a brandy distilled from fermented fruit juice.
2. Mehitabel seems to think that she is merely saying "dear old friend," but vieux as in vieux jeu, means old-fashioned or antiquated.
3. Noblesse oblige refers to the honorable behavior supposedly required of persons of noble birth or rank.
4. Haute classe: high class, noble.
5. See note 1 for September 1, 1916.
6. Marquis was probably referring to the British actress Lily Langtry, legendarily beautiful and notoriously dissolute. Three years before, however, D. H. Lawrence had referred to an actress as "the lily of the stage" in Twilight in Italy.
7. Canaille: French, the rabble, the lower classes.
8. Don is a respectful Spanish form of address, as in Don Quixote.
9. "The Arrow and the Song" is Longfellow's famous poem that in-

cludes the oft-quoted lines "I shot an arrow into the air / It fell to earth, I knew not where."

10. July 1, 1919 was the date on which the War Prohibition Act was scheduled to go into effect.

11. *Toujours joyeause*: always merry, a variation on her usual *toujours gai*.

MARCH 17
Royal Blood and Anarchy

1. The Russian word *bolshevik* originally meant *majority*. Led by Lenin (see January 21, 1921), the radical faction of the Russian Social Democratic Workers' Party gained the political high ground in 1903 when it dubbed itself the Bolshevik Party and its opponents the Menshaviks, or minority. Since the revolution in 1917, the Bolsheviks had eliminated all other parties. In 1918 the Bolsheviks named themselves the official Communist Party, and in 1952 promoted themselves further to the Communist Party of the Soviet Union. In Marquis's time, *bolshevik* was already a common slang term not only for actual members of the Communist Party but also for anarchists, agitators, even labor organizers.

AUGUST 6
A Poem in the Kipling Manner

1. Rudyard Kipling was one of the leading English writers of the late nineteenth and early twentieth centuries, author of *The Jungle Book* and many other volumes of fiction and poetry. He was an enthusiastic apostle of British colonialism, especially in India, where he served in the military and where many of his tales and poems are set. In 1907 he became the first English writer to win the Nobel Prize. Marquis admired Kipling's 1901 novel *Kim* and often reread it. He found a great deal of irresistible humor in his poetic style, however, which this poem beautifully parodies.

AUGUST 14
The Best Thing You Have Done Yet

1. Although smaller venues had been exhibiting contemporary European art for a few years before, in 1913 the Association of American Painters and Sculptors hosted a huge and well-publicized

exhibition of "modern" American and European experimental artworks at New York's Sixty-ninth Regiment Armory. This event is generally referred to simply as "the Armory Show." Featured works included Picasso's then-outrageous 1907 painting *Les Desmoiselles d'Avignon*, which featured highly stylized nude women with distorted heads inspired by Iberian and African masks. In the wake of the Armory Show, many New York galleries began exhibiting such works. As usually happens when confronted with originality, many commentators expressed amusement or annoyance and proclaimed the death of art. Marquis often mocked the pretensions of Greenwich Village "artistes," and in this poem he lampoons the inflated doubletalk that critics and artists fall into. But he also simply resisted change in some fields.

OCTOBER 6
To Settle the Controversy

1. The British writer Margaret Mary Julia "Daisy" Ashford wrote her only novel, *The Young Visiters* [sic] *or Mr Salteena's Plan*, in 1890 at the age of nine. She rediscovered the manuscript and published it in 1919, when she was thirty-eight. Replete with childlike misspellings (as in the title), it is popular for the child's straightforward point-of-view and easygoing humor; it quickly became a stage play and in 2003 became a BBC television drama. J. M. Barrie, the popular British playwright and author of *Peter Pan*, wrote a rather twee introduction to Ashford's little book, passionately attesting to its authenticity and praising the author's style. It was this introduction that inspired the legend that Ashford was in fact a pseudonym for Barrie himself. (See also the previous column and the following.)

2. Although much of Shakespeare's life and career is well documented, there have been countless attempts to attribute his works to someone else. Usually the nominee is a titled personage, such as the Earl of Oxford, or at least someone better educated than Shakespeare, such as the essayist and pioneer scientist Francis Bacon. A passionate fan of Shakespeare and almost entirely self-educated himself, Marquis had little patience with the labyrinthine shenanigans of Baconians and Oxfordians who scorned the commoner who actually wrote the plays and poems.

DECEMBER 3
This Monster Man

1. The Entente Cordiale was a 1904 "cordial understanding" between France and Britain to parcel out colonial boundaries, which Russia joined three years later to form the Triple Entente. Handily for Archy, in lowercase the term applies to any unofficial but well-understood agreement.

2. "Hands Across the Sea" was a term for international cooperation between the United States and Europe. It soon became the title of books and films, and the idea of expressing goodwill with "hands across" something became a running joke.

DECEMBER 12
The Cat Show

1. "Clara Vere de Vere" is a poem by Tennyson, included in his 1842 collection The Lady of Shalott. Cats do not appear in the poem, in which the narrator rejects Clara's high-born charms and guile.

2. The "red star" is actually a planet—Mars. Named for the Roman god of war because of its bloody color, it was once thought to inspire violence and frenzy.

1920

MAY 1
An Archy Drive

1. One luxury Marquis himself almost never experienced was time in which to "think and think and think" before writing. Five years later he abandoned regular columning to pursue fiction and drama.

2. In 1929 Marquis himself spent a few months in Hollywood, but the experience resulted in neither profit nor satisfaction.

OCTOBER 20
Crazy as a Bed Bug

1. The "bed bug," a minuscule insect that nibbles on humans, is Cimex lectularius; it and several kin are members of the family Cimicidae. They flourish in unwashed bedding and are considerably less common in American homes than they were when Marquis

wrote this column. The phrase "crazy as a bed bug" goes back at least to 1832, and refers to the frantic way that these tiny creatures scramble to escape when they are uncovered.

1921

JANUARY 21
This Lenin Person

1. Nikolai Lenin was the pseudonym of Vladimir Ilyich Ulyanov, a follower of Karl Marx's communist economic and political theories who formulated the later Marxist-Leninist policies of Russia and the Soviet Union. He had been a leading figure in the Russian Revolution of 1917 and afterward rose to the position of virtual dictator. He founded the Bolsheviks (see the note for March 17, 1919) and ruthlessly battled opposition and counterrevolution until his death in 1924.

MAY 2
Organizing the Insects

1. Known in English as Tamerlane—or Tamburlaine in Christopher Marlowe's drama—Timur Lenk or Timur-i-Ling was an infamously barbaric Turkish conqueror who sacked great cities from Baghdad to Delhi. His name meant Timur the Lame.
2. In Greek mythology the Myrmidons are a warlike people of Thessaly who accompany Achilles to the Trojan War. Later the term referred to anyone mindless enough to blindly follow another's orders. But Marquis clearly also knew that the bellicose instincts of the social insects had inspired entomologists to dub ants myrmidons and the study of them myrmecology.

MAY 19
The Cockroach Its Life History

1. As you might expect from the specificity, it was a real book, or at least a pamphlet, published by the British Museum.

JUNE 16
My Private Comet

1. People were asking Archy about Comet 7P/Pons-Winnecke, which visits Earth's night skies roughly every five years. It was named for

the French astronomer Jean Louis Pons, who observed it in 1819, and German astronomer Friedrich August Theodor Winnecke, who accidentally rediscovered it in 1858. Based upon these and other observations, astronomers calculated the comet's parabolic orbit and realized that it is associated with the Boötid meteor showers (so called because they seem to radiate outward from the constellation Boötes). Usually this comet is faint, but the 1916 appearance was the most vivid on record.

AUGUST 16
Dodo Birds and Cubist Posters

1. The "twelve mile line" was the offshore border of the territorial waters of the United States, beyond which ships providing hooch (illegal liquor) were not violating Prohibition laws.

SEPTEMBER 13
Ku Klux Klam

1. Archy is mocking the Ku Klux Klan, a white supremacist terrorist organization formed in the southern United States in 1867 to oppose Reconstruction and prevent the enfranchisement of African Americans after slavery had been abolished during the Civil War. Its members engaged in murder, extortion, and robbery to further their fear-driven goals. In 1915 William J. Simmons led the reform of the Klan into an organization that was officially anti-Semitic and anti-Catholic as well as anti-black, and at this time the Klan received a lot of national attention. The Klan faded but was revived in the 1960s to resist the Civil Rights movement.

OCTOBER 5
Krew Krux Kranks

1. See note for September 13, 1921.
2. The Klan called itself an "invisible empire," and its officials were called kleagles.

OCTOBER 14
Cursed Fly Swatters

1. See the note for July 25, 1916, for more on fly swatters.

1922

APRIL 22
Waiting for a Vacant Body

1. Arthur Conan Doyle was a rich source of unintentional comedy to
   a humorist such as Don Marquis. The creator of the always ra-
   tional Sherlock Holmes was in reality one of the most gullible pub-
   lic figures of his time. A tireless advocate of spiritualism, especially
   after the death of his son, Conan Doyle resisted Houdini's claim
   that he was merely an escape artist and insisted that instead Hou-
   dini must have occult powers. *Ectoplasm* was a mysterious sub-
   stance that supposedly emanated from the body of a spiritualist
   during communication with the dead. Conan Doyle even defended
   obviously faked photographs portraying the appearance of ecto-
   plasm around a medium in a darkened room. See also October 19,
   1922 and its note for Conan Doyle's predictably enthusiastic atti-
   tude toward fairies.

APRIL 26
Interviewed the Mummy

1. In a couple of later columns not included in this collection, Archy
   refers to Tutankhamen ("King Tut"), and some commentators have
   speculated that this interview was in response to the Tut fervor. Ac-
   tually Howard Carter and Lord Carnarvon would not open the
   tomb of the boy king until November, so again Marquis was ahead
   of the game.
2. Ra was the Egyptian god of the sun. For several decades *Rah!,* a
   shortened form of *hurrah,* had been a college cheer, and for about
   ten years the term *rah-rah* had been an adjective applied to horta-
   tory boosters. Seti, son of Ramses I, was a Nineteenth-Dynasty
   Egyptian king who reigned from 1290 to 1279 BCE; the mummy's
   yearning for beer must have led him to exaggerate in his claim of
   "forty centuries of thirst."
3. Isis was an Egyptian goddess, mother of Osiris. Some commentators
   think that the traditional Christian representation of Mary holding
   Jesus was adapted from Egyptian images of Isis and Osiris.
4. Phthah, or Ptah, was the Egyptian god credited with shaping the
   material universe. Marquis invented Pish and Phthush, and surely it
   is no coincidence that they sound like skeptical interjections.

MAY 1
Archy to the Radio Fans

1. The message is in Morse code, the dot-and-dash language of telegraphy. Translation: I / GREET / YOU / HOW / IS / YOUR / WAVE / LENGTH / TODAY
2. In this column Marquis also describes how "ten years ago," before he began his signed "Sun Dial" column, much of his best work was ignored because it appeared too far down in the column and in too small a type size. Archy was demonstrating his knowledge of the profession when he struck for a more prominent type. See note 2 for April 26, 1916.

JUNE 21
Once Every Seventeen Years

1. Bacchus was the Greek god of wine and revelry, the convivial deity who had been banished by Prohibition.

AUGUST 2
Warty Bliggens

1. Besides providing the best-named character in the series, this poem encapsulates the favorite target of satirists throughout history—arrogance. "The piece about Warty Bliggens," wrote E. B. White more than a half-century later, "is a brilliant exposure of man's startling assumption about his relationship to nature. I have never read anything to beat it." (From a letter addressed to Edward C. Sampson and dated May 31, 1973, reprinted in Guth, *Letters of E. B. White*, 1976, p. 649.) As one of America's foremost essayists, White was often compared to Michel Eyquem, seigneur de Montaigne, the sixteenth-century Frenchman who founded the modern genre and gave it its name—*essai*, from "attempt." White had read Montaigne, but apparently he didn't remember a famous section in the master's long and wide-ranging essay "Apology for Raimond Sebond." It contains an amusing forerunner of the batrachocentric toad, which is worth quoting (from John Florio's sonorous 1603 translation) if only to place Marquis in a longstanding tradition:

> For why may not a goose say thus? All parts of the world behold me, the earth serveth me to tread upon, the Sunne to give me light, the Starres to inspire me with influence; this commoditie I have of the wind,

> *and this benefit of the waters: there is nothing that this worlds-vault*
> *doth so favourably look upon as me selfe; I am the favorite of nature;*
> *is it not man that careth for me, that keepeth me, lodgeth me, and*
> *serveth me?*

In this essay Montaigne also talks about transmigration, in a re-
mark quite relevant to Archy's daily crisis of identity: "For in the
Metempsychosis or transmigration of soules of *Pythagoras*, and the
change of habitation which he imagined the soules to make, shall
we thinke that the lion in whom abideth the soule of *Cæsar*, doth
wed the passions which concerned *Cæsar*, or that it is hee?" (For
Pythagoras see also the note for September 20, 1922.)

Alexander Pope must have been thinking of Montaigne when he
wrote in his 1734 *Essay on Man*,

> *While man exclaims, "See all things for my use!"*
> *"See man for mine!" replies a pamper'd goose.*

AUGUST 8
My Favorite Poem

1. "Oh, why should the spirit of mortal be proud?" is the first and last
   line of the fourteen-stanza poem "Mortality," written by the Scot-
   tish poet William Knox in 1824. Lincoln did indeed declare it his
   favorite poem; he memorized and often quoted it. Lincoln wrote the
   occasional poem himself, and many people thought he had written
   this one, despite his repeated denials.

AUGUST 12
Always the Lady

1. "Come live with me and be my love" is the fist line of Christopher
   Marlowe's sixteenth-century poem "The Passionate Shepherd to
   His Love."

AUGUST 28
Archy's Own Short Course in Entomology

1. Entomology is the study of insects, a class that technically doesn't
   include either wood lice (arthropods) or spiders (arachnids), but
   Archy is a poet, not a scientist.
2. *Xylophagous*: wood-eating.

3. Presumably the spider's eight legs give her a certain Buzby Berkeley air all by herself. In classical mythology, Terpsichore is the goddess of choral song and dancing; lowercase can refer to any dancer, more often as a *terpsichorean*. Terpsichore is one of the nine Muses, daughters of Zeus and Mnemosyne (goddess of memory); her sisters include Clio (history) and Thalia (comedy).

SEPTEMBER 14
The Most Luckless Creature

1. This was the first Archy appearance after Marquis left the *Sun* and moved to the New York *Tribune*. His column there was to be called "The Lantern," but for two weeks it appeared under the heading of a column that had already existed there, "The Tower," presumably a title designed to ride on the popularity of FPA's "Conning Tower."

SEPTEMBER 18
Low Brow

1. Archy refers to the drawing published as frontispiece in the present volume; a close-up appears on the cover. This illustration, the first portrayal of Archy, appeared several years before George K. Herriman, creator of Krazy Kat, was hired to illustrate the first collection. It was published in the *Tribune* on September 11 in a half-page advertisement welcoming their new columnist and his most popular character. Marquis was always quick to respond in his column to tributes or jibes; it helped keep alive the sense of dialogue with the readers.
2. The term *occiput* merely refers to the back part of the head; it is better known in adjective form, as in the occipital lobes of the brain.
3. *Lowbrow*, describing a nonintellectual person or one with unsophisticated taste, was still a new concept, and Archy refers to it several times. It emerged in the first decade of the century, an inevitable antonym for *highbrow*, which since at least the 1880s had referred to an intellectual or cultured person. Archy certainly regards himself as a mental highbrow, although it's difficult to imagine a creature that could be more physically lowbrowed than a flat-headed cockroach.
4. This kind of joke—as in "I'm sick and dying. Hoping you are the same,"—dates back to before vaudeville.

SEPTEMBER 20
Song of Mehitabel

1. Pythagoras was a Greek philosopher and mathematician in the sixth century BCE. His life is almost entirely unknown and none of his writings survive, yet others recorded enough about his academy in Italy for Pythagoras to greatly influence Greek and Roman thought. His numerological preoccupations included several contributions to geometry. He taught that souls would migrate into a new form after death, and insisted that one's behavior in this life influenced one's likely form after the next roll of the dice.
2. Although it sounds worse, *shoon* is merely an archaic plural of *shoes*.
3. Yes, in 1922 New York City's garbage was already being transported down Long Island Sound on barges.

SEPTEMBER 25
Forgets His Littleness

1. *betelgoose* refers to one of the brighter stars in the sky, the red supergiant Betelgeuse in the constellation Orion. It's pronounced with a long *e*, as in another distortion of the name, Tim Burton's 1988 film *Beetle Juice*.

OCTOBER 19
Fairies

1. Here Marquis parodies another pet delusion of Arthur Conan Doyle, whose notions about spiritualism and ectoplasm he had mocked on April 22, 1922. (See also the note for this date.) The photographs to which Archy refers, published in Conan Doyle's 1922 book *The Coming of the Fairies*, were pictures of two girls interacting with diminutive figures that looked remarkably like illustrations copied from books. In the summer of 1917, nine-year-old Frances Griffiths visited her cousin, sixteen-year-old Elsie Wright, in the village of Cottingley, near Bradford, England. They claimed that they kept seeing fairies in the nearby woodland, and soon they were bringing photographic plates home to Elsie's father for him to develop in his darkroom. The girls insisted that the fairies in the photos were real, and Conan Doyle leaped to their defense. No wonder G. K. Chesterton once remarked of Conan Doyle's legendary gullibility, "it has long seemed to me that Sir Arthur's mentality is much more that of Watson than it is of Holmes."

NOVEMBER 1
The Dactyl Droops

1. The entire poem plays with poetic terminology for aspects of meter. In prosody *meter* refers to the acoustical structure of a line of verse—based upon the number of syllables, the alternation of long and short syllables, the fixed number and positions of both syllable and stress, or merely the fixed number of stresses or accents. In English, which emphasizes at least one syllable in every word, the usual meter is the latter—accentual. Archy plays fast and loose with these rules as with most others. Incidentally, in James Thurber's *New Natural History*, you will find other metrical terms personified, including *spondee* and *trochee* and a charming six-legged beast called a *hexameter*. Thurber mentioned Marquis as an early inspiration.
2. A metrical foot comprising three syllables, with the first stressed and the others unstressed.
3. An *iamb* is a foot of verse containing two syllables, the first unstressed, the second stressed.
4. In poetry, a *foot* is a group of syllables forming a metrical unit such as the *dactyl* and *iambic* above.

NOVEMBER 22
Shakespeare and I

1. This little gem is often acclaimed as the greatest—and certainly the shortest—piece of Shakespearean criticism.
2. Originally *fish wife* merely described a woman who retailed fish, but this profession was not known for its genteel manners.

DECEMBER 13
Archy Is Excited

1. Since the middle of the nineteenth century, *red* had been a usually negative term for *anarchist* or *communist*, because of the original color of the party badge. In 1917 the Russian communists chose red as the color of their flag.

DECEMBER 23
The Futility of Literature

1. Marquis's characters often refer to each other. Archy is joking about the alcohol-weakened, Prohibition-hating Old Soak, Clem Hawley.

2. This spider's ode on her own beautiful works is reminiscent of a
moment in *Charlotte's Web*, when Lurvy first glimpses the web that
will change Wilbur's life: "The web glistened in the light and made
a pattern of loveliness and mystery, like a delicate veil" (New York:
Harper & Row, 1952), p. 77. Charlotte also explains to Wilbur the
morals of fly-eating (pp. 37–40). See the column for July 23, 1918
for the melancholy of crickets in each book.

Acknowledgments

My thanks to those who helped on this project: my wife, Laura Sloan Patterson, for her always insightful critique and advice; Martin Gardner for encouragement and suggestions; Marquis bibliographer John Batteiger for generously lending microfilm photocopies of newspaper files, for serving as the Encyclopedia Marquisiana, and for the photo that provided the cover illustration. I welcome this opportunity to thank the patient and helpful crew at Penguin Classics: executive editor Michael Millman, for starting the ball rolling and for perceptive editorial guidance; his assistant, Elizabeth Yarbrough; assistant editor Carolyn Horst; cover designer Jasmine Lee; and production editor Jennifer Tait.

My thanks also to Laurie Parker for critiquing the introduction and to Jim Young for discussing my idea of an annotated Archy long before I conceived this chronological format. Thanks to the fine staffs of several libraries: the Jean and Alexander Heard Library at Vanderbilt University, especially reference librarian Jon Erickson; the Ben West Public Library in Nashville, Tennessee; the Greensburg and Hempfield Area Library in Greensburg, Pennsylvania, especially reference librarian Jim Vikartosky, and above all the generous director, Cesare Muccari; the Carnegie Public Library in Pittsburgh; the Hillman Library at the University of Pittsburgh; and the many libraries participating in the AccessPennsylvania system of interlibrary loans.

CLICK ON A CLASSIC
www.penguinclassics.com

The world's greatest literature at your fingertips

Constantly updated information on more than a thousand titles,
from Icelandic sagas to ancient Indian epics, Russian drama to
Italian romance, American greats to African masterpieces

•

The latest news on recent additions to the list, updated
editions, and specially commissioned translations

•

Original essays by leading writers

•

A wealth of background material, including biographies
of every classic author from Aristotle to Zamyatin, plot
synopses, readers' and teachers' guides, useful web links

•

Online desk and examination copy assistance for academics

•

Trivia quizzes, competitions, giveaways, news on
forthcoming screen adaptations

FOR THE BEST IN PAPERBACKS, LOOK FOR THE

In every corner of the world, on every subject under the sun, Penguin represents quality and variety—the very best in publishing today.

For complete information about books available from Penguin—including Penguin Classics, Penguin Compass, and Puffins—and how to order them, write to us at the appropriate address below. Please note that for copyright reasons the selection of books varies from country to country.

In the United States: Please write to *Penguin Group (USA), P.O. Box 12289 Dept. B, Newark, New Jersey 07101-5289* or call 1-800-788-6262.

In the United Kingdom: Please write to *Dept. EP, Penguin Books Ltd, Bath Road, Harmondsworth, West Drayton, Middlesex UB7 0DA.*

In Canada: Please write to *Penguin Books Canada Ltd, 90 Eglinton Avenue East, Suite 700, Toronto, Ontario M4P 2Y3.*

In Australia: Please write to *Penguin Books Australia Ltd, P.O. Box 257, Ringwood, Victoria 3134.*

In New Zealand: Please write to *Penguin Books (NZ) Ltd, Private Bag 102902, North Shore Mail Centre, Auckland 10.*

In India: Please write to *Penguin Books India Pvt Ltd, 11 Panchsheel Shopping Centre, Panchsheel Park, New Delhi 110 017.*

In the Netherlands: Please write to *Penguin Books Netherlands bv, Postbus 3507, NL-1001 AH Amsterdam.*

In Germany: Please write to *Penguin Books Deutschland GmbH, Metzlerstrasse 26, 60594 Frankfurt am Main.*

In Spain: Please write to *Penguin Books S. A., Bravo Murillo 19, 1° B, 28015 Madrid.*

In Italy: Please write to *Penguin Italia s.r.l., Via Benedetto Croce 2, 20094 Corsico, Milano.*

In France: Please write to *Penguin France, Le Carré Wilson, 62 rue Benjamin Baillaud, 31500 Toulouse.*

In Japan: Please write to *Penguin Books Japan Ltd, Kaneko Building, 2-3-25 Koraku, Bunkyo-Ku, Tokyo 112.*

In South Africa: Please write to *Penguin Books South Africa (Pty) Ltd, Private Bag X14, Parkview, 2122 Johannesburg.*